Carla Kelly has been writing award-winning novels for years—stories set in the British Isles, Spain, and army garrisons during the Indian Wars. Her speciality in the Regency genre is writing about ordinary people, not just lords and ladies. Carla has worked as a university professor, a ranger in the National Park Service, and recently as a staff writer and columnist for a small daily newspaper in Valley City, North Dakota. Her husband is director of theatre at Valley City State University. She has five interesting children, a fondness for cowboy songs, and too many box elder beetles in the autumn.

Novels by the same author:

BEAU CRUSOE
CHRISTMAS PROMISE
  (part of *Regency Christmas Gifts* anthology)
MARRYING THE CAPTAIN
THE SURGEON'S LADY
MARRYING THE ROYAL MARINE

MARRIAGE OF MERCY

Carla Kelly

Harlequin (UK) policy is to use papers that are natural, renewable and recyclable products and made from wood grown in sustainable forests. The logging and manufacturing process conform to the legal environmental regulations of the country of origin.

Printed and bound in Spain
by Blackprint CPI, Barcelona

First published in Great Britain 2012
by Mills & Boon, an imprint of Harlequin (UK) Limited.
Harlequin (UK) Limited, Eton House, 18-24 Paradise Road,
Richmond, Surrey TW9 1SR

© Carla Kelly 2012

ISBN: 978 0 263 89247 5

MARRIAGE
OF MERCY

Prologue

Robert Inman, sailing master, had a cheery temperament. He had always been inclined to take the bitter with the sweet and chalk everything else up to experience. Still, it was a hard slog to reconcile himself to another year of captivity in Dartmoor, a prison newly built but scarcely humane.

Recently, among the *Orontes* survivors, he had noticed a change in conversational topics. A year ago in 1813, conversation had been almost exclusively of their capture off Land's End, where they had been toying with British merchant shipping.

With a monumental sigh, Captain Daniel Duncan had handed over his letter of marque and reprisal to the victor. The captain of the Royal Navy's sloop of war was a mere ensign, but regrettably had had the weather gauge, so capture had come as a matter of course. Rob had felt a serious pang to see the triumphant crew haul down the Stars and Stripes and fly British colours from the elegant, slanted mast of the privateer *Orontes*.

When the humiliation of capture turned to resignation, tongues loosened up. The powder monkey boasted there wasn't a jail in England that could hold him long. Duncan's first and only mate declared that war would end soon and their discomfort would be a mere annoyance.

Both the powder monkey and the mate had been wise beyond their years, apparently. No jail held the monkey long. He claimed the distinction of being the first to die, courtesy of an infected tooth that the prison governor felt deserved little attention, since it resided in an American mouth.

The first mate's discomfort—indeed, his final one—had proved to be a serious annoyance after rampant scurvy opened up an old wound inflicted by Tripolitan pirates. The scar in his thigh had separated, gaped wider until blood poisoning accepted the invitation and waltzed in, a most unwelcome guest.

As for the war ending soon, no one's expectations were high. The carpenter keeping the calendar had to be reminded to cross off yet another day on the wall, one very much like the day before, with thin gruel for breakfast, and gruel and a crust of bread for supper, and nothing in between.

Earlier conversations had revolved around food and women, as in what each seaman would eat, upon liberation, and just how many women he would sport with at the first opportunity. Food was too tantalising to discuss any more, and women not even a distraction, not to starving men. Rob had spent one fruitless hour trying to remember the pleasures of the flesh, only to realise he had not enough energy for what would follow, even in his generally fertile imagination.

For the most part, everyone sat in silence all the day. Evenings were reserved for night terrors ranging from rats on the prowl to memories of battle, near drownings to other incarcerations during this pesky war brought on by Napoleon. Those were the good dreams. Worse was the reality of scarecrow prisoners crawling among the men, preying on the more feeble.

The eternal optimist, considering his origins, Rob knew things could be worse. He had to say one thing about Dartmoor: the place was built solid, one cold stone on top of another. The wind found its way inside, though, through iron bars that no warden thought should be covered in winter, because that would be too great a comfort for prisoners.

And that was the problem for Robert Inman, sailing master. More than food and women's bodies, he craved the feel of wind on his face, but not the wailing wind that filtered into the prison over high walls. He knew what the right wind could do to a sail. He knew he could stand in one spot on any slanting deck and know precisely what to do with wind. In Dartmoor, he could only dream about wind on his face—the fair winds of summer, the fitful puffs of the dog latitudes, the humid offerings of southeast Asia.

All he wanted was the right wind.

Chapter One

If Grace Curtis, formerly known as the Honourable Miss Grace Curtis, had decided to waste her life in fruitless self-pity, she knew several genteelly poor persons to use as her character models.

Agatha Ralls lived in rented rooms over the Hare and Hound, a steep decline from her childhood in Ralls Manor, a structure built during the reign of one Edward or the other, which now housed bats. Family fortunes had taken a dismal turn when a now-distant earl had backed the wrong horse in the era of Cavaliers and Roundheads. That the family's resounding crash had taken some 150 years was some testament to earlier wealth. Now Miss Ralls lived on very little and everyone knew it.

Or Grace could have looked to the ludicrous spectacle of Sir George Armisted, who maintained a precarious existence on the family estate, when it would have been much wiser to sell it to a merchant with more money than class. Instead, Sir George sat in threadbare splendour in a leaking parlour.

Grace had watched her own father shake his head over Sir George, asking out loud how such a fool justified the expensive snuff he dipped and wine he decanted. That Sir Henry Curtis was doing the same thing never seemed to have occurred to him, even when he lay dying and advised Grace, his only child, to 'make a good match in London during the next Season'.

Grace had been too kind to point out to her father that there were no funds left to finance anything as ambitious as a Season in London, much less induce any gentleman of her social sphere to ally himself with a cheerful face and nothing else. It wouldn't have been sporting to point out her father's deficiencies as he was forced to pay attention to death, as he had never paid much attention to anything of consequence before.

Grace had closed his eyes, covered his face and left his bedroom, resolved to learn something from misfortune and build a life for herself, rather than gently glide into discreet poverty and reduced circumstances. Poor she would be, but it did not follow that she couldn't be happy.

Dressed in black and wearing a jet brooch, Grace had endured the reading of the will. Papa had had nothing to leave except debts. In the weeks before his death, his solicitor had made discreet enquiries throughout the district in an attempt to smoke out potential buyers from among the merchant class who hankered after property far removed from the High Street. He had found one, so Grace had had to suffer his presence as the solicitor read the will.

There had been paltry gifts for the few servants—all of them superannuated and with no hope of other employment—who had hung on until the bitter end, because their next place of residence would surely be the poorhouse. When the old dears turned sad eyes on her, Grace could only shake her head in sorrow, as she writhed inside.

What followed was precisely what she had expected, particularly since the solicitor had told her the night before that the manor and its contents were all going to the new landlord, an enterprising fellow who had made a fortune importing naval stores from the Baltic. With that knowledge, Grace had deposited her amethyst brooch, her only keepsake, in her pocket for safety.

And that was that. Grace had signed a document forfeiting any interest in her home, then had led the new owners through the threadbare rooms.

It was almost too much when the wife demanded to know how quickly Grace could quit the place, but Grace had always been pragmatic.

'I can be gone tomorrow morning,' Grace had said, and so she was.

That she might have nowhere to go never occurred to the new owners, so intent were they to take possession. Her two bags packed, Grace had lain awake all night in her room, teasing herself with the one plan in her mind. She discarded it, reclaimed it, discarded it again, then shouldered it for the final time after breakfast. She straightened her shoulders, picked up her valise and walked away from her home of eighteen years.

Grace had had only one egg in her basket. That it proved to be the right one had given her considerable comfort through the next ten years. It had been but a short walk from her former home to Quimby, a village close to Exeter. The day was pleasantly cool for August, with only the slightest breeze swaying the sign of Adam Wilson's bakery.

She had hoped the bakery would be empty, and it was, except for the owner and his wife. Grace set down her valise and came to the counter. Adam Wilson wiped his floury hands on his apron and gave her the same kindly look he had been giving her for years, even when she suffered inside to beg for credit.

'Yes, my dear?' Mrs Wilson asked, coming to stand beside her husband.

Grace took a deep breath. 'We owe you a large sum, I know,' she said calmly. 'I have a proposal.'

Both Wilsons looked at her, and she saw nothing in their gaze except interest. They had all the time in the world to listen.

'I will work off that debt,' Grace said, 'if you can provide me with a place to live. When I have paid the debt, and if my work has been satisfactory, I'll work for you for wages. I know you have recently lost your all-around girl to marriage with a carter in Exeter.'

To her relief, nothing in Mr Wilson's face exhibited either surprise or scepticism. 'What do you know about baking?' he asked.

'Very little,' Grace replied honestly. 'What I am is loyal and a hard worker.'

The Wilsons looked at each other, while Grace stared straight ahead at a sign advertising buns six for a penny.

'My dear, you have a pretty face. Suppose a member of your class decides to offer for you, and then we are out all of our training?' Mrs Wilson was the shrewder of the two.

'No one will offer for me, Mrs Wilson,' Grace said. 'I have no dowry to tempt anyone among the gentry. By the same token, no man among the labouring class will want a wife who he fears would take on airs and give him grief, because she is elevated in station above him and can't—or won't—forget. I am completely marriage-proof and therefore the ideal employee.'

So she had proved to be. The Wilsons lived above the bakery on the High Street, but had gladly cleared out a small storeroom behind the ovens for her use, a fragrant spot smelling of yeast and herbs. She had cried her last tear, walking to Quimby. Once that was done, she became an all-around girl and never looked back.

The first time one of her acquaintances from her former days had come into the shop, Grace had realised she could never afford to look back. She knew the moment would happen sooner or later; blessedly, it was sooner. The morning that one of her dearest friends had come into the shop with her mama and ignored Grace completely, she knew the wind blew differently. Discreetly put, Grace Curtis had slid.

The matter bothered her less than she had thought it might, considering that she had debated long and hard about throwing herself on the mercy of that particular family. Grace's decision had been confirmed most forcefully a year later. She overheard Lady Astley say to an acquaintance that they had taken in a poor cousin. And there she was, middle-aged and obsequious, always nervously alert in public to do her cousin's bidding, for fear of being turned off to an unkind world. No, Grace knew she had been wise in casting her lot with the Wilsons.

When two years had passed, Mr Wilson declared the family debt eliminated. He seemed surprised when she took a deep breath and asked, 'Will you keep me on still?'

'I thought that was the term,' he told her, as he set yeast to soften by the mixing bowls.

'I hoped it was,' she replied, reaching for the salt, afraid to look at him.

'Then it is, Gracie. Let us shake on it.' He smiled at her. 'You're the best worker I ever hired.'

The years had passed easily enough. After a brief peace, the war set in again. The Wilsons' two sons sailed with the Channel Fleet, one dying at Trafalgar and the other rising to carpenter's mate. Their daughters all married Navy men and lived in Portsmouth. Grace found herself assuming more and more responsibility, particularly in keeping the books.

She had never minded that part of her job because she was meticulous. Her real pleasure, though, came in making biscuits: macaroons, pretty little Savoy cakes, lemon biscuits, all pale brown and crisp, and creamy biscuits with almond icing.

It was these last biscuits—she named them Quimby Crèmes—that had attracted the attention of Lord Thomson, Marquis of Quarle. Mr Wilson always thought he was aptly named, because the old man always seemed to be picking one. Colonel of a regiment of foot serving in New York City during the American War, Lord Thomson suffered no fools gladly, be they titled like himself, merchants with more pretension than the Pope, or the smelly knacker man, who regularly

cleared the roads of dead animals. Lord Thomson
was equally disposed to resent everyone.

Grace was the only person in Quimby who
had a knack for managing the marquis and she
did it through his stomach. She had noticed his
marked preference for her Quimby Crèmes when
he visited the bakery, something he did regularly.

His bakery visits puzzled Mrs Wilson. 'My
cousin is an upstairs maid in his employ and I
know for a fact he has any number of footmen
to fetch biscuits on a whim. Why does he do it?'

Grace knew. She remembered her own treks
to the bakery for the pleasure of the fragrance inside the glass door, and the fun of choosing three
of these and a half-dozen of those. Invariably,
after Lord Thomson made his selection, Grace
watched him open his parcel outside the shop
and sit in the sun, eating one biscuit after another.
She understood.

She probably never would have realised her
eventual fondness for Lord Thomson if he had
not come up short in her eyes. One morning—
perhaps his washing water had been cold—he el-
bowed his way into the shop, snarling at a little
boy who took too long to make his selection at
the counter. He poked the lad with his umbrella.
The boy's eyes welled with tears.

'That's enough, Lord Thomson,' Grace declared.

'What did you say?' the marquis demanded.

'You heard me, my lord,' she said serenely,

adding an extra lemon biscuit to the boy's choice. 'Tommy was here first. Everyone gets a chance to choose.'

After a filthy look at her, the marquis turned on his heel and left the bakery, slamming the door so hard that the cat in the window woke up.

'I fear I may have cost you a customer,' Grace told Mr Wilson, who had watched the whole scene.

'I can be philosophical,' Mr Wilson said, patting Tommy on the head. 'He's a grouchy old bird.'

She worried, though, acutely aware that Lord Thomson didn't come near the shop for weeks. Easter came and went, and so did everyone except the marquis. Quimby was a small village. Even those who had not witnessed the initial outburst knew what had happened. When he eventually returned, even those in line stepped out of the way, not willing to incur any wrath that might reflect poorly on Grace.

With a studied smile, Lord Thomson waited his turn. As he approached the front of the line eventually, an amazing number of patrons had decided not to leave until they knew the outcome. Grace felt her cheeks grow rosy as he stood before her and placed his order.

She chose to take the bull by the horns. 'Lord Thomson, I've been faithfully making Quimby Crèmes, hoping you would return.'

'Here I am,' he said quietly. 'I'll take all you have, if you'll join me in the square to help me eat them.'

She had not expected that. One look at his triumphant face told her that he had known she would be surprised and it tickled him. She smiled again. 'You have me, sir,' she said simply. She looked at Mr Wilson, who nodded, as interested in the conversation as his customers.

To her relief, they ate Crèmes and parted as friends.

Year in and year out he visited the bakery, even when the decade started to weigh on him. When an apologetic footman told her one morning that Lord Thomson was bedridden now, and asked if she would please bring the crèmes to Quarle, she made her deliveries in person.

Standing in the foyer at Quarle, Grace had some inkling of the marquis's actual worth, something he had never flaunted. The estate was magnificent and lovingly maintained. She felt a twinge of something close to sadness, that her own father had been unable to maintain their more modest estate to the same standard. Quarle was obviously in far better hands.

She brought biscuits to Lord Thomson all winter, sitting with him while he ate, and later dipping them in milk and feeding them to him when he became too feeble to perform even that simple task. Each visit seemed to reveal another distant relative—he had no children of his own—all with the marquis's commanding air, but none with his flair for stories of his years on the American continent, fighting those Yankee upstarts, or even his interest in the United States.

His relatives barely tolerated Grace's visits. Her cheeks had burned with their scorn, but in the end, she decided it was no worse than the slights that came her way now and then. She found herself feeling strangely protective of the old man against his own relatives, who obviously would never have come around, had they not been summoned by Lord Thomson's new solicitor.

At least, he introduced himself to her one afternoon as the new solicitor, although he was not young. 'I'm Philip Selway,' he said. 'And you are Miss Grace Curtis?'

'Just Gracie Curtis,' she told him. 'Lord Thomson likes my Quimby Crèmes.'

'So do I,' he assured her.

She returned her attention to Lord Thomson. She squeezed his hand gently and he opened his eyes.

'Lean closer,' he said, with just a touch of his former air of command.

She did as he said.

'I'm dying, you know,' he told her.

'I was afraid of that,' she whispered. 'I'll bring you Quimby Crèmes tomorrow.'

'That'll keep death away?' he asked, amused.

'No, but I'll feel better,' she said, which made him chuckle.

She thought he had stopped, but he surprised her. 'Do you trust me?' he asked.

'I believe I do,' she replied, after a moment.

'Good. What's to come will try you. Have faith in me,' he told her, then closed his eyes.

She left the room quietly, wondering what he meant. The solicitor stood in the hall. He nodded to her.

'Coming back tomorrow?' he asked.

'Yes, indeed.'

Lord Thomson's relatives were returning from the breakfast room, arguing with each other. They darted angry glances at the solicitor as they brushed past him and ignored Grace.

'You'll be back tomorrow?'

'I said I would, sir.'

'Grace, I believe you'll do.'

'Sir?'

He followed the relatives, but not before giving her a long look.

As she considered the matter later, she wondered if she should have stayed away. But who was wise on short notice?

Chapter Two

Mr Selway knocked on the door of the bakery the next morning before they opened for business. Apron in hand, Grace unlocked the door, wondering if he had been waiting long.

He didn't have to say anything; she knew. 'He's gone, isn't he? Mr Selway, I'm going to miss him,' she said, swallowing hard.

'We are the only ones,' he said. 'I wanted you to know.' He put his hand on her arm. 'Please attend the reading of his will, which will follow his funeral on Tuesday.'

Surely she hadn't heard him right. 'I beg your pardon, sir?'

He increased the pressure on her arm. 'I cannot say more, since the company is not assembled for the reading. Be there, Grace.'

And there she was, four days later. The foyer was deserted, but Mr Selway had told her they would all be in the library. She opened the door quietly, cringing inside when it squeaked and all those heads swivelled in her direction, then turned back just as quickly. The family servants stood along the back wall and she joined them. Mr Selway looked at her over the top of his spectacles, then continued reading.

This reading was different from her father's paltry will. Mr Selway covered a wide-ranging roster of properties, even including a Jamaican plantation, part-interest in a Brazilian forest, a brewery in Boston and a tea farm in Ceylon.

'T'auld scarecrow had his bony fingers in a lot of pies,' the gardener standing next to her whispered.

She nodded, thinking about Lord Thomson's generally shabby air. She tried to imagine him as a young army officer, adventuring about the world. Her attention wandered. Before his relatives had descended on him, Lord Thomson had had no objection to her borrowing a book now and then. She thought of two books in her room behind the ovens and hoped she could sneak them back before the new Lord Thomson missed them. Not that he would, but she did not wish to cross him. Grace was a shrewd enough judge of character to suspect that the new Lord Thomson would begrudge even the widow her tiny mite, if he thought it should be his. Books probably fell in that category.

Mr Selway finished his reading of the properties devolving on the sole heir, who sat in the front row, practically preening himself with his own importance. The solicitor picked up another sheet and started on a much smaller inventory of items of interest to other family members, ranging this time from items of jewellery to pieces of furniture. She listened with half an ear.

The servants were given their due next, some of them turned off with a small sum and thanks. Others were allowed to keep their jobs, probably, Grace reasoned, no longer than it would take for the new Lord Thomson to decide them superfluous. Still, a pound here and a pound there could mean the world to people on the level she now inhabited.

Mr Selway put down that document and picked up the last one remaining in front of him. He cleared his throat, looking uncertain for the first time, as if unsure how this final term would be received.

Without a look or a word, Grace knew instinctively that whatever the term was, it would fall on her. She looked around the room in sudden panic. Everyone had been accounted for and Mr Selway had explicitly insisted on her presence. She started to ease toward the door, afraid for the attention soon to be thrust upon her and wanting only to return to the bakery. She stopped moving when Mr Selway looked directly at her.

'There are two final items in the will, recently added, but no less attested to,' he said.

'One is a small matter, the other a large one. Let me mention the small one first. I will read what the late Lord Thomson dictated to me, only one month ago.' He cleared his throat and took a firm grip on the document. 'For the last five years at least, I have been kindly treated by Mr and Mrs Wilson's assistant, Grace Louisa Curtis. She has never failed to bake precisely the biscuits I craved, and—'

The new Lord Thomson groaned. 'Good Lord, next you'll tell me that my uncle is bequeathing her a brewery on the Great Barrier Reef that we have no knowledge of! Let her have it and be damned.'

Now dependent on this new marquis for whatever thin charity he chose to dispense, his relatives laughed. Grace cringed inside and started sidling toward the door again. It looked so far away.

Mr Selway stared down the new marquis and continued. "Knowing of her kindness to me, when none of my relatives cared whether I lived or died, I have arranged for Miss Curtis to take possession of this estate's dower house and its contents for her lifetime."

'Good God!' Lord Thomson was on his feet, his face beet red.

Mr Selway looked at him and then down at the page. '...for her lifetime. In addition, she will receive thirty pounds per annum.'

'This is outrageous!' the marquis shouted.

'It is a mere thirty pounds each year and a small house you would never occupy,' Mr Selway said mildly. 'Do sit down, Lord Thomson, I am not quite finished.' He glared him down into his chair again. 'As I said, this was the easy part.'

Grace stared at the solicitor. The colour must have drained from her face, because the gardener standing next to her guided her towards a stool that a footman had vacated.

'I don't want this,' she murmured to the gardener, who shrugged.

'Since when has what we wanted made a difference?' the man whispered back.

'Go on, tell me the rest,' Lord Thomson exclaimed. 'Lord, this is a nuisance!'

Mr Selway put down the document and folded his hands over it. 'Lord Thomson, it will probably come as a surprise to you that your predecessor had a son.'

'I'll be damned,' the new marquis said. 'A bastard, no doubt.'

'Takes one to know one,' the gardener whispered, but not in a soft voice. The back row of relatives turned around, some to glare, others to titter.

'Yes, my lord, a bastard, so you needn't fear you will lose a penny of your inheritance,' Mr Selway said. 'While his regiment was quartered in New York City during much of the American War, your uncle dallied with one Mollie Duncan, the daughter of a Royalist draper. The result was a son.' He looked at the document again. 'Daniel Duncan.'

'How could this possibly concern any of us?' Lord Thomson snapped.

'Ordinarily, it would not. Through various means, your uncle managed to keep track of Daniel Duncan's career. When this current American war began, Duncan commanded a privateer called the *Orontes*, out of Nantucket.'

'So Uncle's bastard is making life difficult for British merchant shipping,' the marquis said, smirking. 'Why do you think I even care about this?'

Mr Selway picked up the document again, and pulled a thicker packet from a drawer in the desk. 'Because before his death, your uncle arranged for Captain Duncan, currently a prisoner of war in Dartmoor, to be paroled to Quarle's dower house.' He glanced at Grace, his eyes kind. 'He specifically requests that Grace Curtis provide his food and care during his parole here. When the war ends, he'll go free. That is all the connection you will have with him.'

Lord Thomson laughed. 'You can't seriously honour this. The old devil was crazy.'

He had gone too far. Grace could see that in the way the other relatives whispered to each other. The new Lord Thomson seemed to sense their disgust of him. He folded his arms and sat silent, his lips in a tight line. 'Well, he was,' he muttered.

Mr Selway spoke directly to him, leaning forwards across the small desk. 'Lord Thomson, your predecessor would have done this sooner, had he not had this sudden decline that led to his death. Everything has been approved for such a transaction. I tell you that the deceased had friends in high places, whom it would be wise not to cross. You are in no way rendered uncomfortable at an estate you seldom visit, anyway.'

Apparently Mr Selway was not above a little personal pride. He smiled at Lord Thomson, even though Grace saw no humour there. 'I build only airtight wills, Lord Thomson.' He looked down at the document before him. 'Any attempt on your part to alter or in any way hinder the carrying out of this stipulation would be folly. I repeat: Lord Thomson had friends in high places.' Mr Selway folded the will and left the room.

Lord Thomson sat slumped in his seat. After a disparaging glance at her husband, the new Lady Thomson rose and gestured his relatives toward the dining room, where refreshments waited. Grace sidled out of the door ahead of everyone, eager to leave the building by the closest exit. *If I hurry, I can be out of here and pretend none of this has happened,* she thought.

But there was Mr Selway, obviously waiting for her. She sighed.

'Mr Selway, please don't think I need any of the provisions mentioned in Lord Thomson's will,' she told him, even as he guided her into the bookroom. 'I want to go back to the bakery.' She tried to get out of his grasp 'Mr Selway, please!'

'Sit down, my dear,' he said, his expression kindly. 'There is no stipulation that you must remain in the dower house, if you don't wish to. The thirty pounds is yours annually for life, though.'

Grace nodded. 'I want to save money to buy the bakery some day, when the Wilsons are too old to run it.'

'Then this is your opportunity.' The solicitor said nothing else for a long while. When he spoke, his words were carefully chosen. 'Grace, I have observed in life that most of us place our expectations abnormally high and we are disappointed when they remain unfulfilled. Have you placed yours too low?'

She shook her head. 'I have not,' she told him quietly. 'You know as well as I do that thirty a year will not maintain me in any style approaching my former status. It will not induce anyone to marry me. Heavens, sir, I am twenty-eight! I have no illusions.'

'Indeed you do not,' Mr Selway replied. 'You may be right, too.' He leaned towards her. 'Think about this, Gracie: it is 1814. This war with America cannot last for ever. Dartmoor is a fearsomely terrible place. You would be doing a great favour to *our* Lord Thomson to succor his only child, no matter how boisterously he was conceived.'

'I suppose I would,' she said, feeling that the words were pulled from her mouth by tweezers.

'Could I discuss this with the Wilsons? If I have to live in the dower house with a paroled prisoner, I'd like to keep working at the bakery.'

'I see no harm in that, as long as the parolee is with you.'

Grace stood up, relieved. 'Then I will ask them directly and send you a note.'

'I ask no more of you, my dear,' Mr Selway said.

The Wilsons had no objections to any of the details of Lord Thomson's will, so amazed were they that a marquis would consider doing so much for their Gracie, a woman others of her class seemed content to ignore in perpetuity.

'What's a year or less?' Mr Wilson asked. 'You can live in a nice place, take care of a paroled prisoner, then return to us and all's well. Or keep working here, if you wish. Maybe he'd be useful to us.'

'Maybe he would be.' She hesitated. 'And… and might I some day buy your bakery?' Grace asked timidly. 'I'd like nothing better.'

Both Wilsons nodded. 'The war will end soon, Gracie,' Mr Wilson assured her. 'You'll be doing a favour for old Lord Thomson. How hard can this be?'

Grace had sent a note to Mr Selway and was greeted by him the next morning as she opened the shop.

'We'll go at once,' Mr Selway told her. 'I've

heard tales of Dartmoor and how fearsomely bad
it is. Let's spring the man while we can.'

'Must I be there, too?'

He nodded. 'I fear so. Lord Thomson stipulated
there would be three signatures on the parole document. Yours and mine, signed and notarised in
the presence of the prison's governor—a man
called Captain Shortland, I believe.'

'Three?'

Wordlessly, he took the parole document from
a folder and opened it to show her the first signature. Grace gasped. 'The Duke of Clarence?'

'Sailor Billy, himself.' Mr Selway put away the
parole. 'Let's go get a man out of prison, Gracie.'

And they would have, the very next day, if
news had not circulated through all of England—
glorious news, news so spectacular that all of
Quimby, at any rate, had trouble absorbing it.
After nearly a generation of war, it was suddenly
over. Cornered, trapped, his army slipping away,
the allies moving ever closer, Napoleon had been
forced to abdicate.

Mr Selway told Grace he must return to London, muttering something about 'details' that he
did not explain.

'If the war is over, will the American return
home?' she asked, as he came by the bakery in
mid-March. She didn't want to sound too hopeful, but as each day had passed, Grace realised
how little she wanted to honour Lord Thomson's

will, not if it meant the continuing animosity of the new marquis, who still remained in residence.

'Alas, no. That is a separate conflict. We still have a parolee on our hands, or at least, I think we do,' he told her. He nodded his thanks as she put a generous handful of Quimby Crèmes in a paper for him. 'Our recent peace could be worse for the Americans, if better for us.'

'How?' she asked, embarrassed at her ignorance of war.

'Now we can focus all our British might on the pesky American war.' He nodded to her. 'I expect I will be back soon, though. War seems to grind on.'

He was back in less than a week, knocking on the bakery door after they had closed for the night and she was sweeping up. She let him in and he gave her a tired smile.

'I am weary of post-chaises!' he told her, shaking his head when she tried to help him off with his overcoat. 'I just dropped by to tell you that we are going to Dartmoor tomorrow.' He sighed. 'Captain Daniel Duncan is still ours.'

She could not say she was pleased, and she knew her discomfort showed on her face. Mr Selway put his arm around her. 'Buck up, my dear. At least we needn't *stay* in Dartmoor.' He gave her shoulder a squeeze. 'Let's make old Lord Thomson proud of us Englishmen.'

Chapter Three

Grace knew she had a fertile imagination. After only a brief hour in Dartmoor, she knew not even the cleverest person on earth could imagine such a place.

Her mood had not been sanguine, but she credited their first stop of the morning to the lowering of her spirits. Mr Selway had had the key to the dower house and said they would visit her new home first, as he handed her into the post-chaise.

When they had arrived, the solicitor had unlocked the door and they found themselves in an empty house.

'I thought the will mentioned house and contents,' Grace said, as she looked around the bare sitting room, where even the curtains had been removed.

A muscle began to work in Mr Selway's jaw.

'Wait here,' he said. He turned on his heel and left the dower house.

Grace wandered from room to room, admiring the pleasant view from uncurtained windows, even as she shook her head over Lord Thomson's petty nature.

Mr Selway had returned in no better humour. He walked in the door and threw up his hands. 'Such drama! Such wounded pride! Lord Thomson can't imagine what happened to the furniture in the dower house and heartily resents my accusation that he emptied it out like a fishmonger's offal basket.' He shook his head. 'He says all will be restored to its proper place.'

'I won't hold my breath,' Grace said.

'Wise of you. There might be furniture here, but I think Lord Thomson will send his minions to the attics to find the dregs.'

'We don't need much.'

'What a relief. I doubt you'll get much!'

It's good you did not ask me if I am afraid, Grace thought, as they left Quimby by mid-morning and began a steady climb onto the moors. *This spares me a lie of monumental proportions.*

The higher they climbed, the colder the air blew, until she had wrapped herself tight in an all-too-inadequate shawl. Shivering, she looked on the granite outcroppings and the few trees. 'Is it April here, or only April in the rest of England?' she asked.

'Many have remarked that even nature conspires against this place,' Mr Selway commented. 'I have heard complaints about the change in atmospherics around Dartmoor.' He glanced out the window. 'Could England have chosen a more unaccommodating place for a prison? I doubt it, perhaps that is the point.'

They were both silent as the post-chaise wound its way along a dirt track of considerable width, as though armies had marched abreast. *Or prisoners,* Grace thought. *Poor men.*

When she thought they would wind no higher, the fog yielded to cold rain. She peered out of the window as the chaise entered a bowl-shaped valley. And there was Dartmoor Prison, an isolated pile of granite with walls surrounding it like a cartwheel. She looked at Mr Selway. 'Perhaps it's a good thing old Lord Thomson never got here,' she said. 'It would have broken his heart.' *It's breaking mine,* Grace told herself.

'There must be thousands of prisoners inside,' she said, touching the small carton of biscuits she had brought along as a gift, suddenly wishing it were loaves and fishes and greatly magnified.

'The prison's first inmates were Frenchmen, acquired during the war,' Mr Selway told her, his eyes on the tall grey walls as the carriage drew nearer. 'I don't know when Americans started arriving, but I can surmise it was after 1812.'

'I don't want to go in there,' Grace whispered

as the chaise stopped and a squad of Royal Marines approached at port arms.

'Who can blame you?' the solicitor murmured. 'Here we go, Gracie.'

He rolled down the glass and handed over the papers. The corporal took them inside a small stone building by the gate. He was gone long enough for Grace to feel even more uneasy. 'There is nothing about this process to put someone at ease, is there?' she commented to Mr Selway.

'No, indeed, child,' he replied. 'I've been in Newgate—just as a solicitor, mind!—and it's the same there. I don't know why it is that everyone seeking entrance, even by legal means, is made to feel so small.'

The marine returned their papers and hitched himself up next to the coachman. The chaise rolled through the first gate, which led to another gate. There appeared to be three gates and then an interior wall that bisected the circle, with a still-smaller gate yielding to what must be the prison blocks beyond.

Mr Selway eyed the grey government buildings. 'It takes a lot of paper-pushing to run a prison, I suppose. Even misery must be documented.'

'You sound like a radical,' Grace whispered, her eyes widening at her first sight of prisoners, dressed in yellow smocks and unloading supplies into a warehouse.

'Do I?' he asked. 'Fancy that.' He tightened his grip on her hand as the chaise slowed and stopped, and the coachman set the brake. 'End of the line. We walk from here.'

The marine jumped down from his perch and opened the door, holding out his gloved hand for Grace. She took a deep breath and regretted it immediately. A foul stench rose from the very stones of the prison. Grace put her hand over her nose, but it did little good.

They were led immediately into an office on the second floor of a building that looked out on to the prison yards, as though the caretakers of misery felt they would be somehow beyond the noisome odours, sights and sounds below. She looked out of the window in horrified fascination. The prison appeared to be divided into pie-shaped wedges with high walls around each three-storey building.

After a long wait, she and Mr Selway were ushered into the prison governor's office, a comfortable haven with sweet-smelling fragrances in bowls on every table. The governor introduced himself, holding a scented handkerchief to his nose, then took their papers. He spent a long time looking at the signature that had surprised Grace yesterday.

'Imagine,' he said at last, flicking his handkerchief at them, as if they smelled bad, too. 'What possible interest his Grace has in this one, I can't understand.' He waved his handkerchief again.

'Go on. Take him. Take them all! What an argumentative, carping lot.' He looked at the letter again, then at the clerk hovering at his elbow. 'Daniel Duncan, captain of the *Orontes*. Building Four. Keep an eye on him, for God's sake.'

He turned back to the paperwork in front of him. They were dismissed. Mr Selway lingered a moment. 'Captain? Could Miss Curtis remain here while I fetch the prisoner?'

Shortland frowned at Grace. 'No. This damned document specifically states she is to accompany you to retrieve the prisoner.' He looked at the corporal at attention in the open door. 'Send a squad. She'll be safe enough.'

'Safe enough doesn't thrill my bones,' Mr Selway muttered as they followed the marine downstairs. 'Still… Chin up, Gracie. This shouldn't take long.'

Surrounded by a squad of marines, they entered the prison courtyard. 'Don't look at anyone. Eyes ahead,' Mr Selway murmured, keeping a tight grip on her hand.

She did as he said, taking shallow breaths as the stench grew the closer they came to a single prison block. Two men in plain uniforms stood at the entrance, blocking it with their muskets. As the squad advanced, one of them stepped forwards.

'We're here for Daniel Duncan of the *Orontes*,' the corporal said. 'Produce him at once.'

One of the warders shook his head. 'Can't.

He's ill. You'll have to fetch him out.' His eyes stopped on Grace and she felt her face begin to burn. 'Good Lord deliver us! He's halfway back. Stall Fourteen, I think.'

The squad of marines pressed closer to Grace and Mr Selway as they entered Block Four. Even above the odour of too many unwashed bodies, Grace could smell mould and damp. As dark as it was, the walls seemed to shine and drip. *Dear God, how could anyone survive a day in this place?* she thought, trying not to look at the misery around her: men lying on the rankest straw, others huddled together, one man muttering to himself and then shrieking, someone else coughing and coughing and then gasping to breathe.

'We've passed into hell,' she whispered to Mr Selway, who clung tighter to her hand.

Guarded by the marines, they walked half the length of the building, which appeared to be comprised of open compartments that reminded her forcibly of the stalls in her father's stable. Ten or more men appeared to be crammed into each stall, sitting or standing cheek by jowl.

''Twas built for far fewer,' the marine next to her said.

Grace's feet crunched over what felt like eggshells. It might have been glass; she was too terrified to look down. She walked on what she fervently hoped was nothing worse than slime and mould. The straw underfoot was slippery with it.

'Here,' the corporal said, and there was no denying the relief in his voice. 'Daniel Duncan? Captain Duncan?'

Grace screwed up her courage and peered into the enclosure. A man lay on the odourous straw, his head in someone's lap. All around him were men equally ragged, some barely upright.

'There he be,' said one of the scarecrows, gesturing to the man on the filthy floor. 'What can thee possibly do more to him that hasn't already been done?'

His voice was stringent and burred with an accent she was unfamiliar with. Grace looked at him and saw nothing in his expression to fear. She looked at Daniel Duncan and her heart went out to him. She came closer, the marines right with her, which forced some of the prisoners to leave the enclosure. She knelt by the still form.

'Captain Duncan?' she said. 'Can you hear me?'

After a long moment, the man nodded. Even that bare effort seemed to exhaust him.

'Mr Selway and I are here to parole you to Quarle, the estate of the late Lord Thomson, Marquis of Quarle. Do you know that he was your father?'

Another long pause, as her words seemed to seep into his tired brain, and then another nod. 'I know,' he whispered. She had to lean close to hear him. 'I'm dying, though. Best you leave me alone to do that.'

'You can't die!' she exclaimed and the prisoners close around her chuckled.

'Like to see you stop him,' a Yankee said. 'It's the only right we have left and, by God, we're good at it.'

'But we're here to parole him,' Grace said. 'Mr Selway, do something!'

Oddly, Mr Selway backed away, as though he hadn't the stomach for such desperation. She hadn't expected that of him, but then, he was a gentleman, and not the baker's assistant she had become, used to throwing slops on middens.

'I don't know what I can do,' he said.

She shivered, then knelt in the straw. 'Maybe we can help you,' she said.

Duncan shook his head. 'Too late, miss.' He turned his head slightly. 'Choose another.'

'But...'

She stopped, listening to another commotion near the entrance to the prison block. The prisoners started to hiss in unison, which made her jump in terror. She looked at the enclosure entrance to see a warden carrying a cudgel. He spoke to Mr Selway, who looked at her.

'I am to go with him and sign yet another infernal paper.'

'Don't leave me here!' Grace said, her hand at her throat.

'I'll be right back, Gracie,' Mr Selway said uncertainly. 'You're safe with the marines.' He hurried after the warden. 'I'll bring a stretcher,' he shouted over his shoulder, as the hissing started again.

'Thee is safe with us, miss,' said the first prisoner who had spoken to her. 'We mean thee no harm.' He chuckled. 'Besides, thee has marines and we don't.'

She jumped again as Daniel Duncan reached out slowly to touch her arm. One of the marines moved closer, but she waved him back. 'Please, miss,' Duncan whispered, 'I have an idea.'

He looked into her eyes, then up at the marines. He did it twice, and she thought she understood. Grace stood up. 'Would you mind giving this dying man some room?' she asked the corporal. 'I'd feel a great deal braver if you would guard the entrance to this enclosure. You can face out. It might be safer for all of us. I don't trust the ones roving in the corridor.'

'Nor I,' the corporal said. He glared at the prisoners in the enclosure. 'No trouble, mind, or you'll be taken to the *cachot* and left there to rot!'

Can there be a worse place than this? Grace thought. With an effort, she turned her attention back to the dying man. 'Captain Duncan, what can I do?' She knelt again, taking his hand. His bones felt as hollow as a bird's.

'Take someone in my place,' he said again. He coughed and Grace wanted to put her hands over her ears at the harshness of the sound. 'Now! Choose!'

He closed his eyes in exhaustion, coughed again, took a gasping breath that went on and on, and died. His hand went slack in hers.

Horrified, Grace sat back on her heels. She looked around her, but all the prisoners were looking at their captain, the man who must have led them well, because they were in tears. Two men—mere boys—sobbed in earnest.

She glanced at the marines, who were facing out, concentrating on the prisoners milling in the passageway. *Lord Thomson would want me to honour his son's dying wish,* she thought.

'Quickly now, who should it be?' she whispered, as one of the men rolled his captain to the side of the enclosure and shrouded him with a scrap of burlap. No one came forwards to be chosen. They were stalwart men—that she knew without knowing more. *Choose, Grace,* she ordered herself. *Just choose.*

She knew then who it would be. He was sitting on the foul floor, leaning his head against the rough wood of the enclosure, eyes half-open. He looked as starved as the others, no healthier or sicker than his mates. What she saw in him, she could not tell, except that he was the man who would take his captain's place.

Grace touched his arm. His eyes opened wider; they were blue as the ocean.

'Who are you?'

'Rob Inman,' he said. His mates quickly moved him forwards to lie down where his captain had died.

'I choose you, Rob Inman.'

Chapter Four

The whole business was deceptive in its ease. In less than a minute, Grace received an education in how desperation can grease the wheels. The only one who seemed to harbour any misgivings was the chosen man.

'Don't do this,' he said, not opening his eyes. 'Surely someone else is sicker.'

'Nope. Thee is our ideal candidate,' said the sailor who had spoken to Grace first.

He did something then that touched Grace's heart and assured her she had nothing to fear from these rough, stinking men: he kissed Robert Inman on the forehead. 'Thee is a sailing master fit to fight another day.'

'No. No.'

'Aye, lad. No argument now. We'll see thee again in Nantucket.' The man—he must have been a Quaker—transferred his gaze to Grace. 'Keep him safe, miss.'

'I will. I promise,' she whispered.

She rocked back on her heels, ready to stand, when she heard the prisoners in the passageway hissing again. The warden with the cudgel reappeared, followed by a very concerned-looking Mr Selway and other marines carrying a stretcher.

Mr Selway sighed with relief to see her safe and looked at Rob Inman. Grace held her breath. In the gloom of the stall and his obvious eagerness to be gone, would he notice?

He didn't. Mr Selway motioned to the stretcher bearers, who were none too gentle as they picked up the sailing master and plopped him on a stretcher marked with yellowish stains. Inman groaned and opened his eyes, reaching out for his mates, who gave him three feeble cheers and sent him on his way. Grace looked at the Quaker. 'Thank you for doing that,' she whispered. 'I could not have thought so fast.'

'Nothing to it,' he whispered back. 'Dartmoor sharpens the intellect.'

She had to smile at that. *And England thinks to defeat these men,* she told herself. *Think again, Johnny Bull.* 'I wish I could help you,' she whispered.

He indicated Rob Inman with his eyes. 'Thee has.'

There was nothing more to say, not with Mr Selway looking at her with such a worried expression, and the prisoners starting to shift about, as though wishing her gone, and with her, their sailing master. *I'm sorry we were too late to save your son, Lord Thomson,* she thought, near tears. 'Let us leave this place now, Mr Selway,' she said.

She experienced momentary terror when the warden made them stop at Captain Shortland's office again. 'Can't we just leave?' she asked Mr Selway.

'You have to sign the document releasing Captain Duncan,' the solicitor said. 'I signed when I was in here earlier.'

Anything, anything to get away, she thought, glancing at Rob Inman on the stretcher. He had shielded his eyes against the glare of the sun. She looked around quickly; everyone looked alike: thin, yellow-smocked, with hollow cheeks. She doubted the governor of the prison could tell any of them apart. Still…

She willed herself calm. 'Mr Selway, do get… Captain Duncan in the chaise. The light is bothering his eyes.'

She held her breath. Surely no one would have any need to examine Rob Inman closely. To her relief, the solicitor indicated the post-chaise and addressed the marines. 'Lads, help the captain into the chaise.'

Grace hurried up the stairs to the governor's office. Handkerchief still to his nostrils, Captain Shortland stood at the window, watching the marines deposit Inman in the chaise. He returned to his desk, his lips tight together with every evidence of displeasure.

He pointed to where she should sign. 'He'll be nothing but trouble to you, I warrant, although he looks harmless enough now. Damned Americans.'

Grace signed her name, wondering if she would end up in a place like Dartmoor if anyone got wind of her deception. She signed more documents, the last of which the governor folded into a pouch. 'This is the parole,' he told her. 'You are to keep your eyes on this man at all times. If he escapes or leaves Quarle without you, he will be shot on sight.' The governor breathed deeply of the handkerchief. 'One less rascal for me.'

He handed her the parole with a short laugh. 'One less, but now we can turn our full attention to the United States. What with Boney soon to be exiled, this prison may harbour more of those damned Americans!'

Please, God, no, Grace thought, alarmed. *They are already so mistreated.* She opened her mouth to tell the prison governor precisely that, but closed it. He didn't seem like someone concerned with the death of Americans.

He turned to a clerk, handing him the documents she had falsified by carrying out Captain Duncan's death wish. *What will come of this?* Grace asked herself, as the clerk took the papers to his own high desk in the next room. *Thank the Almighty no one knows Rob Inman from a watering can.*

* * *

It wasn't until they dropped off the marine at the final stone gate that Grace drew a regular breath. She could not help the sigh that escaped her.

'I'm sorry you had to be there, Grace,' Mr Selway said. 'Well, the worst is over. Captain Duncan, lean forwards and I'll cut those bonds.'

'No need, sir,' the man said, as he worked the knot with an expert's skill and slipped his thin wrists out of the rope. 'Marines may sail on ships, but no one said they can tie a sailor's knot.'

Grace couldn't help smiling. Rob Inman watched them, alert, his blue eyes sunken, but glowing with fever.

Impulsively, Grace leaned forwards and touched the back of her hand to his dirty forehead. 'You're burning,' she said. She looked at the solicitor. 'Mr Selway, perhaps we should stop here in Princetown and get some—'

'No!' Inman interrupted, his voice weak but emphatic. 'Drive on. I want out of this damned cold valley more than I want fever powders, miss. Just drive on. Please.'

Mr Selway nodded. 'Good enough, lad,' he murmured.

With a sigh of his own, Inman leaned back. He wrapped his arms around himself, shivering despite his fever. Without a word, Grace took her lap robe and covered him. Eyes serious, he nodded his thanks. In a moment, he slept.

'I'll summon the physician as soon as we have the captain in bed in the dower house,' Mr Selway whispered to her. 'That is, if Lord Thomson—bless his tiny, atrophied heart—has thought to return the beds and linens.'

Leaning against the side of the chaise, Inman had slept. He opened his eyes now and then, looking around in surprise each time. Grace had watched his hands. For a good hour, he kept them balled into tight fists. After one time when he opened his eyes, his startled expression unmistakable, Grace covered one fist briefly with her hand. He looked into her eyes as an abused pup would, wondering what she would do to him. When he closed his eyes this time, she noticed that his hands opened and he relaxed.

'We mean you no harm, Captain,' Grace murmured.

As soon as they had left the bowl-like valley cupping Dartmoor Prison, the sun shone again. The grass even seemed greener and hawthorn hedges sprouted white blossoms all along the highway. *This place is so evil even spring stays away,* Grace thought, with a shudder.

The coachman stopped by a river, shady and overhung with branches already leafing out. 'Time to water t'horses,' he called down to the occupants of the chaise.

Inman opened his eyes no more than part way, as if even that much exertion was nearly beyond him. As Grace watched him, he gazed with growing interest at the stream. In mere seconds, the parolee shrugged off the lap rug and threw open the door. He was a tall man and did not need the step to be lowered to hurtle himself from the chaise.

'I say there!' Mr Selway called after him.

He didn't even look back. With a stagger, he righted himself and plunged into the stream as Grace stared, then leaped to her feet, too, ahead of Mr Selway.

'Please don't run away!' she shouted after him as she jumped from the chaise.

Ignoring her, he waded into the water. Grace stood on the bank, ready to leap in after the parolee. She raised her skirt and petticoat—she could see that the stream came barely above the tall man's knees—then lowered them as she watched the sailing master, her mouth open.

He had stopped by a bright clump of greenery growing in the water. With an audible sob, Inman grabbed a handful of the greens and stuffed them in his mouth. He chewed and swallowed, then snatched another handful, and then another.

'My God, what is he doing?' Mr Selway said, standing beside Grace on the bank.

Grace felt her heart go out to the thin prisoner. 'I believe it's watercress,' she whispered, her eyes still on the man she had chosen. 'Mr Selway, he's starving.'

They watched him as he moved to another clump of watercress. Bits of greenery clustered in his beard as he picked one more handful and walked back to the bank. Mr Selway gave him a hand up and he stood there, watercress in hand, like a man with springtime posies.

'Do you want to take them with you?' Grace asked. 'You needn't, really. There is lots of food at the dower house—or at least there will be—and those will only wilt.'

She tried to take the watercress from him, but he shook his head and stepped away from her.

'Let him be, Gracie,' Mr Selway murmured. 'Let him be.' He took the parolee by the elbow and guided him back to the chaise. 'Let me help you in, Captain. There's a good lad.'

They resumed the journey. Grace's eyes filled with tears as she watched Inman admire the watercress he clutched to his chest, unmindful of the damp. Several times before he slept again, he raised the little handful of greenery to his nose, just to smell its peppery fragrance.

He grew alarmed when they stopped in Exeter near a group of red-coated militiamen, laughing and joking with each other. 'Easy, lad,' Mr Selway said, a hand on his arm. 'I'll send Gracie into the public house here for some broth and maybe a pasty. Nothing too rich, mind,' he warned her as he handed over some coins.

As she waited for the food, Grace stood by the window, watching Rob Inman in the chaise. His eyes never left the militiamen. He looked solemn anyway—his mouth was slightly downturned by nature—but there was no disguising the fear on his face. *And what was Dartmoor prison like for you, Rob Inman, turned Duncan?* she asked herself, unable to help the shiver that travelled her spine like a bird on a wire.

Inman wanted to gulp down the broth, but Mr Selway was firm on insisting that he sip instead. The solicitor thought to limit him to half a pasty, until the parolee fixed him with a glare that would have cut through lead, something surprising in one so weak.

'On the other hand, maybe you know what's best,' Mr Selway said smoothly, as the parolee refused to relinquish the remainder of the pasty.

Grace couldn't help a smile. 'Mr Selway, the governor of the prison did say he would be a lot of trouble.' It was only the mildest tease, but Rob stopped chewing and looked at her.

'I'm no trouble to anyone, miss,' he said around the pasty in his mouth. 'Well, maybe just to those who get between me and a good wind.' He was so serious. 'Aye, that would sum it up.'

Listening to him, Grace realised she had never heard an American accent before, if that's what this was. There was just the faintest sound of vaguely familiar diction, and then the careful, clipped words originating from a distant shore. She liked the stringent sound.

Then he was asleep again, the food barely swallowed, crumbs lodged in his beard to keep the watercress company. *That will all come off to-morrow,* Grace decided. *And from the way you're scratching your head, I'll get a servant to shave you bald. And if not a willing servant, then I will do it.*

They arrived at the dower house after dark, with only the moon to show the way. There were so few lights burning in the manor house that she wondered if Lord Thomson was still in residence. Mr Selway had his own opinion about that. 'What a miser he is,' he said, making no effort to hide his disdain. 'I just can't bring myself to trust people who sit in the gloom to save a groat.'

'Do you think he intends to remain long?' Grace asked. 'He could be a trial.'

'I am certain he will be, Gracie. No, I think Lord Thomson will stay long enough to make himself thoroughly unpleasant, then return to London. He will probably pop back unexpectedly every now and then, yearning to catch us in some misdeed.'

Grace shivered. 'I wish him gone now.'

'So he will be soon! Patience, my dear.'

She couldn't help her audible sigh of relief to see furniture in the dower house. On closer inspection, it was much as Mr Selway had feared: Lord Thomson had emptied out the manor's attics. As she gazed at the mismatched chairs in the breakfast room and the rump-sprung sofa in the sitting room, Grace couldn't say she was surprised.

While Rob Inman swayed at the foot of the stairs, holding on to the railing, Grace hurried upstairs. Beds had been returned to all four bed-chambers, complemented by bureaus with drawers missing and a leg gone and propped nearly level with a chunk of wood.

She glanced in the smallest chamber she had designated for herself, surprised to see a small fire in the grate and shabby curtains returned to the window. She heard a noise across the narrow hall and peeked into the chamber she had thought to reserve for Captain Duncan.

She didn't recognise the man, but he must have been one of the old retainers who did odd jobs around the manor. Dressed in a nondescript pair of trousers and a smock, he shook out a patched coverlet for the bed.

Grace cleared her throat. 'And you are...?'

'Emery's my name,' he told her, as though she should have known. 'You don't remember me? I rake the ground after the sheep have grazed.'

'Emery?' she said. 'I don't recall...' She blushed and stopped herself. 'And now I am being foolish. You must remember, I've only been coming to Quarle for the last few months, when Lord Thomson could no longer walk to Quimby.'

'Aye, miss, and I work on the grounds. That explains it.' He indicated the partly made bed. 'I thought to have this all ready, Miss Curtis.' He peered beyond her into the hall. 'Did the prison release Captain Duncan?'

'Yes, indeed. He's downstairs and he's so tired. I thought I would have to hurry up here and make the beds. It appears you have beat me to the effort.'

Emery bowed, which made Grace smile. 'Gracie, I think I am destined to be your butler.'

'Emery, Lord Thomson would never allow us a butler, even if you are just a gardener,' she said quietly.

Emery spread out the coverlet. 'True. He turned me off the estate. Considering that I have no place to go, I thought I would appoint myself butler.' He tucked in a neat corner. 'It's about t'only job I haven't held here, so why not, says I?'

He seemed to be imperturbably ignoring her, which amused her. 'Emery, there can't possibly be any provisions for a butler in Lord Thomson's will,' she told him.

'Then I will fit right in, Miss Curtis. I have very few needs and I've always wanted to buttle. How about I lend you a hand with Captain Duncan?'

Grace nodded, relieved to find so willing an ally, where she had expected none. 'Yes, by all means, lend a hand.'

Rob Inman seemed determined to make his own way up the stairs, pausing once or twice with Emery hovering by his elbow, and Mr Selway watching his progress from behind, ready to catch him if he stumbled.

With an exasperated groan, he stopped at the top of the stairs. 'Honestly,' was all he said and his gaze seemed to take them all in. He did not object, though, when Emery took him by the arm and steered him slowly into his chamber. He looked back at her, a quizzical expression on his face. 'Miss, I'm being abducted. Granted, it's happening at glacial speed,' he declared, which struck her as the funniest thing she had heard in weeks.

Grace laughed out loud, which brought a fleeting smile to his face. 'Thank the Almighty,' he said. 'Glad to know you have a sense of humour. We might need it.'

Emery seemed determined to be of service, which touched Grace. He helped Inman off with his shoes, shaking his head. 'Lad, it's been a rough time, eh? No stockings and no shoelaces, and not much leather.'

'I think the rats were as hungry as we were,' Inman said. He yawned and looked at Grace. 'Pardon me, miss, but I'm lousy and fleabitten and not worth an "Ave". Just give me a sheet and I'll sleep on the floor.'

Grace shook her head. 'You'll sleep on the bed, Captain. Tomorrow's soon enough for delousing. You won't object if I cut your hair?'

'Shorter the better,' he said after another yawn. He lay down and turned toward the wall, as Emery hitched the coverlet higher and rested his hand briefly on the parolee's shoulder. 'Goodnight, all you nursemaids.'

The three of them left the room. Mr Selway spoke first on the landing. 'Our Captain Duncan seems not to mind taking charge. I think we've been told what to do.'

They went down and sat belowstairs while Emery took some food from a basket. 'Mrs Clyde had me bring over this basket. She said it's no trouble to prepare a little more for the dower house.'

'It won't be until Lord Thomson gets wind of his staff's philanthropy,' the solicitor said. He bit into a beef sandwich. 'Grace. Emery. I do have some modest discretionary funds for the maintenance of Captain Duncan here in the dower house. I was going to hire a cook, but if you will do the honours, Grace, then we can stretch the budget to include our new friend Emery.'

'I certainly can cook,' she replied, on firm ground now. 'And bake. I think that must be why Lord Thomson wanted me here in the first place. I can think of no other reason.'

Mr Selway smiled. 'Actually, Grace, before he died, he told me he hoped you and the captain would fall in love and marry.'

Grace laughed and then sobered as she remembered the scene in the prison, the one Mr Selway had not witnessed. *The captain is dead,* she thought with a sudden pang, as the two men chuckled and then conversed with each other. *And here is Rob Inman.* She had to smile again, thinking of Lord Thomson with real fondness. 'He was a funny old stick, to get such a notion,' she told her companions. 'Pigs will probably fly first, wouldn't you agree?'

Chapter Five

'I suppose stranger things have happened, Grace,' Mr Selway teased. He took another sandwich out of the basket and wrapped it in a napkin. 'I'm going to that closet off the sitting room that I have dubbed the dower-house bookroom—my, aren't I grandiose?—to make a careful scrutiny of Captain Duncan's parole and Lord Thomson's whimsical will.' He stood up, nodding to Emery. 'If Grace agrees, I believe you will be a welcome addition to our staff.'

She nodded. 'Our staff? What an exaggeration! Mind, Emery, this position only lasts until the war ends and the captain returns to America.'

Emery winked elaborately. 'If you're man and wife by then, I can be your butler in the United States. I don't much fancy the workhouse.'

Mr Selway laughed and left the kitchen. Her eyes merry, Grace finished her sandwich while the old man swept up the crumbs from the table and carefully deposited them in the basket.

'Mrs Clyde said she'll give us a pot of porridge with lots of sugar and cream,' Emery told her.

'After the captain has been deloused and shaved, I'll go to the greengrocer's in Quimby,' Grace said. 'He is so thin. I can certainly feed him back to health.' She shook her head. 'As for the other matter, we'll let Captain Duncan decide whom he marries.'

'Aye, Gracie.' Emery yawned elaborately. 'Now, if we can't think of anything else to rescue, I'll find my bed.' He stood up and stretched, then walked to the door off the servants' dining room.

'I only wish we could pay you more than the barest pittance.'

''Tis enough. This will be interesting.'

I don't doubt that for a moment, Grace thought as she climbed the stairs. She opened the door quietly to Rob Inman's room, listening to his even breathing. She closed the door softly behind her.

A lengthy bath won't come a moment too soon, she thought, as she went to her own room. *He smells worse than a kitchen midden in August.* She would probably have to burn everything he was wearing and his bedding, too. *The least I can do is return him to America in better shape than Captain Shortland gave him to me,* she thought.

She stood in front of the fire in her room, hands outstretched, wondering why she had ever agreed to any condition in Lord Thomson's will.

'Emery is right. It will be interesting,' she murmured, as she folded her clothing on the battered bureau, with its mirror in dire need of re-silvering. 'Thank God for Emery.'

Grace burrowed under her covers, pulling her knees close to her chest for warmth, missing the yeasty fragrance that permeated the bakery. *Grace, at least* you *are not incarcerated in Dartmoor Prison,* she reminded herself. 'Maybe it's best not to think about such things,' she murmured into her pillow.

Her sleep had been troubled. She kept seeing the real Captain Duncan, his eyes closed in death, his silent, stinking men grouped about him. Over and over in her dream, she looked at Rob Inman, then chose him. Why him and no other? She had no idea, but there he was in her mind's eye as she tossed and turned, waiting patiently as he had probably waited since the *Orontes* was captured. What else is there to do in prison but wait?

She wasn't sure what woke her hours later. She wasn't perfectly convinced that she had even been asleep, not with her mind still filled with the horror that was Dartmoor, contrasted with the unexpected kindness in the eyes of Rob Inman's shipmates, as she knelt in the odourous straw by their dead leader.

She sat up, listening. There was no mistaking it. Someone was moving down the narrow hallway to the stairs.

Her heart hammering in her breast, Grace threw back her covers and reached for her shawl. She opened her door to see Rob Inman walking quietly down the stairs.

'Rob Inman, you had better not be planning an escape. You're taller than I am, but I think I could stop you.'

He stopped and looked around, startled at first, then amused. 'You probably could,' he told her, then sank down on the step. 'I tried to wrestle a rat last week and ended up losing my shoelaces.'

She sat beside him, but not too close. 'Are you hungry?' she whispered.

He nodded. 'If my left leg didn't smell so bad, I'd probably gnaw on it. D'ye think there's anything edible in the kitchen besides that old man who thinks he's a butler?'

Grace put her hand to her mouth to stop her laugh. 'I think there's another sandwich or two in the basket. Shall we find out?'

He nodded and tried to rise, then shook his head. 'Best you go on and save yourself, miss. I think I'm done for.'

'Spare me the drama,' she teased as she started down the stairs. 'Promise you won't jump parole, and I'll find you a sandwich.'

'I can't make a promise like that,' he said quickly.

'You must, on your word as a gentleman,' she replied just as quickly. 'You will be shot dead if you break parole. I'm not quizzing you.'

He gave her a long look, as if weighing the

very marrow of her bones. 'If I must, I will. But know this—Captain Duncan may have been a gentleman, for all that he was a bastard. Rob Inman is no gentleman and never was.'

'I suppose that will have to do,' she said dubiously, puzzled about this man old Lord Thomson had foisted on her. No, that she had foisted on herself in Dartmoor. 'But I have questions.'

'I imagine you do.' He grinned. 'And I'm still hungry.'

She found the basket easily enough in the dark kitchen and tiptoed with it upstairs, after pausing a moment to smile at the sound of Emery's snoring. She handed the captain the remaining sandwich; he waited not a moment to demolish it and look around for more. She followed it with one of her own Quimby Crèmes. The cook at the manor house had obviously visited the Wilsons' bakery a few days ago. Grace had made these just before the visit to Dartmoor.

'I could eat more of these,' he said, his mouth full.

'You will. I made them,' she said proudly. 'My own recipe.'

He looked at her, a question in his eyes.

'I'm a baker for the Wilsons in Quimby,' she told him. 'Well, I was, and I will be again once you are sorted out.'

'You're going to sort me out?' the parolee asked, humour in his voice. He might have been hungry and weak, but he wasn't slow. 'How on earth did you end up as Captain Duncan's keeper?' He popped the rest of the biscuit into his mouth. 'If that's what you are.'

'I suppose I am, in a way. Your keeper now,' she mused. 'The old Lord Thomson—I wouldn't give you a penny for the new one—used to visit the bakery shop regularly and he liked my Crèmes. He was full of crochets, but I never paid his ill humour any mind.' She couldn't help the tears that welled in her eyes and hoped they didn't show. 'I think I was almost his only friend.' She also couldn't help the way her voice hardened. 'His own relatives were just waiting for him to die. Shame on them.'

'I don't see the connection, Miss…Grace.'

'Nor do I. For some reason, Lord Thomson provided me with the dower house to live in and thirty pounds a year. I suppose that will last until the new Lord Thomson works out some way to stop it.'

'I gather you could use the money,' he commented.

'I could, indeed. I intend to buy the bakery some day.'

'But you don't sound confident Lord Thomson's kindness will continue.'

'I'm certain it won't,' she replied, with no qualms. 'People like that generally get their way, or haven't you noticed?'

'Aye, lass, I've noticed.' He lowered his voice.

'Why did the old man parole Captain Duncan? I know his origins. Dan was never shy about them. Was it a case of the old rascal wanting to help his bastard son from America?'

'I suppose that was it,' she replied. 'You'll find this amusing, but Mr Selway told me that Lord Thomson had some vision of Captain Duncan and me falling in love and marrying.'

'Then you would have had to reckon with the captain's wife and two children on Nantucket!' He sighed heavily then. 'Wish I could get word to them about what has befallen as good a man as I ever knew.'

'I suppose it will have to wait until the war is over and you go home,' she said. To lighten the moment, she added, 'And I suppose you have similar entanglements to prevent my falling in love with you!'

'Well, no,' he said quietly. 'I did have a wife, but she died. A Nantucket girl, like Captain Duncan's Bess. She understood the sea. They do, on Nantucket.'

'I'm sorry for your loss,' Grace said. 'I didn't mean to make light of it.'

'How were you to know? It's been almost four years, but I am sorry, too,' he told her. He turned reflective then, leaning on his elbow on the stairs. 'What with the sea and then the war, I reckon I spent more time on the *Orontes* than in my own bed on Orange Street. Oh, and let's not forget the attractions of Dartmoor.'

She thought about the seafarers Rob Inman

had left behind. Something about the man beside her seemed to loosen her tongue. It couldn't have been an air of capability, not with him so weak he had to prop himself up on the stairs. Still, she wanted to talk to him.

'Tell me. The sailor in that dreadful stall. He said "thee" and "thou".'

The expression in Rob's eyes seemed to soften. 'You have to know Nantucket. It's an island of seafarers, many of them Quakers.'

'Are you...?'

'Not I. Most of my neighbours back home are.'

He was silent, probably thinking of his island. She touched his arm lightly. 'I've never quite been able to understand why things happen the way they do. Maybe people have to be really old to understand.'

They were both silent. She reached for his hand. 'Let me give you a hand up, Captain Duncan,' she said. 'Remember, you *are* Captain Duncan, you must be. Maybe you can sleep, now that you've had something to eat. Tomorrow comes early and we have quite a morning planned for you.'

'Eh?' He was shaky on his feet, so she held his hand until he regained his balance.

'It involves a bath and pine-tar soap and short hair again and no beard. Even if you're truly attached to prison yellow, your clothes are going in the burn pit.'

'You can have them and gladly, too, but I don't

have anything else to wear,' he reminded her. 'Prisoners don't come with wardrobes.'

'Mr Selway is two steps ahead of you,' she assured him, as they slowly walked up the stairs and to his room. 'Whether you like it or not, he's acquired shirts and trousers from Royal Navy stores in the Plymouth navy yard.'

'The Royal Navy? Oh, foul!'

'It's no more than checkered shirts and dark trousers. Probably what you wore on the *Orontes*.'

He smiled. 'Very much like. Will I fit them?'

'Eventually.'

He went in his room and she stood at the door. 'I have to ask, do all Americans sound like you?'

'Nay, lass,' he replied and put his finger to his lips. 'I *know* this should also be our little secret, I was born and at least partly raised in a very poor part of London. I'll tell you more tomorrow, if you're interested.'

'You're English?' she asked, surprised.

'Not any more,' he assured her. 'That's what you British don't understand, once an Englishman doesn't mean *always* an Englishman.'

'I could never be anything but English,' Grace declared.

'You're so certain?' He sat down on his bed then, as if too tired to stand. 'You speak good English for a baker's assistant. You seem a bit refined. What has England done for you lately? For me, nothing. Goodnight now.'

Chapter Six

Grace hated to admit it, but Rob Inman was right: England hadn't done much for her lately. She thought about his words long after she should have been asleep.

It was one thing to be suddenly poor. It was quite another to be treated by former friends as though she did not exist. She lay in bed, feeling her cheeks burn as she remembered the smarts and slights that came her way in the bakery, as former friends looked right through her.

And here was Rob Inman, an unwilling parolee who was making her ask questions of herself. *He's a challenge. Maybe I shouldn't have chosen him,* she thought, punching her pillow a few times in the hope of finding a comfortable spot.

But the fact remained that she *had* chosen Robert Inman and old Lord Thomson had chosen her to watch him. Her eyes grew heavy, but she had to smile at the absurdity of it all. *Lord Thomson, I fear your good intentions are going to be a lot of trouble to me,* was her last thought before she slept.

Emery was as good as his word. In the morning, he brought breakfast from the manor house and a daunting-looking cake of pine-tar soap.

'If this doesn't scare away fleas and lice, then we haven't a prayer,' he told her as they carried hot water to the tin tub he had set up outside in the overgrown garden. 'While he's soaking, I'll strip off the bed clothes and burn sulphur in that room, same's as if it was the hold of a ship after a long voyage.'

The parolee required no coaxing to adjourn to the garden for the cure. With some dignity, he wrapped a sheet around himself after Emery commanded him to drop his pathetic clothing by the rose arbour. Rob frowned to see Grace standing by the tub, testing the water.

'I don't require your services,' he protested. He wrapped the sheet tighter around his thin body.

'My thoughts precisely!' she said. 'I'm just making sure the water isn't too hot. My assignments in this endeavour are to bag your sheets and burn your prison clothes.'

Trying not to laugh, she left Rob in the garden at the mercy of Emery and his pine tar.

* * *

Mr Selway found her in the upstairs hall with the sheets and blankets bagged in a canvas sack. He followed her as she deposited the bedclothes by the garden path, next to the captain's discarded prison yellow.

They sat on a bench by the kitchen door. The solicitor opened a folder. 'Here it is, Grace, all of our restrictions dealing with a paroled prisoner of war.'

She scanned the document. 'The upshot appears to be that Captain Duncan must never be out of our sight.' She looked up. 'He can leave the estate with one of us?'

Mr Selway nodded. 'Apparently, yes, but we must sufficiently impress upon him that he is not to escape. If he does, under penalty of our own incarceration, we must immediately notify the justice of the peace and he will be shot on sight.'

'Where would he go?'

'Down to the sea. I imagine Captain Duncan could easily blend in with the seagoing crowd in Plymouth and ship out on any merchant vessel in the harbour. The fleet's always hungry for crew.'

Grace thought about that as she listened to the captain's protests at having his hair washed yet again, from the other side of the shrubbery. 'Surely Lord Thomson didn't want his only son to use a parole to escape?'

'I don't know what he intended. Indeed, he never knew his son, did he?' Mr Selway said, his voice troubled. 'The burden of this falls on you, Grace, I fear. I will check in with you now and then, but I have business elsewhere.'

'I understand, Mr Selway,' she said, feeling alone in the venture. 'At least there is Emery to help me.'

'True. We're fortunate there.' He handed her the papers. 'Here is the parole for Captain Daniel Duncan, age thirty-six.' He stopped and looked in the direction of the garden. 'I must admit, the captain looks younger than I would have thought…' His voice trailed off; he shook his head. 'Who would have supposed that incarceration in Dartmoor would render a man younger looking?'

Grace held her breath. Mr Selway was right; Rob Inman was younger than his captain. 'May… maybe it's all that good sea air,' she said, trying not to stammer.

Mr Selway shook his head. 'Gracie, sea air usually makes a man older.' He gave her a generous smile. 'Maybe it is all that healthy *American* air! My dear, I've arranged *carte blanche* for you with Quimby's merchants. You can order anything—within reason, of course—and I will get the bills in Exeter. Send them to this postal-box number.' He handed her a note. 'Cheer up, Gracie. What can go wrong with so prosaic an arrangement?'

It was on the tip of her tongue to blurt out that Captain Duncan was dead, but she stopped. Why, she wasn't sure, except that she had made a promise to the real Daniel Duncan, and felt honour-bound, even if he was an American and a prisoner. Besides that, how well did she even know Mr Selway? This had better be her secret with Rob Inman.

Emery called to her to fetch the new clothes that Mr Selway had left in the bookroom. She took them to the kitchen garden, where the captain sat in the tin tub with his bony knees close to his chin, as tight as a whelk in a basket. His back was turned to her; she gaped at the lash marks on his back. They were fading, but the harsh Stockholm pine tar brought them out in raw relief.

Grace stared at his back another moment, then retreated to the house. Her mind on the man in the tub, she stirred a pot of thick porridge, lacing it liberally with sugar. She pronounced it a success after the addition of a touch of cinnamon and set it to the back of the range to cool slightly.

As Grace stood there, a maid from Quarle tiptoed down the stairs, holding a wicked-looking pair of shears. Gingerly, she held them out to Grace. 'Emery said I was to give you these for serious work.'

'Oh, he did?' she asked, amused. Smiling to herself, she went upstairs. 'The maid said you need me,' she told Emery, holding out the shears.

'*I* need you,' Rob Inman said. 'Please.' He grinned at the old man. 'Emery is a dab hand at scouring my skin raw, but we both agree that a steady hand close to the scalp and face fall in your territory.'

'Aye, aye, Captain,' she said, stepping closer for a good look at the task.

The captain was dressed now in canvas trousers and a checked shirt, looking much like the seamen she had seen in and around Devon's seaports. Emery had already draped a towel around the man's shoulders. Clean now, his hair was a handsome reddish-gold, long on his shoulders and mingling with his beard, which Emery must have dragged a comb through, because it flowed in waves to his chest.

Grace walked around him several times. 'This is daunting,' she murmured under her breath. 'Do I tackle your head first, or your face?'

'It's all the same to me, just as long as your hands don't shake,' he said cheerfully. 'I suggest whacking off my hair first. Get as close to my scalp as you can. I like to wear it short.'

She stepped in closer, tongue between her teeth, frown on her face, and pulled up a handful of still-damp hair. 'No sudden moves, now.'

She hacked at his hair. 'I had no idea it was this colour,' she commented, as she worked her way around his head. Emery had vanished and the maid watched—her eyes wide—from the security of the shrubbery.

'It hadn't been washed in a year,' Rob said, 'Cut it closer. Don't be afraid.'

Grace concentrated on the task, then glanced at the maid. 'What do you think?'

'I think 'e's 'andsome.'

Rob laughed out loud, which sent her running up the steps and into the house, her apron clutched to her face.

'You've embarrassed her, Captain Duncan,' Grace said severely. 'And no, you're not handsome.'

Maybe he could be. Grace cut closer to his scalp, flicking her fingers against his head when he moved. 'Stop that, unless you want me to inflict a serious injury.'

As soon as she said that, Grace thought of the marks of the lash on his back, covered now with a respectable shirt. 'I doubt anything I do would trouble you much,' she amended. 'Still, behave yourself. Mr Selway is gone and you must mind me.'

'Mr Selway spoke to me earlier. I'll tell you what I told him, I cannot promise good behaviour,' he replied, serious now. 'What's to prevent me, once I get my strength back, from just walking away from here? You don't appear intimidating. I could knock over Emery with a mere backhand.' He chuckled. 'That maid is usually at Quarle, but she thinks I'm 'andsome, so she'll give me no grief.'

'Mr Selway said you will be shot on sight,' Grace protested.

'An irate husband said that to me once,' he mused.

Grace flicked her fingers against his scalp, harder this time.

'Ow!' He put his hand to his head. 'D'ye have steel splinters for fingernails?' He turned serious then. 'They'd have to find me to shoot me.' He shrugged and shook the hair from the towel. 'Careful around my ears.'

Swallowing the irritation she felt, Grace did as she was bid, admiring his hair. It seemed a shame to cut it so short.

The captain fell silent then. She hummed as she worked, looking at him objectively. The maid might be right. When Rob was allowed to eat in peace, the bony lines of his face would certainly fill out. His nose was straight and his lips full enough for all general purposes.

She stood back a moment, looking at him, before she started on his face. 'I'll trim your beard with the shears, then you can get close to it with a razor.'

Rob Inman did look better, despite his emaciation. She could hardly avoid noticing how blue his eyes were, maybe almost as blue as Plymouth Sound on a good day with no overcast. Intent upon her business, she trimmed close to his high cheekbones. He did have long lashes, the kind a woman would envy. *She* would, at any rate, if she bothered to invest much thought in the matter.

When his face was trimmed to within shaving

distance of a straight razor, she crouched a little to tackle his neck. He turned his head to oblige her. After a few snips, she stopped and stared.

'My God,' she whispered.

Rob frowned, then must have realised what she was staring at. 'It's not that bad, Grace. It didn't hurt for long.'

She couldn't help her tears, but wiped them away with her apron, even as she knelt in the grass by the stool. 'Why would anyone do that?' she asked, when she could speak.

Her question seemed to embarrass him. His finger went to the black imprint of the letter *R* in his neck just below the hinge of his jaw. 'I don't think the British penal system has much fondness for runaways, Gracie. At least that's what we figured it stood for. Or maybe *rascal,* or *wretch,* except I think that's spelled with a *w.* Think what a permanent memory I'll have of your island.'

Chapter Seven

'They did that to you in Dartmoor?' Grace asked. She just held the scissors. Her hands shook, and she didn't trust herself to continue.

'Who can blame them?' he asked. 'I did a runner, and had the misfortune to be caught and hauled back. When Captain Shortland grew bored of his goon lashing my back, he brought out the iron. Grace, it was seven or eight months ago. Now I just have a souvenir.'

'That doesn't make it right,' she said, wondering why she wanted to argue this kind of logic with a prisoner, someone who had done her country harm.

He tried to smile, but she saw how tired he was. 'Grace, there's no accounting for war. It's a nasty business, better not engaged in, but once you're caught in its grip, you realise how small a cog in the great wheel you truly are. Admiral or powder monkey, it hardly matters. Just cut me close,' he told her; now there was no mistaking the exhaustion in his voice. 'I'll shave myself, if you trust me with a razor.'

'Of course I do. And while you're doing that, I'll bring out some breakfast.'

'Music to my ears,' he said with a conscious effort.

She hurried as fast as she could, because he seemed to wilt before her eyes. She wished she had brought him breakfast even before the bath; it was all he could do to sit upright. 'I'll send Emery out with a razor, soap and hot water.'

Rob shook his head. 'Food first.' He could barely keep his eyes opened. 'Anything.'

'I'll hurry back,' she said, irritated with herself for not noticing how weak he was.

When she returned with a tray of well-sugared porridge and two hard rolls stuffed with butter and marmalade, her charge lay asleep on the ground. He had pillowed his head on his arms and his breath came slow and peaceful.

'Drat!' Grace said under her breath, guilty she had not thought to bring him food sooner. She set the tray beside him in the grass and sat cross-legged next to him under a hawthorn tree, which was shedding its white blossoms.

Perhaps he had smelled the food. Rob opened his eyes and reached for a roll, almost in one motion. He moved onto his back, chewing and swallowing with the same singleness of mind she had seen yesterday, when he had devoured the watercress. The other roll went down faster than the first.

'Can you help me sit up? It's a pain to be so useless.'

She did as he asked. In another moment, the bowl of porridge was just a memory. He looked around for more.

'Emery is afraid you will vomit if you eat any more right now,' Grace told him.

'Emery can take a flying leap off a quay,' Rob said. 'You're a baker's assistant? At some point in your life, maybe you knew what it's like to be hungry.'

'I've been lucky,' she said, too shy to tell him of her plummet from her station in life and her rescue from a worse fate by the Wilsons.

By the time Rob had finished shaving—he took his time, stopping to rest—Grace had to agree with the maid who had brought the food from the manor. The man was at least a little handsome, discounting the high relief of his facial bones, a defect that time and food would soften.

'I don't think you'll scare horses,' Grace said, handing him a warm towel, which he draped over his face with an audible sigh.

'I hope to heaven not,' he replied and swabbed the warm towel across his face and neck, where the prison brand stood out in stark relief.

Shaved and shorn, the captain looked so different. She wished she had not cut his hair so close, because it was a beautiful shade of reddish-gold. His eyes were as nicely blue as she had noticed earlier and his nose was straight, even if it did appear etched into his face, because of his total lack of body fat. There was something about him—she had noticed it last night on the stairs: an air of capability she did not expect to see from a man who was a prisoner and weak from hunger and ill use.

She wondered if that was an American trait. Even with a brand on his neck and too few pounds on his body, her parolee did not look like a man who knew his place.

How do Americans do that, I wonder? Her next thought: *Can I possibly keep him on this estate, if he chooses not to be here? Lord Thomson, what have you wished on me?*

'Will I do?' the captain asked, catching the eye of the little maid who still stood there.

The child nodded. Grace doubted anyone in recent memory—maybe ever—had asked her opinion, much less with a smile.

Grace touched her shoulder. 'He's teasing you.'

'I think you'll do,' the maid said, then ducked behind Grace, overcome with shyness.

'I think so, too,' she told her. 'If we do our duty—as Lord Nelson admonished all Englishmen—and fulfil our charge from old Lord Thomson, we'll send him back to…to…'

'Nantucket.'

'…to Nantucket healthy.'

'Your country is counting on you,' he said gently.

The appeal to patriotism brought the maid out from behind Grace. Still unable to speak, she bobbed a curtsy and dashed for the manor.

The captain watched her go. 'You realise, of course, that I will be able to inveigle anything I want from the big house, if she is my go-between.' He handed back the empty porridge bowl. 'Now, if you will help me upstairs, I hear my bed calling me.'

Grace did as he asked, uneasy at his exhaustion and the way he had to literally pull himself up the stairs. He stood at the top of the landing for a long moment, teetering there until he had his balance. She wondered what he was thinking, unable to really know if his startling change of circumstance had even registered completely.

He headed towards his chamber, but Grace put her hand against the small of his back and steered him to the next room. 'Emery is fumigating the chamber where you slept last night,' she told him as she opened the door. 'This is where you will be staying.'

He stood in the doorway, just looking at the simple but pleasant room. 'Believe me when I tell you it is humiliating to be full of lice and fleas. I haven't been so uncomfortable since my childhood.'

Her curiosity piqued, Grace had to know more. 'Fleas and lice on Nantucket?' she teased in turn.

The amusement in his voice was evident. He laughed softly, even as he sat down heavily on the bed. 'Nantucket? Comes with sand fleas, too. But I told you last night I was born in England. I'm one of those Americans that England insists can only be English, because I was *born* here. This is what you get for choosing Rob Inman, officially branded a troublemaker. You may wish to surrender my parole to someone else.'

'How could I possibly collect my thirty pounds a year, if I did?'

'Only thirty pounds to watch me?' The captain's eyes were closing. 'I fear you are not being paid well enough for the aggravation I will be.'

It was a disquieting thought. She watched him as he drifted to sleep, wondering just how much trouble one parolee could be.

She left him then, sound asleep. It troubled her to watch a man wilt so fast and so she told Emery belowstairs, as he continued to unpack the shabby goods Lord Thomson thought should furnish the dower house, now that a prisoner of war lived there, along with a baker's assistant awarded the princely sum, per annum, of thirty pounds.

'Why is Lord Thomson so intent upon punishing me for a mere thirty pounds?' she asked Emery.

The old retainer only shrugged and folded another tattered dishcloth into a drawer.

She toyed with the idea of telling Emery of the

switch in Dartmoor Prison, then decided against it. It would serve no purpose to tell anyone who 'Captain Duncan' really was. She wouldn't tell the Wilsons, either, she decided, as she walked to Quimby, knowing Rob would sleep through the afternoon.

'He is rail thin and weak,' she told them both as she stood at the familiar kneading table again.

'Worms, more like,' Mrs Wilson said. 'I have a dose of black draught that will shift 'im.'

Grace smiled, her equilibrium restored by the mere act of stirring a recipe she knew so well. 'I'd rather wish the black draught on Lord Thomson! He took everything out of the dower house before Mr Selway and I returned from Dartmoor and replaced it—when forced to—with the worst rubbish from the attics!'

'A *double* dose of black draught for Lord Thomson,' Mr Wilson said with a laugh as he watched her. 'Enough to keep him in the necessary and out of your business!'

Trust the Wilsons to cheer her up, she decided as she hurried to the greengrocer to buy food to tempt the American's appetite. Mr Selway had smoothed her path with the local merchants. She ordered food and timidly told the proprietor to direct the receipt to Philip Selway, Esq., Exeter, Postal Box Fifteen. The man didn't even blink. 'Aye, Gracie,' he told her. 'That solemn-looking solicitor gave us strict orders about your invoices.'

So it went at each store she visited; everyone was curious about Captain Duncan. Grace resigned herself to being part of the most interesting thing that had happened in Quimby since Quentin Markwell, Exeter's own notorious highwayman, had galloped through town a century ago, pausing to steal the vicar's smallclothes from his washing line.

She returned to Quarle in good humour, at least until she saw Lord Thomson watching her out of an upstairs window, his glare evident even from some distance. 'Surely it is but a matter of months until this poor man is gone,' she muttered. 'Lord Thomson, be a little less odious, if you can.'

Grace's irritation at the marquis did not improve when she entered the dower house. Emery was waiting for her, sitting on one of the rickety chairs in the small foyer and looking uncharacteristically glum.

'We've lost him already, Gracie,' he said.

'Impossible,' Grace retorted, trying to hide her sudden fear. 'I left him asleep upstairs before I went to the Wilsons. He was too weak to move.'

'He's moved, Gracie. Trouble is, where?'

Chapter Eight

Why in heaven's name did I ever agree to this parole? Grace asked herself as she quickly set down the purchases she had brought with her—choice dainties to tempt that wretched man's appetite. *The constable will shoot him on sight? Only if I don't beat him to it,* she thought grimly.

'He can't have just vanished, Emery,' she stated, hands on her hips. 'He could barely walk!'

'Perhaps we are underestimating him,' Emery offered.

'Or he's only trying to fool us so he can escape,' Grace snapped back. 'Where on earth would he go?' She sat down on a rickety chair in the entrance hall. 'Is there not a chair in this silly house that doesn't list?'

She was silent then, listening to herself: querulous, testy and complaining. She sighed. 'Emery, I wish you would smite me when I complain.'

He recoiled. 'Never! That would go against every bit of butlering I can think of. Which ain't much,' he added philosophically.

She couldn't help smiling, despite her worries. 'Don't you know you should humour a lunatic?' she teased. 'If I am not imposing, would you please even off these chair legs?'

'Consider it done,' the old retainer told her.

She stood outside for a long moment, wishing herself calm, even as she wanted to smack Lord Thomson and throttle Rob Inman. Where *was* he? She berated herself again for choosing Rob Inman, out of all the miserable American prisoners she could have selected. She walked to the modest circle drive in front of the dower house, totally at a loss. Emery had thought the parolee would have no trouble blending with the seamen that walked about Plymouth, but he would have to get there first. Plymouth was not close, especially for someone teetering just this side of starvation.

If you're found, you will be shot, you wretched man, she thought, walking into the road, but not ready to pass the manor house again, not with Lord Thomson watching her. She rubbed her arms, chilled at what would happen to him if the marquis had even an inkling that the captain had left the house unaccompanied.

'Where would *I* go, if I were you?' she asked out loud. 'You've said you like the wind on your face.'

And then she knew and realised she had better

be right. Looking about to see if Lord Thomson was in sight, Grace hiked up her skirt and ran towards the highest point of land on his property. It wasn't much of an elevation, but just enough of one to tempt someone homesick for the sea, who might think he could see Plymouth Sound from its height. She used to walk there occasionally with old Lord Thomson, when he'd had the strength, because he or one of his ancestors had put a bench at the top.

Sure of herself now, she hurried to the high point, rehearsing in her mind what she would say to Rob when she found him. To her amazement and growing fear, he was nowhere in sight. She even stood on top of the bench, the better to scan the countryside.

Defeat settled on her shoulders like a blanket. He hadn't been in her charge for much more than a day and she had already lost him.

The strength of her anger surprised her, until she realised that for the past ten years, she had maintained a steely, bloodless sort of calm—something to insulate her from slings and arrows. As she scanned the countryside, she was acutely aware that she was feeling stronger emotions than she had dared invoke earlier, even though she suspected Rob Inman was going to prove a challenge.

'If I cannot find you, it's your problem,' she muttered out loud. Even as she said the words, she knew it wasn't true. He was her stewardship now and she had come up short far too soon. It was a daunting thought and she took several deep breaths, trying to calm herself. How far could a barely functioning man go?

The answer came to her with even more certainty than her last guess. She based it on something old Lord Thomson had told her, as he'd reminisced about the war with the colonies. 'When I was garrisoned in New York City, I was so hungry for the sight of my estate and lands here that I used to stand by my window on Wall Street and turn north and east,' he told her simply. 'I was homesick and only the points of the compass helped.'

'Rob Inman, you are looking south and west now, I vow,' she murmured as she stood up and turned about. She started moving in that direction, knowing there was a small knoll, practically on the edge of Quimby, at the furthest corner of Lord Thomson's land. 'Not that you will know just where the boundaries are,' she grumbled out loud as she ran.

And there he was, lying down. Quietly she sank into the grass beside him, wondering if he was asleep, or even if he was dead. Gently she put her fingertips on his neck to find his pulse. Just as gently, his hand came up to cover hers.

'I'm still alive, Gracie,' he said. 'I should have known you would find me. Maybe I hoped you would. I'm not certain I can stand. I'm a baby, I overdid it.'

More relieved than she had ever been in her life, she let her breath out slowly, pulled her hand away and made herself comfortable beside him. 'First I thought you might have gone to the high point by the bench, maybe thinking you could see Plymouth Sound.'

He turned onto his back, opened his eyes, then closed them again, as though the effort taxed him. 'I did. What a disappointment. The wind felt good though.' His eyes remained closed. 'How did you know I was here?'

'I remembered something your captain's father told me about just wanting to stand somewhere and look in the direction of England. I…I thought maybe you had done the same thing, in the other direction.'

'He did that, too? I'll be damned. I thought maybe I could see just a sliver of the Atlantic. Just some tiny bit of the ocean that I know washes against Nantucket.'

He couldn't say any more. 'What a damn fool you are in charge of, Grace,' he whispered. 'I want to go home so badly.'

She didn't say anything and debated a moment whether to take his hand. *Perhaps I must earn my thirty pounds a year,* she told herself as she put her hand in his and rested them both on his chest.

'Tell me about your part of America. I know it is a large country.'

'Very large. My part is Nantucket, not so large.'

Only a hugely insensitive person could have

failed to hear the way he caressed the word. *Nantucket.* Grace rolled it around in her mind, liking the sound of it. Maybe it was an Indian word.

'Nantucket is a small island off the coast of Massachusetts. My home…' He couldn't speak for a moment. 'My home is on Orange Street. I bought it for Elaine before we married. I can see the bay from my second storey.' He smiled then, his eyes still closed. 'Salt marsh and tar—what a lovely fragrance.'

'I doubt it,' she said, laughing.

'Aye, it is, Gracie Curtis,' he assured her. 'I like it probably as much as you like the fragrance of those Quimby Crèmes.'

She could understand that. 'How long have you lived in America? Why did you ever leave England?'

Grace hoped he would talk. If they were gone long enough, Emery might come looking for them and he could help her get the parolee back to the dower house. Besides, she wanted to hear why someone would leave his home and cross an ocean.

'I can't say I had any choice,' he told her after a long pause, when he seemed to be gathering his thoughts. 'I was seven years old. At the time, I thought my father was doing me a terrible injustice. I see now his only crime was to want me to live.'

'What did your father do?'

'He had me indentured to a sea captain in

the Pool of London. Captain Duncan's father, actually.'

'But Captain Duncan's father was old Lord Thomson,' Grace said.

'True. His mother was Mollie Duncan, quite a sprightly lady,' Rob Inman said. He lay still on the grass, holding his hand up as hawthorn blossoms settled around him. 'After the British army evacuated New York City, she married David Cameron, a ship's captain from Nantucket.'

She could tell the memory was a good one, because Rob smiled. 'He was a hard man—I suppose that's the nature of the business—but he was always fair to me.'

'How did your father meet him?'

He eyed her for a moment, as if wondering what she would think. 'My father was a thief. My ma, too, I suppose. I come from a family of thieves.'

'Oh,' was all Grace could think to say, which made Rob laugh.

'Nowhere near as respectable as a baker's assistant,' he told her. 'As far as I can recall, we lived on the lee side of a warehouse in the Pool. Ever hear of it?'

She had and not in glowing terms. 'I…I thought it was just wharves and warehouses. People actually *live* there?'

She had embarrassed him; she could tell by the blush that crept up his face. She started to apologise, but he stopped her.

'No fears, Gracie. It was what passed for living, I suppose,' he said. 'I don't remember a day when I wasn't hungry.'

'I'm sorry.'

'No fears!' he said again, regaining some of his equilibrium. 'What happened to me was dumb luck. All I can tell you—I was only seven—is that Da and Mama had been whispering together for several days. I remember that we were on the run from someone. Da had been jailed a time or two for petty theft, but this must have been more serious. I think he feared the drop.'

Don't stare, Grace, she scolded herself. *He probably thinks this is your background, too.*

'And your mother?'

'She was no better. I do remember a neighbour woman scolding her for feeding me gin. It put me to sleep, so Mama and Da could thieve in peace.' Rob held out his hand to catch the blossoms. 'I can only suspect there was just enough family feeling for Da to want me out of there. One morning he dragged me to the wharf. I remember he looked at several merchant vessels— a Russian flag, a ship from the Ottoman Empire, another from Denmark. When he saw the Stars and Stripes, he hauled me up the gangplank.'

'The sailors didn't just throw him off?'

'Dumb luck again. Captain Cameron happened to be on deck. So was Dan Duncan. I believe Dan was sixteen or so. My father plunked me down in front of them, said I'd be a good cabin boy and hightailed it off the ship. Last I saw of him was a clean pair of heels.' He chuckled. 'More like, a dirty pair.'

'They could have just thrown you off the ship,' Grace said.

'Certainly.'

'Did you cry?'

He regarded her more seriously. 'Is that what you would have done?'

Grace shrugged. When Papa's solicitor had sold their estate and bid her good day, he had not made the smallest enquiry into her future. Perhaps Rob Inman's father was kinder. At least he left his son with people. Still, this was a man far below her in status—she smiled inwardly—if status mattered to her any more. 'What did you do?'

'Before I left our warehouse lean-to, Mama had put a handkerchief in my pocket,' Rob said. 'It must have been one they picked from someone, because there was lace on it. I took that, crawled on my knees to Captain Cameron and started polishing his shoes.'

Grace felt her heart crack a little around the edges, imagining a child with a strong instinct to live, grovelling at the feet of a sea captain who could easily have thrown him off the ship.

Maybe Rob Inman knew what she was thinking. There was an element of disbelief in his voice, even though the incident had obviously happened years ago. 'He could have done anything to me. God only knows why he didn't just kick me aside. He had Dan take me below, give me ship's biscuit and assign me the duty of keeping their cabin clean.'

'That was it?'

'Almost.' Rob blew at the blossoms in his hand. His breath carried them to her lap. 'Captain Cameron followed rules, but he could bend them, if needed. That evening, I put my X to a document that indentured me to him for eight years.'

'Do they still do that in America?' Grace asked.

'No. The practice ended a few years later.'

'What happened to your parents?' she asked, holding her hand out, too, for the blossoms that drifted around them.

'Who knows? On a voyage before this war, we docked near the Pool. Dan was captain by then, and we looked. I couldn't find the warehouse. Maybe it burned down.'

'So that was it.'

'Not quite. Captain Dan was a bit like his stepfather, not a man to leave stones unturned, if the mood was on him. Dan found a minor clerk in an office in the maritime services. We checked manifests for prison ships to Australia. Found a Matilda Inman in the 1795 convoy. She might have been my mother. I never knew her Christian name. No other Inmans, though. My father probably found a noose that fit his neck, right here in England.'

Grace shuddered.

'D'ye know where your parents are?' he asked.

She nodded, unwilling to tell him her story, mainly because it paled in comparison to his. *I only had to grovel to people I knew,* she reminded herself, *not some stranger who could just as easily have sent me to a workhouse, or left me on the dock.* No wonder Rob Inman felt no particular tie to the land of his birth. 'Mama died when I was fourteen and Papa died ten years ago, when I turned eighteen.' She saw no need to tell him of her gentle, if debt-filled, upbringing.

'We're the same age, Gracie,' Rob said. He smiled at her, a soft, slow smile that had shyness in it and just a touch of something that felt like friendship. 'Has life been kind to you?'

She could have said no. Maybe she would have only an hour ago. She looked at him lying on the grass, too weak to stand. *Until peace is declared, I can be your friend,* she thought.

'Life *has* been kind to me,' she said. 'Very kind, actually.'

Chapter Nine

She meant it. As onerous as her current station in life, at least she had not been raised in one of London's worst districts, pitchforked into an indenture, or left to rot in prison. Still, Grace could see no reason to get too involved in his story. *I'm a lady,* one side of her brain seemed to be telling her, while the other side just laughed and said, *Not lately.*

She looked at Rob Inman again, wondering, if, torn from her corner of Devon, she would ache to see it again. 'Well, what *has* England done for me lately?' she murmured, reminded of his earlier question.

He made a weary attempt at a smile. 'Forgive that, Grace. I'm rude and crude,' was all he said.

There was a more important question: how to get this exhausted man back to the dower house? As she sat there with the afternoon waning, Grace hoped Emery would come looking for them when she didn't return.

Lord Thomson did the honours, to her dismay.

Sitting there, she felt the drumming of horse's hooves before she saw the marquis. As displeased as she was to see him top the small rise, she had to hide a smile at the inelegant way he sat a horse. 'You look like a sack of meal, Lord Thomson,' she said as she watched him approach, rising and plopping down in his saddle.

He thundered closer and closer and Grace stood up, planting herself in front of the parolee. Surely even so distasteful a specimen as Lord Thomson would not run down a helpless man. *Or me,* she thought grimly.

'For God's sake, help me up,' Rob Inman said behind her, the alarm in his voice unmistakable.

With one eye on the approaching horse, Grace did as he asked, tugging him to his feet until he swayed beside her. He put a hand on her shoulder to steady himself.

With a curse, and considerable sawing at the reins, Lord Thomson managed to stop his horse. She pursed her lips tight together to keep from laughing, when the horse stopped suddenly and Lord Thomson pitched forwards, hugging the animal's neck.

Such a clumsy approach didn't sweeten his mood. He righted himself and gave the old horse a clout to the head, then shook his finger at the two of them.

'You don't have the right to tramp about on my land, you bastard!' he shouted. 'Captain Duncan, you are the leavings of a British officer and colonial trash!'

He was taunting Rob. Grace swallowed her own hot words, wondering when she had suddenly become so combative. She yearned to yank the man from his horse and thrash him until his teeth rattled.

Rob Inman stiffened. *Don't say what you want to,* Grace pleaded silently. Suddenly she wished Mr Selway were there with his calm air. *Maybe I need a keeper more than Rob. This situation is bringing out the worst in me.*

Rob merely bowed slightly. He wasn't strong enough to release her, but his voice lacked nothing. 'My lord, let me assure you—thanks to poor food in Dartmoor Prison, I am not leaving much of a footprint on English soil right now. Your grass is quite safe.'

The marquis's face turned red, but what could he say that wouldn't sound childish? He turned his attention to Grace, jabbing his finger at her this time. 'Keep a better eye on my uncle's bastard. I know he wandered away. I've been watching. If he does this again, I'll shoot him.'

'He was trying to see the ocean,' she said quietly. 'Now he knows he can't see it from your land.'

Maybe even as dense a soul as Lord Thomson began to grasp how foolish he sounded. He tried to urge his old horse closer to the two of them, to force them to back up, but it wouldn't budge. He sawed at the reins to turn away, which made the nag roll the whites of her eyes and step in a clumsy circle.

'If you want to see any of that idiotic legacy my addled uncle left you, Grace Curtis, you had better not let this man out of your sight again.' It was his parting shot, delivered as querulously as though he were a spoiled child denied a bauble.

With a vicious whack of his whip on the horse's hide, Lord Thomson got her in motion, but just barely. Taking her sweet time as the man on her back seethed, the horse took her deliberate way slowly down the knoll.

Rob laughed softly. 'That was worth the insult,' he commented. 'Call me vindictive, but I do love to see small men made smaller.' He leaned on her more heavily. 'Gracie, I just can't manage that walk back and I suppose you daren't leave me to get help.'

'We'll just have to wait here until someone more reasonable comes,' she replied as she helped him down again. 'Lord Thomson would shoot you, if I left you here alone.'

He sank down, real relief etched on his fine-boned face. 'No, he'd have someone else shoot me. Men like that seldom do their own dirty work.'

'All the same, we won't depend on any charitable bones in his body. I'm certain he has none,' she said.

* * *

It was nearly dark before Grace heard Emery calling to them. She stood up, relieved. 'Over here!' she called, jumping and waving.

She stood there impatiently, wanting to run to the old man and hurry him along, except some instinct told her not to leave Rob.

Odd. Just below the brow of the hill, when he was still out of sight, she heard Emery talking to someone. She took a step forwards, but Rob was quicker, grabbing the hem of her dress as he lay on the ground.

'Stay here, Gracie,' he said in a whisper.

She did as he said. In a moment, her heart slid into her stomach as she heard a rider gallop away and Emery top the rise, muttering to himself as he carried a basket. She felt her face drain of all colour as she glanced at the captain. 'You're right about small men,' she murmured. 'Someone was waiting there to kill you, if I had left your side.'

He nodded. 'You're going to have to earn every penny of that legacy.'

When Emery joined them, he looked back in the direction he had travelled. 'Did you know one of Lord Thomson's men was just waiting there? He had a brace of pistols.' He managed a little smile. 'Emery to the rescue.'

Rob laughed. 'And you brought me some food. One would think you really *were* a butler, to anticipate my needs.' He glanced at Grace. 'Now, this part of life in England I could become accustomed to!'

Rob ate quickly, pausing only when he was done. 'Could it be that I have been paroled to an estate where the owner is so patriotic that he cannot bear the sight of an American?'

'I think it rather that he doesn't like either of us,' Grace said.

'Such a relief to know it isn't just because I am American.' He accepted another sandwich from Emery. 'Some day, we Americans and you British may have to cooperate on the world stage. Don't laugh! Anything's possible.'

When he finished, Emery handed him a bottle of cream. 'The cook at the manor house thinks you need fattening.'

Rob looked at it dubiously. 'Strawberries would help.'

'Too early,' Grace said, amused. 'Drink it, Captain.'

He did as she said, then regarded the empty bottle philosophically. 'If I balloon into Gargantua, I'll never fit through a hatch again.'

'It will take more than cream, Captain,' Emery said gravely. 'Up now, one hand on me and one on Grace.'

He did as Emery said.

By stopping every so often, they had made it back to the dower house as darkness fell. Inside the front door, Rob shook his head over the stairs. 'May I just stay in the sitting room to-night?' he asked. 'Cover me with something and leave me be.'

Grace left him in the sitting room. By the time she had covered him with a blanket, he was asleep. She watched him for a moment, her eyes going first to the brand on his neck, then to his fine-veined hands, which he had crossed on his chest in a protective gesture.

'How is it that you are even alive?' she asked softly, thinking again of the little boy crawling across the deck. 'How different we are.'

To her surprise, he opened one eye. 'I told you it was dumb luck,' he whispered back as she laughed softly. 'I had the best hearing on the *Orontes*, by the way.' He winked at her then, a slow wink. 'Maybe we're not so different.'

She woke long before the sun was up, lying in bed and wishing herself back in her fragrant room behind the ovens. She tried to compose herself for sleep again, but she knew she should check on her parolee. Putting a shawl around her shoulders, she padded quietly down the stairs and went into the sitting room.

The sofa was empty, the blanket flung aside. 'Dratted, dratted American!' she said through clenched teeth. 'I will have to tie a cowbell around your neck!'

At a complete loss this time, she returned to the foyer and noticed the front door was slightly ajar. She opened it and sighed with relief to see Rob sitting on the steps.

'Take another step and I swear I will thrash you!' she exclaimed, plumping herself down beside him. 'You probably do not come when you are called, either!'

He chuckled. 'Only when it's the captain.'

'Why are you making my life so difficult?' she asked, irritated with him.

'I really wasn't going to budge, Grace, honestly. Then I heard the wind come up and I had to feel it on my face. Really, where would I go? I'm a stranger here.'

She knew the feeling. Grace had a sudden yearning to tell him how drastically her own life had changed years ago, and the early months after her father's death as she dreaded facing anyone in Quimby, especially the tradespeople who would never recoup the debt her father had incurred. She had paid back what she could, but it would never be enough. Even more humbling had been the kindness with which she had been treated by the ordinary folk.

'A penny for your thoughts,' the captain said.

She looked at him, not realising he had been watching her. 'It's nothing,' she said.

'You just looked a little forlorn.' He laughed softly. 'You must wish I'd stay put.' He leaned back, resting his elbows on the top step. 'After I crossed the Atlantic that first time, I ran away when Captain Cameron's ship—the *Maid of Nan-*

tucket—docked in the bay. He found me fast enough. Where did I think I would hide on an unfamiliar island? He gave me such a tanning.'

'I didn't think he would do something like that,' she said, surprised.

'I told you he was a hard man. But fair. He reminded me that he had bought me for eight years, and that it could be a bad eight years or a good eight years. That's a lifetime when you're only seven.'

'Where did you stay?'

'In port, I had a small room in the attic of his house, but we were mostly at sea. I slept on the deck amidships, right in front of his cabin.' He smiled. 'Slid around a bit in bad weather, but I was never seasick.'

It was a life of such harshness that she could hardly imagine it. He seemed to sense her distress.

'Mostly I worked hard and did what the captain asked. I never had to go without food again, even if it wasn't very good after months at sea. Steady meals and work to do. In exchange, Captain Cameron taught me to read and cipher. That's when things changed.'

'How?'

'I discovered a gift for numbers and geometry. Captain Cameron said so. I don't think I ever made a mistake when he showed me how to use a sextant. And then when he set me to learning the sails and studying the wind, I was in high cotton.'

'High cotton?' she asked, mystified.

'An expression I picked up in Georgia. Nothing's better than high cotton.'

She listened to his enthusiasm, glad he wasn't dwelling on what had happened that afternoon, or maybe, for a few moments, thinking of Dartmoor.

'Do you have a gift for something, Grace?'

'Quimby Crèmes,' she said promptly and he laughed.

'I love wind and angles!' His expression was thoughtful. 'And now I make you rush downstairs and hope I haven't done a runner.'

Grace stood up, wrapping her shawl tighter around her. There was still a chill in the April air. She held out her hand to Rob Inman.

'Up you get, sir,' she told him. 'I am going back to bed and you are returning to the sofa. Before I tread the stairs, I will visit the kitchen and ask Emery to bring you some porridge. I cooked it last night and sugared it well, so it will go down much easier with cream, rather than cream by itself.'

'You intend to feed me back to health?'

'It is not a mere intention,' she told him, pinking up because he did have a nice smile. 'It is a promise.'

Chapter Ten

Perhaps Rob Inman's hillside encounter with the goodness and hospitality that was Lord Thomson had unnerved him sufficiently. He made no more attempts to 'do a runner', as he expressed it. Grace was wary enough not to expect too much, but she did find herself looking forward to the parolee's cheerful good morning from the breakfast room each day.

Grace knew she was a good cook. She couldn't have had a happier charge than her parolee, who grew healthier by the day. The proof came after a visit by the village surgeon, who thumped Rob's chest, listened to his heart, probed at the additional flesh covering his still-visible ribs—so Emery informed her—and pronounced him sound as a roast.

'Grace, this is a signal triumph,' the doctor told her, as he walked down the stairs, Rob following behind and buttoning his shirt. 'All latent signs of scurvy are gone. He tells me he sleeps all night and his legs no longer look skinny as a marsh bird's.'

'I am certain that is more than Gracie ever wanted to know, sir,' Rob said in good-humoured protest.

'Then I shan't mention that your piss is a right fine yellow again,' the doctor said. 'Ah, yes, I thought that would stop you, you rascal!'

'Nothing is sacred for a parolee,' Grace said, amused more than embarrassed, since the parolee had such an easy way about him.

'True, Grace,' he said. 'My life is certainly not my own.'

She stopped smiling, because he was serious. In quick time, he heaved a small sigh, glanced out of the window as if looking for something he could not see, then returned to the present, as if determined to make the best of things. She didn't know what to say.

She thought about the matter through luncheon, which Rob ate with his usual gusto, even though he returned only monosyllables when Grace tried to make conversation.

Exasperated, she tapped her spoon against the glass to get his attention. The gesture made him smile.

'Aye, Gracie,' he said, 'I'm paying attention.'

'No, you're not. You're miles away and I am

getting weary of you!' she declared. 'You're worse than a bored child.'

He startled her by slamming his hand on the table. The glasses jumped; so did she.

'How would *you* feel if a man you admired had to die so you could be in a warm place with food?' he snapped, his face red, his lips a tight line.

Grace leaped to her feet, feeling the blood drain from her face. Hotheaded, her first instinct was to snap back and assure him her life was no holiday on the seashore. Some kindlier angel of her own nature seemed to hush her then. She was silent in the face of his terrible loss and at such a price.

'I apologise,' she said finally, when her own temper subsided. 'I should have thought before I spoke. Let me leave you alone for a while.'

Perhaps his own kindlier angel was hard at work, too, because he sighed. 'Nay, Grace, sit down.' He looked into the distance, a place she had no wish to visit, because she had spent an hour of her life in Dartmoor and that was enough. 'Why did you pick me?'

Because I hadn't a brain in my head, she thought, irritated again. Calmer in another moment, she sat down, but not as close as before. 'I can't answer that.'

'Nor should I have asked.' He returned to that distant landscape, then visibly roused himself. 'Give me something to do, then,' he told her. 'Anything.'

She considered the matter calmly. This parolee was obviously her trial to bear, and she had to do better. 'Very well, sir. Since you are mine until this war is over, apparently, we are going to the bakery.'

Quimby was no more than a mile away, but she couldn't help but notice how he flagged as the village came in sight.

'Maybe this wasn't a good idea,' Grace said, slowing down and feeling her own guilt at rushing him.

'It's an excellent idea, Gracie my keeper,' he assured her. 'How will I ever get strong again if I don't exert myself? Uh, is the bakery on this side of the village?'

Thankfully, it was. 'Right there,' she told him, 'where all the people are.'

He eyed the small crowd with some wariness. 'Are the natives friendly?' he asked, only half in jest, from the sound of his voice. 'When we were captured off Plymouth Sound, the Royal Navy paraded us through the streets of Plymouth. Ever have a chamber pot dumped on your head, Gracie? I thought not.'

She gasped. 'They didn't!'

'They did, on more than one street.'

'That's terrible!'

He chuckled. 'We thought so, too.'

'Surely you were allowed to wash when you got to Dartmoor.'

'My, but you have an exalted opinion of a prison,' he told her. 'They really aren't that accommodating.'

She hadn't meant to pull such a long face, but he had noticed.

'Buck up,' he said, still eyeing the citizens. 'I don't see anyone with a pitchfork.'

Pitchforks, no, but she couldn't overlook the wary faces as she came to the bakery. *He's harmless,* she wanted to tell them. *He's not so different from us: just an ordinary man caught in an extraordinary situation.*

The afternoon was warm and the door to the bakery stood open. Grace took a deep breath of yeast and spices, which never failed to put the heart in her body. She smiled at her neighbours. 'This is my parolee, Captain Duncan. He's a good man and he's far from home.'

Her words sounded silly to her ears. What was she thinking?

'And you know me,' she added almost unnecessarily, because they did know how far she had fallen. Those of her own social sphere didn't concern themselves with her on any level now. Standing there, Grace suddenly realised she preferred it that way.

'Aye, we know ye!' someone called, the words cheerful. Others laughed and stepped away from the door to let them enter.

Her parolee let out a quiet breath when they entered the shop. Mrs Wilson stood behind the

counter, arranging two loaves of potato bread
in a string bag for the vicar's maid of all work.
Her eyes lit up when she saw Grace. 'Well, there
now,' she said in her gruff voice. 'Look what you
dragged in.'

Grace laughed. 'He won't eat much and I
promise to take care of him. May I keep him?'

Everyone in the shop laughed. Rob relaxed no-
ticeably.

'Only until the war is over, Gracie,' Mrs Wilson said. 'So you're Captain Duncan? I wondered
when she would bring you here.'

'Aye, I'm Daniel and I'm bored, Mrs Wilson,'
he said frankly.

Mrs Wilson called over her shoulder, 'Mr Wilson! Front and centre! Gracie's brought us another stray!'

'Another one? Mrs Wilson, has she harboured
other felons and miscreants of the American variety?' Rob teased.

'Cats, mostly,' the woman replied, 'which I
admire, because we're free of mice.'

'I'm hardly that useful,' Rob said.

Mrs Wilson shrugged. 'You're a man, I don't
expect much.'

Grace had to turn away because she knew she
could not hide her smile, or her relief. Mrs Wilson was treating her prisoner like every other man
who entered the shop.

'All right, you two, no more wrangling,' Grace
scolded with mock severity.

'My thought precisely,' Mrs Wilson said. 'Time to make yourself useful, young man.'

She had opened her mouth to give him orders when Mr Wilson came into the bakery from the storeroom, a sack of flour on his shoulder. Like his wife, he shook hands with Rob Inman. His eyes were lively with curiosity. He stood there with the heavy sack on his shoulder as though it weighed nothing, listening to Grace explain her parolee's presence in the bakery.

'He's bored of the dower house, but I must accompany him everywhere he goes, Mr Wilson,' Grace explained. 'If I don't, Lord Thomson will shoot him on sight, according to the parole. Since he is my responsibility, I want Mrs Wilson to put him to work.'

'What better place to regain your strength than a bakery, eh, Captain?' Mr Wilson asked. 'Lead on, Mrs Wilson!'

Mrs Wilson set Rob to work at the bread trough, stirring the mass of flour as Grace added more, then poking and prodding at it with the heels of his hands until it turned into bread dough. Mrs Wilson supervised, watching the dough and then watching the captain. Grace had already set herself to work at a smaller trough, preparing a batch of Quimby Crèmes, alert for the tinkle of the shop bell, so she could serve customers.

Grace hardly had to pay attention to her own labours; they were second nature. She found herself touched by Mrs Wilson, a no-nonsense woman who never suffered fools gladly. When Rob started to flag, she ordered him to sit down and crack walnuts as Mr Wilson took over at the trough. It was done so smoothly that Rob never had a moment to be embarrassed about his weakness.

Grace couldn't help her feeling of relief. *Good,* she thought, as she rolled out the dough. *Let us send you back to your Nantucket healthy and alive. Thirty pounds a year, Gracie,* she reminded herself. *You can tolerate even an American for thirty pounds a year.*

They made the walk to Quimby every day that week, and then the next, as Rob's strength gradually returned. It became his job to add flour to the big troughs where Mrs Wilson and Grace kneaded the yeasty dough into bread. Mrs Wilson was never shy about splitting open at least one hot loaf a day, slathering on butter and handing him the heel, after she discovered how much Rob liked that slice. At first Mrs Wilson dared him with her eyes to make much of what she did. Once she saw that he earned that heel and more by relieving Mr Wilson, who suffered silently from arthritis, Rob Inman became a welcome part of her day.

Grace wished that the residents of her little town could understand that Captain Duncan— she had to think of him as Captain Duncan—was not a man to fear, even though he was American at heart, if not by birth. The Wilsons saw his kind character revealed every day in small ways. Grace wanted others to see this, too, but maybe it was too much to ask of folk who had known a generation of war.

After the Wilsons, Quimby's children were the next to succumb to the American prisoner's curious charm. It didn't happen right away. When they walked from the dower house to Quimby, the children often delighted in calling him 'Foul Yankee,' or chanting, 'Prisoner, prisoner'.

Rob took it all in his stride, though, wearing an amused half-smile on his face, while Grace wanted to thrash each child. Once he had even gently squeezed her shoulder, telling her to cool off. 'Gracie, Gracie, this is nothing,' he murmured, his lips close to her ear. 'Remember the chamber pots?'

The change came when he did a kindness to Bobby Gentry. The boy's father had not returned from Trafalgar, never to even know he had a son. It was the smallest kindness. Grace watched the whole event from the bakery window.

The week had been a stormy one, with rainfall marring the beauty of Devon in late June. The rain had cancelled most of the bonfires lit all over the shire, to celebrate the end of war and the arrival of the Allies in London, and no one was happy about it, especially the children. They took out their disappointment on Rob Inman, pelting him with mud as they walked to Quimby. When Grace tried to stop them, Rob just shook his head and good-naturedly told her to move away so she wouldn't be a target, too.

He had been sweeping out dried mud in the shop, while Grace arranged the week's stale bread in the bin, ready for the poor of Quimby tomorrow. She looked up to watch Bobby Gentry coming for his mother's weekly loaves. He was picking his way through the puddles in that light-hearted way of children. This time, he misjudged the depth of a puddle and sank to his knees.

'Bobby!' Grace exclaimed. Through the window, she watched him check his pockets in growing alarm, scrabbling in the mud. 'I think he lost his penny.'

Rob leaned the broom against the counter, his eyes on the little boy in such distress. 'Then there'll be no bread in Bobby's house this week?'

'And little else.'

'Find me a penny, Grace,' he said, holding out his hand to her without even taking his eyes from Bobby, in tears now.

Without a word, she took a penny from the change box and gave it to him. He was out of the door moments after his fingers closed over the coin.

Grace watched, a lump in her throat, as Rob skirted the larger puddles, then walked directly into the one where the little boy was mired. Without a word, he picked up Bobby Gentry and set him on comparatively dry ground, then returned to the puddle, running his hand in the mud, his face firm with concentration, until he held up the penny from the till.

Bobby clapped his hands, his own mud and misery forgotten when he saw the penny. Rob handed him the coin, then made him stand still as he took out a handkerchief and wiped down the boy's trousers and shoes. Grace noticed with a pang that the captain was barefoot now, his old shoes trapped in the mud.

Bobby had noticed the same thing. His lip began to quiver again, until with a comical face, Rob began to root around in the mud again, searching for his wretched shoes. He brought them out of the mud hole with a crow of triumph that made Bobby laugh. When the little boy came inside the bakery for his stale bread, Grace took the penny with a flourish and returned it to the change box. Mrs Wilson insisted on adding half-a-dozen Quimby Crèmes, an unheard-of luxury for the Gentry household.

The captain's ruined shoes remained outside the bakery door that evening as they walked home. 'I'll write to Mr Selway in Exeter and send him a tracing of your foot, so you can have new shoes,' Grace said. 'I should have done that weeks ago.'

'No hurry,' Rob said. 'It's summer.'

In the morning, his muddy shoes were gone and he went barefoot.

* * *

Two days later, they had been replaced by a new pair of shoes—not fancy, but respectable, such as a workman would wear—with a cryptic note stuffed in them. 'We liked Bobby's da.' That was all. The American held the shoes in his hands for a long moment, then spent a longer moment in the back room, until Mrs Wilson began to mutter, 'What a soft touch he is', even as her own eyes glittered with tears.

The children of Quimby never teased Rob again as he walked into town with Grace, especially after Bobby Gentry—one of the original tormentors—walked beside the captain and took his hand.

What won over Quimby entirely was the day Lady Adeliza Tutt nearly came to an untimely end in the bakery.

Chapter Eleven

Not that anyone had any real love for Adeliza Tutt—quite the contrary. She had worn out many a welcome in Quimby. But she was the widow of Barnabas Tutt, a local butcher. Tutt might have started as a butcher, but he'd had a knack for property. His prodigious acumen had earned him a fortune and a knighthood from the Regent, who had borrowed extensively and found this a convenient way to pay the debt. Until that event, the Tutts had been as common as ditch water. They still were, but Lady Tutt had been 'elevated', and she let no one forget it.

Rob had asked about Lady Tutt after other Quimby residents had begun to thaw, following his rescue of Bobby Gentry. 'Some people are warming to me, but not her,' he commented, once her ladyship was out of hearing.

Lady Tutt had declared in round tones for everyone in the bakery to hear that she couldn't imagine why loyal English folk like the Wilsons would tolerate his presence. Wasn't he a pirate, after all?

'A privateer, Lady Tutt,' Grace had said. 'There *is* a difference.'

Lady Tutt had fixed her with a lengthy stare. 'Grace Curtis, we all know you have slipped, but you're going too far to champion someone your father never would have even noticed.'

'It's not you, Rob,' she said later, as they walked home, hoping he hadn't heard, or didn't understand, Lady Tutt's comments directed at her. 'She's pretentious. I suppose that happens to people elevated to a title, rather than born to one. You're fair game.'

'I certainly am,' he replied cheerfully.

Maybe Rob saw Lady Tutt's continuing disapproval as a challenge. Grace smiled at his obvious attempts to please the old ruin. He couldn't even coax a smile from Lady Tutt's companion, a mousy creature with one sole aim in life: to remain employed without suffering too many slings and arrows from an exacting employer who considered herself vastly superior to everyone.

'Should I tell Lady Tutt how divine she looks in…in… What is that dreadful colour she wears most often?' Rob asked her one morning.

'Puce,' Grace whispered.

'Sounds vile. Calling it plain brown would be more charitable.'

'I dare say it would,' Grace agreed as she held out her hand for the slab of dough he had sliced off for the bread pan. 'Lady Tutt will always prefer the French word.'

He came closer so no one in the shop could overhear. 'Maybe I will comment favourably upon the fact that, for a fat lady, she doesn't sweat much.'

Grace turned away and put her apron to her mouth.

'You know, if you keep that expression too long, your face will freeze,' he said.

'I wish this war would end, so you would go away,' Grace scolded, when she could talk. 'You are vulgar and useless.'

He grinned and returned to the bread he was kneading, lifting up a great length of it and whacking it on the table so hard that Lady Tutt's companion jumped in fright.

Not Lady Tutt. She fixed him with a stare. 'Rudesby,' she declared, then, 'American.'

Grace greased three more bread pans, idly watching Lady Tutt go through her typical ritual of squeezing off bits of bread to taste without having to pay for them. She was walking into the back room for more yeast when she heard a gasp and a gargle. Grace whirled around to stare at the spectacle of Lady Tutt clutching her throat and turning a mottled colour that contrasted un-favourably with puce.

Grace stood there, stunned, but not Rob. 'You, there!' he shouted to Lady Tutt's companion. 'Slap her on the back!'

The companion gasped, 'I dare not!' then turned horrified eyes on her employer, who had sunk to her knees. 'She would turn me off with-out a character!'

'Not if she's dead, you ninny,' Grace heard him growl under his breath.

The other customers in the bakery were equally inept, whether from fear of the wrath of Lady Tutt, or from surprise. No one did anything. Grace started towards the counter.

'You know, you British will never win this war,' Rob muttered as he vaulted over the coun-ter with one hand, pushed the lady's companion aside, grabbed Lady Tutt around her considerable girth and administered a sharp smack to her back at the same time as he squeezed below her ribs.

Nothing happened, except that the compan-ion slid to the floor in a graceful faint, unable to bear the sight of her mistress so manhandled. He smacked Lady Tutt again. With an audible pop, a ball of purloined bread shot from her mouth and landed next to the cat in the window display. The cat arched its back, hissed and leaped onto the still form of the lady's companion. Grace shooed it away and waved smelling salts under the com-panion's nose, until she began to sputter.

Rob kept his grip on the knight's widow. 'Breathe in and out now,' he ordered.

'I. Am. Perfectly. Capable,' Lady Tutt began, gasping between words. 'Unhand. Me. You. Brute!'

Without a word, Rob plopped her on the floor unceremoniously. 'Lady Tutt, that's what happens when you pinch bites of bread you haven't paid for,' he said as he left her there. In another moment, he was kneading dough again.

The other customers in the store couldn't leave fast enough. *I give this incident three minutes to be all over the High Street,* Grace thought. She helped the companion to her feet, then turned her attention to Lady Tutt, still sitting in the middle of the bakery.

With an awful expression, the widow stared holes through Rob's back as he worked the bread dough. Hiding her smile, now that the emergency was so quickly over, Grace followed her basilisk gaze. *Admit it now, Lady Tutt,* she told herself. *He has a wonderful pair of shoulders, now that there is flesh on his bones again.*

Lady Tutt held out her hand imperiously and Grace helped her up. The woman's turban was askew and favouring one ear over the other. When the companion did nothing but stare, Grace took a deep breath—Lady Tutt had always frightened her, too.

'There now, Lady Tutt. I suggest you go home and lie down,' she said.

To her relief, Lady Tutt signalled to her ad-dled companion. 'Hand me my parasol,' she com-manded, not quite up to her usual strength, but intimidating enough to elicit an audible gulp from her employee.

'And that is that,' she told Rob when they started back to the dower house that afternoon. 'I doubt you will ever receive a word of thanks.'

She was silent a moment, digesting again the whole frightening business of Lady Tutt. She laughed, which made him stop in the road, put his hands on his hips in that lazy way she rather liked and tip his head slightly to one side.

'All right, what's the joke?' he asked.

'Heaven forgive me, but while you were pound-ing her back, I thought of six or seven people who would love to have done that.'

'Grace, you are a rascal!'

They had come to a crossroads and the rustic bench that served as a waiting place for the local bonecracker that travelled at a sedate pace be-tween villages. He took her hand and pulled her down beside him.

'I've been meaning to ask you—recently, Lady Tutt said something about you "slipping".' He didn't quite look at her. 'What did she mean?'

'I don't have to tell you,' Grace said quickly, angry at him.

'Damn right,' he replied agreeably. 'It's not my business.' He took her hand. 'But I have

some idea, and, well, your English is so good.'
He chuckled. 'It can't be worse than my story.'

She turned her hand and he released her immediately. *You have some nerve,* she thought, wondering why his good opinion mattered even slightly to her. *Mind your tongue, Grace,* she told herself, after another long minute. As she sat there, Grace realised that she had never told her story to anyone, not even the Wilsons—at least, not the whole story.

Maybe it boiled down to this: she could say nothing and the social disgrace would be her uncomfortable secret from a man she would never see again after a few months. Or she could speak, with courage. He had done that—couldn't she be as brave?

'Not worse, just humiliating,' she said finally. 'Papa was a baronet and he had a lovely estate mortgaged to the hilt. Retrenchment was not in his vocabulary. He could have sold his estate and lived quietly in Bath on the proceeds, after paying his debts.' She stopped, unable to continue.

Rob put his arm around her, and she didn't pull away this time. 'You could see every red flag and he could see none, I suppose.'

She nodded, dabbing her eyes with her apron, breathing deeply of its comforting yeast and cinnamon. 'I would suggest some economising measure and he would give me such a wounded look.'

Suddenly shy, she glanced at Rob. There was nothing on his face but concern. 'Mama died years earlier. I can't help wondering if she felt some relief…'

'Go ahead, Gracie,' he said, his eyes kind. 'There were probably moments when you hated your father for being so careless of your own future.'

'I did! I did!' she burst out. 'I wanted him dead so I could try my hand at salvaging the family name, at least. If we had sold some land and practised strict economy, I would still have a home.' She scrubbed at her eyes fiercely, almost daring him to say anything. 'Perhaps I could have married…' She let the thought drift away, because it was too intimate to share with a man.

He remained silent, his arm firmly about her shoulders. For the smallest moment, Grace wondered what it would be like to drop her burdens at someone's feet other than her own. It passed.

Her offhand remark must have puzzled him. 'You can't marry?' he asked. 'Seems a waste of a pretty woman.'

She glanced at him, pleased and shy at the same time. Her mama had called her pretty, but that was what mothers did.

'Rob, just think, no one from my original social sphere would ever stoop to marrying me, because…because I have "slipped", as Lady Tutt so crudely put it. And no one from the sphere I live in now would ever assume to court someone from the gentry. It isn't done.'

'I see what you mean,' Rob said, after considering the matter. 'You'd fare a lot better in America.'

'Dan, I am twenty-eight, here *or* there!' she declared, laughing at the absurdity of it.

He slapped his forehead in mock vexation. 'An antique! What was I thinking?'

She never anticipated what he would do next. Without a word, he kissed her so quickly she almost wasn't sure he had done it.

'No problem there,' he said. 'Your lips work. You'd do well in America.'

'Don't do that,' she said as her face flamed.

'Am I too coarse for a baronet's daughter?' he asked just as quickly. 'I'll watch myself.'

Grace sighed inwardly, uncomfortable. How to whitewash over a kiss? 'And I'm a dunce,' she said, keeping her voice light. 'What's so special about America?'

'Name me another place where a poor wretch from the Pool of London could ever be a sailing master who owns his own home.' His smile was tinged with sadness. 'Or where said indentured servant—I was a slave!—could ever hope to marry a merchant's daughter.'

'That's what Elaine was?'

'Aye.' His shoulders slumped. 'I caught her fancy. What a blessing she was.'

It was simply said and told her worlds about his heart. They continued walking in silence, shoulders touching occasionally as they strolled along.

* * *

The silence lasted through dinner, a simple
meal of soup and rolls brought from the bakery
and eaten belowstairs. *I have slipped, indeed,
Lady Tutt,* she told herself, as Emery ate with
them. She looked at him with satisfaction, counting the old yard man safe because she had helped
him avoid the workhouse.

Her satisfaction would have continued all evening, if Lord Thomson hadn't banged on the door
with his walking stick.

Grace opened the door. 'Lord Thomson?'

'The only one.'

She couldn't bring herself to invite him in, but
he came in, anyway. 'Where's my uncle's bastard?' he asked, with no preamble.

'Right here,' Rob said, coming to stand beside Grace.

Lord Thomson drew himself up. 'Most people
address me as "my lord".' He glanced at Grace—
just a quick glance, but she felt suddenly unclean.
'Even bakery drudges.'

'You'll wait a long time for me to say milord,'
Rob replied. 'And she's no drudge.'

Don't, she wanted to warn Rob, but he didn't
need a warning. He stood there, eyeing the marquis, until the smaller man looked away.

Neither man spoke and no one moved, until
Lord Thomson reached into his inside pocket.
'What should appear upon my doorstep a few
minutes ago but a missive from Lady Tutt,

Quimby's biggest mushroom. She labours under the misconception that Lord Thomson harbours bastards under his roof. Stupid woman.'

Rob frowned at the marquis's vulgarity. 'Ladies present,' he murmured.

'No, there aren't.' Lord Thomson opened the letter. 'It seems she wants your attendance upon her tomorrow afternoon, to thank you for saving her life.' Lord Thomson looked at Rob through his quizzing glass. 'I heard about that little charade from my butler. Really, was it necessary for you to save her life? Think of the years of pretension we could have all been spared, if you had let her choke.'

He was trying to get a rise out of his poor relation, but Rob ignored it. 'I may be a bastard, but I don't read other people's mail,' the parolee said.

It was said cheerily enough, but Grace clearly heard the steel behind the words. Lord Thomson did, too, evidently. He threw the letter at the American, turned on his heel and left. The effect was muted somewhat by the fact that the front door he had left open behind him had quietly closed during his brief audience in the foyer. He hit the door with a smack and sat down abruptly.

Rob was too wise to laugh. He picked up the letter. 'Stay as long as you like,' he said. 'It's your dower house.' He left the foyer whistling 'Yankee Doodle'.

Lord Thomson leaped to his feet and yanked at his waistcoat, which had ridden up. He put a

shaking hand to his nose, which was beginning
to bleed. He gave a plaintive bleat at the sight of
his own blood, then twisted the doorknob, jerking it viciously until it opened.

'Some day you'll wish that hadn't happened,'
he snarled and slammed the door behind him.

'I'm ahead of you, Lord Thomson,' she murmured as she heard him stomp down the grav-
elled driveway. 'I *already* wish it.'

Chapter Twelve

It must have been the marquis's parting shot. Lord Thomson and the marchioness were gone the next day, leaving only a skeleton staff, according to Emery who announced their departure. 'I have my sources,' was all he would say, which amused Grace.

'Is this better or worse?' Rob asked, as they stood in the driveway, watching the carriage. He shook his head. 'Captain Cameron used to tell me, "Don't poke the bear", whenever I was inclined to get into a brawl with someone who could thrash me.'

'We didn't poke the bear,' Grace argued. 'He poked himself.'

'It's all the same, to a ninny like that,' the parolee said. 'What should we do? I am uneasy.'

They looked at each other. 'You need a haircut,' Grace said, after a long perusal.

Rob smiled at that. 'What an adroit change of topic, Gracie!' He reached over and touched the worry lines between her eyes. 'And you need not fear so much for me,' he told her. 'It's not worth thirty pounds of anxiety per annum. Tell you what, cut my hair and I'll shine my shoes and we'll visit Lady Tutt after work.'

She nodded, shy again. 'Maybe we should visit Mr Selway in Exeter. I would like his opinion about the odious Lord Thomson.'

'I've been wondering why we have not heard from him. Maybe you're right. Haircut first, then Lady Tutt and maybe Mr Selway, if we're still worried.'

His hair was easier to cut this time; not that it had changed much, but she felt more relaxed, so close to him. They went onto the lawn by the kitchen garden again and Grace snipped away, enjoying the opportunity to stare at his face, under the guise of making sure he was even on both sides. She tugged on the hair by both ears to make sure it matched. He sat still as she evened up the red-gold hair by his ears. 'I never move when women fidget around my ears with sharp objects,' he told her.

She tapped his cheek with the flat part of the scissors. 'How often has that ever come up in your life?' she teased back.

'Alas, not often enough,' he said. He started to take her hand, then must have changed his mind. 'You never finished your story yesterday.

Did you just go to the Wilsons and offer to work for them? Tell me.'

There was a low stone wall by the chair. She sat there, the shears in her lap. 'The lawyer read the will and, in almost the same breath, sold the house, its contents and the land to a brewer from Bristol. And there I was, homeless.'

'No relatives? No one?'

She shook her head. 'Mama's family had disowned her when she married Papa. She was the daughter of an earl and no one on that side of the family ever enquired after me.'

Rob tipped his chair back. 'It's hard enough for a young man to strike out on his own. You were eighteen?'

She nodded. 'I thought about throwing myself on the mercy of the district's better families, but I just couldn't.' She shrugged. 'The Wilsons had always been kind to me, even when I couldn't pay their bills. I went to them and offered to work for nothing, to pay off Papa's debt.'

'You indentured yourself.'

She glanced at him, startled. 'I suppose I did. I worked for two years, then Mr Wilson pronounced the debt paid. He was kind enough to hire me then.'

'You just walked into the bakery and laid it all out?'

She looked him in the eye then, admiring the brightness of his blue eyes, and the intelligence— or was it shrewdness?—that gazed back at her.

'Not as dramatic as crawling across a deck to wipe a captain's shoes, I suppose, but there was a similar measure of desperation…' She couldn't say any more.

'Neither of us had anything to lose, did we?' he asked, but his question didn't need answering.

He held out his hand to her and she took it. Again she had that curious feeling of laying her burden down, even if Rob Inman was as powerless as she was; more so, even, because he was a prisoner of war. She squeezed his hand, released it and stood up. *Better not get used to his kindness, Grace,* she told herself. *It can't last beyond a peace treaty.*

They were both quiet on their walk into Quimby. Halfway to the village, he took her hand, which made her heart hammer in her chest.

'I have a confession, Grace,' he said. 'Ever since I started working at the bakery, I've been wondering how I could escape and make my way to Plymouth.'

She stared at him. He released her hand. 'It's true. I'm desperate to shake the dust of England off my shoes. When you chose me in Dartmoor, I knew I could escape, especially after I saw the only things standing in my way were you, a doddering old man and a maid from the manor who thinks I'm handsome.'

Grace swallowed. *So do I,* she thought.

'But I can't. Lord Thomson would come down

on you like a mallet on a teacup. You'd lose your thirty pounds a year and…'

'I will probably lose that anyway,' she said.

'Maybe, maybe not.' He took her by both shoulders, after looking around to make sure no one watched. 'I can't promise I won't run. Who knows what might happen? But you chose me, Gracie, you're stuck with me until this war ends.'

He pulled her close then, doing it gently, gently as though he wasn't sure what she would do. She hesitated only a second, then gratefully rested her head against his chest.

'You can lean on me, Gracie,' he told her. 'You've been managing alone for too long and I know that gets tiresome. Comrades, then, until this war is over?'

She closed her eyes, breathing in the fragrance of his shirt, and nodded. 'Until it's over.'

'And I promise not to kiss you again,' he told her. 'After all, you're a baronet's daughter and we know where I came from.'

But how do you un-choose someone, when a war ends? Grace asked herself as they worked side by side in the bakery that day. She glanced at Rob occasionally, noting how serious he was. He chewed on his lip as he kneaded the bread, banging it harder on the boards than usual, and looking at her now and then, a frown on his face.

I must assure this good man that I really don't

require looking after, Grace thought. *He needn't worry about me, after he is back in America.*

The thought of America made her pause, hands wrist-deep in the dough. Was it really possible to start from scratch there? It was on the tip of her tongue to ask if Nantucket had a bakery, but she stopped herself in time.

It was almost a relief when she took off her apron after the last batch of bread was cooling and told Mrs Wilson that she and Rob had been invited to Lady Tutt's house. 'She only invited Captain Duncan, but I am his keeper and must attend, too.'

'If her high-and-mighty ladyship is feeling any remorse for all the bread she has pinched in past years, you might appeal to her better nature to pay me,' Mrs Wilson said. She made a shooing motion. 'Go on! If you keep her waiting, you'll never hear the end of it.'

Meekly, Rob took off his apron, too, and ran his fingers through his hair.

'You already look splendid, Captain,' Grace teased.

He could tease as well as she. 'I'm hoping she wants to put me in her will,' he said. He licked his finger and smoothed down his eyebrows, which made Grace laugh. 'Or, at the very least, do odd jobs for her.'

'She cannot ask you to do odd jobs, Captain, because I am your keeper.'

He grinned. 'Gracie, even Elaine never called me her keeper.' He shook his head, his eyes merry. 'She knew better!'

'That is the first time I have ever made a joke about my wife,' he said later, as they walked toward the Tutt mansion. 'It felt good, Gracie. Maybe that's how it happens. At first, it was too painful to even mention her name. Once in Dartmoor, I thought I had forgotten the colour of her eyes. I hadn't, of course. But now…' He stopped, giving her arm a slight tap. 'It's fun to remember the good times.'

It was so personal, so intimate, but Grace was growing used to Rob Inman's utter transparency. 'I'd like some day to think of my father in a kind light,' she said.

'You will,' he assured her. 'Maybe not tomorrow, maybe not for years.'

'I think too much anger turns a person bitter,' she said, as they started walking again.

'It can.' He took her hand and she could think of no objection. 'We're a strange pair. Maybe only someone who has crawled across a deck on his knees can understand what courage it took for a baronet's daughter to walk into a bakery and pledge to work off a debt.'

She nodded, unable to blink back the tears. His arm went around her shoulder then. 'You're ambitious, Grace, and I like that.' He chuckled.

'I don't even mind that I'm worth thirty pounds a year to you, which makes me valuable to you.'

'Am I crass?' she asked, embarrassed.

'Ambition is crass? Oh, it is not, Gracie! You want to own the Wilsons' bake house. More power to you.'

She took his hand this time. *He understands,* she thought, excited. 'I have ideas! I would bring in more sweets and more flavours of bread.'

'Cinnamon bread with raisins. Have you ever tried it?'

She shook her head.

'Oh, this is a deprived little island,' he said, shaking his head. 'I had no idea.'

She started to laugh then, realising in her heart that she had not laughed like that in years, if ever. Years of worry and work and anger seemed to turn into smoke and blow away. She stared at Rob Inman for a moment, then laughed again when he started to laugh.

In another moment they were both sitting on the roadside, back to back, leaning against each other as their laughter gradually subsided into isolated bursts of merriment and then just a general shoulder-shaking.

'This is absurd,' she managed to say finally. 'I'm not certain why we're laughing.'

'I know something even better than cinnamon bread. We'll try it tomorrow.'

'We're going to Exeter tomorrow,' she reminded him. 'To find Mr Selway.'

'The day after, then. This will make the Wilsons a fortune.'

She looked over her shoulder, interested. He looked at her, too, until they were cheek to cheek. He was so close; he smelled lovely of cinnamon and yeast. She kissed his cheek impulsively. 'Cinnamon drives me wild,' she whispered and he started to laugh again.

He stood up and pulled her to her feet. 'Gracie, you're amazing. Behave yourself and let's visit Lady Tutt.'

She was blushing furiously now, grateful only that no one else was on the side road to watch such total foolishness. 'Thank goodness no one saw that.'

He grew suddenly serious and held her off. 'Don't be certain. Did I mention to you that I think we're being watched all the time? I thought not.'

Chapter Thirteen

Grace looked around, her eyes wide. 'Are you certain? Who? Why didn't you say something?'

He shrugged, as serious as she was, even though his face was still ruddy. 'Maybe because it seems silly. It's Emery.'

'Why would he do that?'

'Remember that henchman of Lord Thomson's who was waiting for us on the other side of that little knoll?' he asked, as they resumed walking. 'The really ugly customer?'

'Yes. I think Lord Thomson called him a butler, but between you and me, I've never seen a butler who looked like a road mender.'

Rob nodded. 'I see him around Quimby, whenever we are there.'

'I don't doubt you,' she replied. 'But Emery?'

'I think he's watching Ugly Butler—that's

what I have been calling him—who is watching us.'

'Then thank God for Emery!' Grace lifted the door knocker.

Lady Tutt received them in her best sitting room. They knew it was her best because her butler told them so.

'Amazing,' Rob whispered, looking around a room overstuffed with furniture in the Egyptian style.

'Hush, I am admiring the wallpaper,' Grace said. It was an Italian scene, with coy flirtations between shepherds and shepherdesses who looked too overweight to cavort much.

'Good God,' he whispered back.

Lady Tutt swept into the room with the triumphant air of a spider who had captured a multitude of moths in her web.

'What do you think of my wallpaper?' she asked the parolee.

'Words fail me,' he said.

'Nothing like this in your country, is there?' Lady Tutt positively crowed.

'Not that I have seen,' he told her, 'and I've been to Boston, New York, Philadelphia and Baltimore. Charleston, too. But I live among pretty ordinary folk on Nantucket and we're not given much to…uh…the finer things.'

With a gesture—probably as well practised as her entrance—Lady Tutt had them sit. In a moment, there was a clanking from the hall as a maid struggled with a tea cart of majestic proportions. Grace glanced at Rob, who smiled even more broadly.

'Lady Tutt, you know how to entertain,' he said, with what sounded like total sincerity to Grace. 'Are those…could they be….éclairs?'

Before she replied, Lady Tutt glowered at Grace. 'He looks a trifle thin, Grace. I'd have thought you would prepare a more lavish table for someone compelled to eat so poorly on an American vessel. I realise he was subsequently lodged in one of our most enlightened prisons, but obviously not long enough for his own good.'

Grace couldn't think of a reply that would do such a stupid sentence justice. She should have trusted Rob Inman. He could lie about wallpaper, apparently, but that was all.

'Lady Tutt, I was fed well enough on the *Orontes*,' he told her. 'It's a ship and had its own challenges, I assure you. The problem came in Dartmoor, which *everyone* in England ought to be ashamed of.'

Lady Tutt frowned. 'Impossible! Only last week, the administrator of prisons visited our ladies' society—we go about doing good now and then. He assured us it was a modern facility in every way. Practically new.'

'I'm not mistaken,' he told her, trying to sound both apologetic and emphatic at the same time. 'I lived there a year and would have died, if Lord Thomson hadn't sprung me.'

Lady Tutt still didn't look as though she believed him, but graciously chose to soldier on. She indicated the overloaded tea cart. 'Have whatever you'd like, Captain.'

Rob needed no urging to eat. He loaded his plate, then popped an éclair in his mouth. 'Excellent, Lady Tutt. I will rescue you any day of the week, if éclairs are involved.'

Lady Tutt tittered. 'I cannot imagine what I choked on.'

Umbrage and purloined bits of bread, Grace thought grimly, as she selected an éclair.

She sat back and watched Rob Inman calmly eat his way through the tea cart, modestly deflecting Lady Tutt's effusive thanks for her survival as she poured tea from a hyper-ornate silver pot, and sent the maid running for more éclairs.

When she had finished—Rob had discovered caramel-coated biscuits and showed no signs of stopping—Lady Tutt folded her hands in her lap. 'There now. Since you were so quick-witted to save me from a terrible death, as—'

'I was,' Rob said earnestly, which made Grace press her napkin hard against her lips.

'...from a terrible death,' Lady Tutt continued inexorably, 'I invited you here to show you that I bear no hard feelings over America's cruel perfidy in so underhandedly attacking British shipping, with no provocation.'

Grace pressed harder and glanced at Rob again.

'Uh, Lady Tutt, I think you have that backward,' he said, after another longing look at the caramel biscuits. 'Was your source the same prison administrator?'

'Heavens, no!' she declared. 'It was a member of the Admiralty. We believe it is the duty of every benevolent society to know what is going on in one's country. At least, what is approved for ladies to know.'

'Um, aye,' he replied. 'Actually, the Royal Navy has an ungentlemanly habit of snatching American sailors off their ships and impressing them.'

'They would never,' Lady Tutt said, all complaisance. 'The Admiralty officer said the Royal Navy was only guiding home Englishmen who got mixed up in America, somehow.' She patted his hand. 'That's why you're confused.'

Rob struggled on doggedly. 'Lady Tutt, there is also the matter of British fur traders inciting Indians to burn and loot American settlements along the frontier, and scalp my countrymen.'

'Surely nothing more than a rumour, young man. Your president is such a hothead.'

You might as well urge the tide not to go in and out, Grace thought, amused.

'President Madison has been called many things, but not generally a hothead,' Rob said, but Grace could tell he was weakening under Lady

Tutt's barrage of misinformation. He took a sip of tea to fortify himself. 'At any rate, I was glad to render you a service in the bakery. We can both agree that was a good thing.'

'Indeed we can, Captain Duncan,' Lady Tutt said, sailing serenely on, convinced of her facts. She indicated Grace with a nod. 'Grace, it wasn't necessary for you to accompany the captain here today. I don't recall inviting you.'

Grace felt her face grow warm. 'You didn't, Lady Tutt,' she managed to say.

'That is the term of my parole,' Rob said quickly. There was an edge to his voice that Grace knew was not her imagination. 'I cannot leave Lord Thomson's estate without Grace Curtis, or I will be shot. That is a fact. I need Grace Curtis.'

'What a silly rule,' Lady Tutt said. 'I believe I will write to the Lord Admiral and have you released to *my* custody.'

The captain shook his head. 'The condition must stand, Lady Tutt. I know you are impervious to any possibility that England could be at fault in this war—'

'She is not,' Lady Tutt interrupted.

'Ah, yes. I promise faithfully not to ruin anyone in Quimby with my republican sentiments. You'll have to excuse us now.' He glanced at Grace. 'It's getting dark and I turn into a werewolf once a month.'

Grace stifled her laughter by holding her lips tight together and looking across the room. Lady

Tutt didn't even blink. She held out her hand and
Rob took it, giving it a firm, republican shake,
and not a kiss.

'Dear, misguided boy. If you ever need anything, I would be happy to oblige,' she said, as
she rose as gracefully as her bulk would allow
and walked them to the door of the sitting room.
'I owe you my life, after all. Good day, Grace.'

'She didn't listen to a single word I said,' was
his first comment as Grace hurried him from the
mansion so she could laugh. He shook his head
and ducked theatrically when she pummelled
him. 'What? Maybe I *could* turn into a werewolf.
Never tried it.' He shook his head. 'I'm sorry she
was rude to you.'

Grace shrugged. 'I'm never used to it, but it
bothers me less and less.'

He took her arm. 'You're a terrible liar. It bothers you.' He shook his head again. 'Grace, if I had
stayed there one more minute, my head would
have exploded!'

'Or your stomach,' she teased. 'I gave up counting the éclairs.'

'Wise of you.'

Twice, Rob had taken her arm and stopped on
the way back to Quarle, listening to other footsteps, which had finally stopped, too. 'Ugly Butler,' he had whispered both times.

'I can't keep calling him that,' he said finally,

as they came onto Lord Thomson's estate again, once they were through the vicar's orchard.

'I rather like it,' Grace said. 'Ugly Butler.'

'Grace, you're a rascal,' Rob teased. 'Why didn't I notice that before?'

'You were too busy looking around for something to eat,' she retorted.

Emery came into the kitchen as she finished preparing dinner, offering no explanation for his tardiness. She smiled at him, touched by his willingness to keep an eye on Ugly Butler for them and his modesty in not admitting it. *I suppose we all like a little drama in our lives,* Grace thought, as she watched with appreciation as he set the table.

'Emery, maybe you *should* have been a butler,' she told him. 'You're good.'

He gave her a slow wink, which made her laugh.

'Emery, do you want any help with the dishes?'

He shook his head. 'I think you'd rather be sitting with the captain than drying a plate or two,' he observed.

She could have been embarrassed, but what was the point? 'Emery, you are wise beyond your advanced years,' she teased.

Rob was sitting on the front steps, which he seemed to prefer, even though it struck Grace as strange. *What would my father say?* she asked herself, as she watched him a moment, then joined him. *Do I even care?*

'Do you sit on your front step in Nantucket?' she asked.

'I have a nice porch with chairs,' he told her. 'I like to watch the sun go down over the bay. Elaine would knit and I'd prop my feet on the porch railing and howdy my neighbours.' He sighed. 'I wasn't home much.'

'Who lives in your house now?'

He shrugged. 'No one. Maybe some spiders and mice now. Of course, Elaine's father was my agent for the house, so it is probably let. I want to go home.'

She heard the frustration in his voice and the longing. *Would I miss Quimby if I left it?* she asked herself. Better not to even think about it. She was here and that was that. Still… It was impulsive, but how to ask him?

'Rob, suppose someone from England wanted to settle in America. Wouldn't they shun…that person…because she—or he—was British?'

He thought about that, shaking his head. 'Nantucket has its fair share of Lady Tutts, I assure you. But if you can do something well, no one would disparage you. We look out for each other.'

She was sitting a step down from him. He eased himself down and sat next to her. 'You—or someone like you—could start with nothing and become something. I did.'

Grace shook her head, exasperated with herself. 'Why am I even asking this?'

He leaned against her shoulder, just a brief pressure. 'Maybe it's time for a change, Grace.' He smiled. 'Or…someone you might know, of course.'

She thought about what he had said as she brushed her hair and braided it, sitting crosslegged on her bed in her nightgown. Summer was in full bloom and the room was warm. She had opened the windows in hopes that a breeze would pass her way, but nothing stirred outside.

Her head told her that no place could possibly be as perfect as Nantucket. Rob Inman was just homesick and glorifying his small island. Her heart wanted to see it through her own eyes—the beaches, the grey-shingled houses, the sea gulls.

Rob knocked on her door and her heart jumped a little. She knew it wasn't Emery, who had retired an hour ago. She tugged her nightgown down around her ankles and reached for her shawl.

'Yes?'

'May I come in?'

He was still dressed, but he had pulled his shirt tails out of his trousers and removed his shoes. He closed the door and pulled a chair closer to the bed.

'Grace, if we go to Exeter, I'm certain we're going to be followed by Ugly Butler.'

'Why?'

He shrugged. 'Why is he following us now? Be sure to take along that parole document. Lord Thomson would like nothing better than to shoot me, or, at the very least, return me to Dartmoor. I'm not in favour of either scenario.'

She put her brush in her lap, wondering why she had worried about him seeing her in her nightgown. He was all business. 'Then let us do this, the local bonecracker stops at that junction where we sat the other day. The first one comes by before the sun is up. Let's take that one to Exeter.'

'And we won't tell Emery.' In answer to her look, he held up both hands. 'Honestly, Grace. The less he knows, the less danger we will cause him.'

'True. I hadn't thought of that. We'll tiptoe out of the house like thieves in the night.'

'I like that plan.' He frowned then, and she saw his embarrassment. 'I don't have a penny to my name for the carriage.'

'Mr Selway left some money with me,' she said. 'It's not much, but it will get us to and from Exeter, and buy a sausage or two for a noon meal. Mr Selway will furnish us with more when we visit him.'

He nodded. 'You're a sensible soul, Grace, and quite fetching in flannel.'

She made a face at him.

'I admit I want to see Mr Selway, too,' he told

her. 'Ugly Butler makes me uneasy and I wonder when Lord Thomson will show his nasty vis-
age again. I'd also like to hear a little news about
the war.'

Grace laughed. 'You mean Lady Tutt's views
aren't enough?'

He just rolled his eyes, then held out his hand.
'Give me your brush, Grace, and undo that particular braid. You missed a hunk of hair in the back.'

She knew her mother would have had spasms,
but she handed him her brush, then untied the
braid, running the hair through her fingers. He
was right; she had missed a hunk of hair.

'That's better.' He sat on her bed and she obe-
diently turned her back to him, enjoying the unheard-of pleasure of someone brushing her hair,
something that no one had done for her after
Mama had died.

'I used to squirm when my mother did that,'
she said, surprised how breathless she sounded.
'She would usually rap me on the head with the
brush and tell me that if I didn't behave, Napoleon would get me.'

He laughed and rapped her head lightly with
the brush. 'In Massachusetts, the threat is Indians.' He brushed in silence until her hair began to
crackle. 'You have beautiful hair, Gracie.'

She didn't want him ever to stop. 'It's just
brown. You're the one with lovely hair.'

He braided her hair expertly and she knew,
with a pang, that he must have done this many

times for his Elaine. How had that ended each evening? she wondered. Would he turn her around and kiss her? And where did it go from there? And what would she do if he kissed her now?

She felt his breath on her neck, but nothing else, which she told herself was a relief, after he said, 'Nice braid, Gracie', wished her goodnight, and left her room. She lay awake a long time, seeing a handsome man sitting on a porch in Nantucket, feet up and visiting with his neighbours as a sweet-faced woman knitted.

'Why couldn't that have been me?' she asked softly, her hand gentle on the braid he had created so handily.

Chapter Fourteen

Grace woke early, squinting to see the little clock that Lord Thomson must have missed when he plucked the dower house clean. Four-thirty. She tiptoed to the door, knowing which squeaky floorboards to avoid.

She let herself into Rob Inman's room. He was breathing evenly; she listened for a moment, enjoying the homely sound. As she stood in his room, she thought about all the years in her little room off the bakery ovens, hearing no one else, because the Wilsons slept upstairs. *I have lived too much in solitude,* she told herself. *I have also been angry for too long. Rob is right. I don't want to be angry any more.*

But now it was time to wake the parolee. She leaned over him, reaching out to tap his shoulder. Instead, his hand went around her wrist. She gasped and clutched his bare shoulder.

'I'm awake,' he whispered. 'Didn't mean to knock ten years off your life.'

Startled, she blurted, 'Did we never see that you had a night shirt? I can remedy that.'

He chuckled. 'What would I do with a night shirt?'

'Wear it at night,' she replied, feeling as stupid as she sounded.

'Never wore one before,' he said. She heard him sit up and realised she still had her hand on his warm shoulder. 'You have a choice, Gracie, either close your eyes, or exit the room. Or leave them open if you wish. I don't think I've ever startled horses.'

Good thing the room was dark and the parolee couldn't see her fiery cheeks. 'Mind your manners! I think I will tiptoe quietly out,' she whispered.

'Good choice. Let's meet outside the front door. The side door is too close to the kitchen and Emery might hear us.'

She dressed quickly, lighting a candle only to find the parole Mr Selway had left with her. She had decided it was safest to keep the document in her room, hidden in a pouch behind her aprons. She hung the pouch around her neck and out of sight.

Rob was sitting on the front steps when she quietly opened the outside door. She could just see him in the moonrise.

'Ready?' he whispered.

He surprised her by picking her up and carrying her across the gravel of the curved driveway, then setting her down on the grass. 'Quieter,' he said. He took her hand. 'Let's walk in the borrow pit.'

A single lamp burned in an upstairs window as they silently passed the manor house. 'Ugly Butler keeps early hours,' she whispered.

'Or he's scared of the dark.'

Grace put her hand to her mouth to stifle a laugh. Rob held tight to her hand as they walked to the junction, waiting with a woman and two cages of chickens. Grace recognised her as the wife of one of Lord Thomson's crofters.

Grace exchanged pleasantries with the woman. ''Tis market day in Exeter,' the tenant said.

So it was. The local carriage to Exeter was already full of hopeful people like the crofter's wife, carrying goods to market. The driver assessed them. 'Sonny, you'll have to put your wife on yer lap,' he told Rob, then laughed. 'This doesn't mean she's merchandise to sell in Exeter!'

'I wouldn't dream of such a thing,' Rob said, doing a creditable imitation of Grace's own West Country burr, 'even if she is as sweet as a basket of strawberry tarts.'

Everyone laughed. Grace's cheeks flamed. Rob squeezed himself between the woman with the chickens and a man with a single pig. The parolee patted his lap and she sat down, with nowhere to put her arms but around his neck. Both of his arms went around her waist.

'Gracie, you're an everlasting temptation,' he whispered.

'And you are just shy of certifiable,' she whispered back, which made him chuckle.

The other passengers in the crammed conveyance beamed at her. The man seated next to Rob nudged him in the ribs. 'She's a tasty morsel, lad,' he boomed out, which made the pig squeal.

'Sir, you have no idea,' Rob replied. Two geese flapped their wings and honked.

'You're determined this is going to be the hardest thirty pounds I have ever earned,' Grace whispered in his ear, under the noise of the poultry.

'Gracie, don't blow in my ear,' he said. 'It's almost more than a man a year in Dartmoor can stand.'

I have said enough, she thought. Still, Rob Inman was comfortable to sit on, now that a few months of good food had filled him out. And there was still that wonderful fragrance of cinnamon and yeast from his shirt, and his own pleasant odour, nothing more than sun, newly washed hair and whatever it was that made him Rob Inman: sailing master, widower from Nantucket, enemy of the crown and her own parolee.

Her silence must have inspired some remorse from her charge. 'I shouldn't be such a tease,' he whispered practically in her ear.

'And I should play along better,' she whispered back. 'I can do that, you rascal.'

With a small sigh of her own, she rested her head against the captain's chest and closed her eyes. His arms settled around her more gently and he seemed to naturally lean his head on hers. *I wish I had your confidence,* she thought, and then she slept.

The seagulls woke her; she sat up on Rob's lap, wondering if she was still dreaming.

'I think this must be the market square,' he said. 'It's as noisy as Nantucket's harbour. Do we get off here?'

Grace nodded. She felt his sigh, then he surprised her with a kiss to the top of her head.

'My legs have gone to sleep,' he told her. 'On the way back, I'll sit on *your* lap.'

She laughed, waiting until the others with chickens, geese and one amazingly out-of-place cockatoo left the carriage, intent on their modest commerce. Looming above all was Exeter Cathedral. Beyond that, she knew, was the city's Chancery Lane, where the barristers and solicitors competed for business.

Business. That was it. Time to get off Rob's comfortable lap and find Mr Selway. She left the carriage, shaking the wrinkles from her dress and looking at the cathedral, one of England's loveliest. 'I doubt you have anything to compare with this in Nantucket,' she said to Rob.

He shook his head. 'I know we're not here to gawk and sightsee, but can we go inside?'

His open-mouthed reaction inside the cathedral gave her a warm glow. He stared at the intricate ribbing overhead, turning around to admire the building's magnificence.

'Amazing,' he murmured. 'I go to meeting in a little shingled church just off the bay. Sometimes we sing louder than the seagulls caw, sometimes we don't.'

He walked further into the cathedral, eyes up mostly.

'You there! Shoo! Shoo!'

Startled, Grace turned to see a deacon coming toward them both, making motions with his hands, as though he would sweep them from the building. Rob moved quickly toward her, as though in her defence. His face was alert, with a determined set to his jaw that boded considerable ill will to the deacon, even if he was a man of the cloth.

Grace clamped her hand on his arm and stepped in front of him. 'Rob has never seen Exeter Cathedral before and we were—'

'Go on now!' the clergyman exclaimed. 'There is a wedding in an hour of people far above you two! Go away.'

After a long look, Rob turned on his heel and left the cathedral, Grace right behind. He didn't stop on the steps, but took long strides on to the lawn, where he stood finally, his hands tight into fists, his face grim.

'I will stick with my grey-shingled meeting house,' he said when he could speak. He held up his hand. 'Grace, don't apologise for your countrymen! There's no excuse.'

He was right; she had been about to offer an excuse for rudeness that had no excuse, except that they were poorly dressed. She looked away, unable to bear the hurt in his eyes. As she stood there, so embarrassed, another thought crossed her mind, one that took some of the sting away. A year ago, she would have thought little of the deacon's rudeness. She knew she had slipped and had no place in the more privileged world. Now she was embarrassed, because she saw the incident through Rob's eyes. He might have been a prisoner of war and a not-so-distant inmate of Dartmoor, but he knew he was the equal of that rude man—certainly his superior in manners. No wrong had the power to dismiss what he was— an American.

She couldn't put all that into words because she wasn't sure how. Grace raised her eyes to his, saw the wound there, but no loss of dignity. She touched his hand lightly, not certain how he would take it.

'Let us go and find Mr Selway,' she said simply.

They crossed the lawn in silence. Rob slowed

down as his anger cooled and he realised she was hurrying to keep up.

'I want to go home so badly,' he said.

'Perhaps Mr Selway can tell us of any progress.'

Perhaps. The problem? No one in Chancery Lane had ever heard of Mr Selway.

Grace had been to the rabbit warren of streets only a few months before her father's final illness, when she had almost convinced him to see a solicitor to discuss selling his estate. As they had approached the office, Sir Henry had exclaimed, 'Daughter, I am a baronet!' as though that would make him immune from his own self-induced ruin, not to mention hers.

Grace went to that same office because she remembered its location. She asked as politely as she knew how, short of grovelling, if the clerk could direct her to the office of Mr Philip Selway.

After a long stare, the clerk had condescended to ruffle through the pages of the magistrate's directory on his high desk. 'No one by that name in Exeter,' he said, still staring at the pages, probably hoping something would appear, so she would leave. 'I cannot find what isn't there.'

Grace turned away. After the rudeness in the cathedral, Rob had waited for her outside. He frowned when she shook her head.

'Not there?' he asked.

'Apparently not anywhere. The clerk looked

through a directory of some sort. There is no solicitor of that name in Exeter.'

They started down the street. He stopped after a while. 'I'm lost, Grace. Is there a straight thoroughfare in this entire town?'

'Probably not. Let's go back to the market square. You're probably famished. Eat away troubles, I always say.'

They found a stall where sausages snapped in the grease. Grace bought three and a grease-soaked packet of pasties. They walked to a low wall beside the River Exe and sat there, eating in silence.

'We've been diddled some way or other,' Rob said finally, wiping his hands on the grass. 'Didn't Mr Selway give you an address where the merchants in Quimby could forward the receipts for any purchases you made?'

She had forgotten that. 'He did. Should I go to the greengrocer tomorrow and ask if he has been paid for what I have bought?'

'I think so,' he said, his uncertainty evident. 'Surely you would have heard by now, if there were bills outstanding.'

She nodded. 'I will ask, but perhaps we should write to Mr Selway ourselves. He told me that letters are to go to Philip Selway, Esq., Postal Box Fifteen, Exeter. Mr Selway—'

'—or whoever he is—'

'—would have to retrieve any mail himself, but

we have no idea where he really is,' she finished. 'This makes me uneasy.'

'Aye. Maybe we misunderstood him. Maybe it wasn't Exeter.'

'It was Exeter, Rob.' Grace shivered, in spite of the summer's warmth. 'I don't understand what is happening. He prepared and read Lord Thomson's will, arranged for us to retrieve you—or at least, Captain Duncan—from Dartmoor, set up your maintenance in the dower house...'

'...and then he left, trusting you with everything,' Rob continued. He looked at her half-eaten pasty. 'I know this makes me as rude as the deacon at Exeter Cathedral thinks I am, but I could eat that, if you don't want it.'

He finished her pasty and wiped his hands again. 'Let's go back to Quimby and write to Mr Selway, or whoever he is.' He stood up and pulled her up with him. 'I'm going to look for a newspaper first, if you'll spot me a penny or two.'

She looked in her reticule and looked again, as if hopeful something would appear. 'Better see if you can find a paper left in a dustbin. I thought we could get some money from Mr Selway today, so all I have is coach fare.'

He grinned. 'I'm resourceful, Gracie. I should find something easily enough. I can't quite believe that Lady Tutt's interpretation of the war is the last word in accuracy. Wait here.'

She nodded, sitting on the low wall again to watch the River Exe, until she remembered the danger of letting Rob Inman out of her sight. She leaped up and ran after him as he crossed the market square.

'I can't leave you alone!' she said, breathless, when she caught up to him.

'Don't you trust me by now?' he asked, chiding her gently.

She tugged at his arm. 'You don't understand! Suppose Ugly Butler followed us? I have to go where you go because I hold your parole. Someone has to worry, if you won't!' It all came out in one breath.

He took her by both shoulders. 'Slow down, Gracie! We haven't been followed today.'

She couldn't help the tears that welled in her eyes. 'I couldn't bear it if you were hauled away or shot.'

He pulled her close, unmindful of the people in the marketplace. 'Grace, I'll be fine. Hey now, don't waste a tear over a Yankee sailing master!'

She sobbed and clung to him. 'Oh, Gracie,' he crooned. 'We'll figure this out. Don't be so fearful.' He tipped her chin up. 'Or tearful. There's not a man alive who has any defence against that, no matter what his nationality.' He clapped his arm around her shoulders and started moving again. 'I reckon you'll have to come with me behind that public house there, so I can search through a dustbin. Maybe the deacon in the cathedral had us pegged. Grace, you're consorting with low company.'

'I am not!' she said, indignant.

'Are too,' he contradicted. 'Wait here at the top of the alley...I'm in plain sight!'

She did as he said, fingering the strings of the little pouch around her neck holding the parole papers, as he searched through a dustbin, then another. He stopped finally and shook off what looked like bread crumbs.

'Success. Let's see what Lady Tutt has not told us.'

He read the odourous paper as they waited for the conveyance, frowning over the news. 'What day is it, my dear parole officer?'

'July 25,' she said promptly. 'I am *not* your parole officer.'

'Bow Street Runner, then,' he teased. He folded the paper and set it beside him. 'Six-week-old news is hardly better than Lady Tutt.'

'Bad?'

'We were not prepared for this war,' he said. 'Now that Napoleon is on Elba, your army has turned its full attention to my country.' He frowned at the paper. 'Now the redcoats are raiding up and down the Atlantic coast, burning, pillaging and raping. Or they were six weeks ago.' Looking grim, he rested his elbows on his knees. 'This hasn't been much of a cheerful outing, has it?'

She shook her head.

'I learned today that we're not good enough for Exeter Cathedral, Mr Selway doesn't exist and my country could be in ruins,' he said, his eyes on the approaching conveyance. 'Learn anything today, my dear Gracie Curtis?' he asked.

My dear Gracie Curtis. She closed her eyes, wishing he would not tease her. 'Mostly I wish I knew what was going on,' she said, digging in her reticule for carriage fare. 'Maybe I wish you were home in Nantucket.'

Maybe I wish I were there, too, she added in her heart.

Chapter Fifteen

The carriage was empty on the return journey. In solitude, Grace searched her mind for any information about Mr Selway that she might have remembered. All she could dredge up was a mild-looking man who had assured her that watching Captain Duncan would be easy and rewarding.

You've been nothing but trouble, but what can I do? she asked herself, glancing at Rob, who slept. *If I give up and return to the bakery by myself, you'll be sent back to Dartmoor.*

She looked away. It was almost tempting never to think of Rob Inman or Nantucket again. She leaned back, her eyes closed, struck with the notion that maybe Lady Tutt was right: she *had* slipped. The worst of it wasn't the decline in her social status, but the death of hope, which had perished with her father. How a prisoner on parole—and not even the right one—could bring that back, Grace had no idea. But he had. Maybe hope was more uncomfortable than social slippage. Something heavy in her heart told her that if she lost hope again, it would never return.

She looked at Rob again. His eyes were open now.

'You look like you're carrying the weight of the world,' he said.

'I don't know what to do,' she replied frankly.

He took her hand and looked at it, as though he wanted to kiss it. 'You've kept me alive. You've given me something to do. I've done nothing in return.'

He didn't release her hand until she moved her fingers. Suddenly it was too much. She moved closer to her side of the carriage, away from him. 'Rob—Daniel—Captain—what you've done is make me vastly discontent with my lot!'

He looked away. 'I didn't mean to.'

'Well, you have,' she said, trying to control the shaking in her voice. 'I'm living on sufferance in a dower house, worrying over thirty pounds per annum—thirty pounds!—and you tell me how wonderful Nantucket is. I could thump you for that!'

'Thump away,' he said softly, moving closer and turning his shoulder to her.

Aghast at herself, she burst into tears, covering her face with her hands and trying to make herself small in the carriage. Rob reached for her.

She slapped his arm as hard as she could, then did it again.

'Shame on you, Rob Inman!' she declared, wondering where all this anger came from. 'I was going to work, buy that bakery and then work harder, with no more expectations.' She stopped for breath.

'What happened?' he asked.

She punched him again. 'You made me think, even for a tiny moment, that I should want more than that.' She scrubbed at her eyes, wishing her tears would stop. 'That there is a place where people would accept me for who I am, not remember who I was!'

She knew she should stop, but she plunged on, scarcely aware of what she was saying. 'That maybe someone—who, I don't know—might even marry me.'

'Someone might,' he said. 'It's quite likely.'

'Stop it!' she said, her hands over her ears. 'You're just a prisoner of war. A…a mere sailing master! What do you know about *anything?* I *am* a baronet's daughter! You're nobody, from the Pool of London!'

What she had said was so rude that it took her breath away. The smallest glance in Rob's direction showed how hurt he was. Appalled, she at last had the wit to be silent.

The bonecracker stopped then, letting them out at the junction where their journey had begun that morning. It was dark now. Too embarrassed to wait for the coachman to help her down, Grace leaped from the carriage and ran. She couldn't remember a time when she had shed so many tears and showed off her own arrogance so thoroughly, she who had nothing left to be arrogant about. She had insulted the one person, aside from the Wilsons, she could rightfully call a friend.

I'm a fool, she told herself, as she pounded along the footpath by the highway. Maybe before she threw herself on her bed for a good cry, she would write to the elusive Mr Selway and demand that he take Captain Duncan off her hands. 'He can find another keeper,' she muttered. 'I can't do this. Rob Inman brings out the worst in me.'

That wasn't it, she had to admit. Whether meaning to or not, her parolee had made her think that she could be more, when she had lost hope. She sobbed out loud. *And I insulted him so cruelly,* she thought, flogging herself mentally. *What was I thinking?*

Grace stopped suddenly. She had left the captain by the junction and it wasn't Lord Thomson's land. Anything could happen to him. She started back down the road, her heart in her mouth.

There he was, trudging along the footpath, his head down. Ashamed of herself for her outburst, she waited for him. He didn't see her yet, but there he was, making his way back to the estate of someone he despised, to continue his parole in a country he couldn't wait to leave, at the mercy of a rude woman, one who had no business being pretentious, who had flung his own low origins in his face. Her face burned with shame.

Something happened to her heart in that small space between the time she watched and the time he saw her. She could have explained it to no one, because she didn't understand it. Rob Inman was more than someone she had grudgingly agreed to help until a war ended. He had become the only man she would ever love in her whole life. Maybe it had been coming on gradually; she didn't know, because she generally kept too busy to indulge in idle fancy. But there he was, still on the thin side: a man who had dropped into her life, because of an impulsive decision on her part.

He didn't know it, obviously, but she did. *And here it ends, because I am the fool,* she told herself. *I doubt he can forgive such rudeness. I know I couldn't.*

She stood still, overriding emotions she had never expected to feel, wondering if there were enough words in the English language to take away the hurt she had just hurled at a decent, kind man.

'I am so sorry,' she said, her voice small, when he came to her. 'It's not your fault that you miss your home and you'd rather be away from this wretched island. I shouldn't have said what I did. It was inexcusable.'

He raised his head to look at her and Grace was mortified to see tears in his eyes.

'I had no call to behave that way. Forgive me, Rob.'

If he had walked on past her, she wouldn't have been surprised. If he never said another word to her, she would have understood. Instead, he put his hands gently on her shoulders and drew her close to him. With another sob, her arms went around him and she clung to him, racked by those horrible deep sobs again.

'Gracie, you're my only friend,' he said finally, making no effort to distance himself from her misery. 'Don't make it so hard.'

Your friend, she thought. *I will learn to be content with that, because I must. How could you possibly forgive what I said?*

Grace said nothing. Rob kept one arm protectively around her shoulders and walked with her. *This man is powerless and he is protecting me,* she thought in awe.

Silent now, they passed the manor, where more lights burned than this morning. Ugly Butler was outlined in the window, watching the road.

'Fooled you this time,' Rob said. He had the effrontery to wave, which made Grace swallow in sudden fright. The silhouetted figure at the window turned away quickly. 'Oops, made him angry. I'm all a-tremble, Gracie.'

She looked at him, her frown back, her fear

there again. 'Let's not make him angrier than he already is,' she suggested.

'You're probably right. I mean, he might send me back to Dartmoor.'

'Don't even tease about that!' Grace said.

He squeezed her shoulder. 'A minute ago, you stormed off and left me to my fate at the junction,' he reminded her.

'I still want my thirty pounds a year, because I'm ambitious,' she said gruffly, which made him laugh, to her relief. She had ruined things, but there wasn't any need for him to know how badly.

Emery wasn't laughing. Grace had never seen a more wounded expression and, underneath it, more irritation than worry, or so it seemed to her.

'I didn't know where either of you was,' he said, as he gestured toward the kitchen, trying to look dignified.

'We went to Exeter to find Mr Selway,' Grace said, as Emery dished out the ragout she had made yesterday.

'What did he have to say?' Emery asked, sitting down with his own bowl.

'We couldn't find him. No one has heard of him,' she said.

As she spoke, she glanced at Rob, who was seated beyond Emery. He gave an almost imperceptible shake of his head.

'I'll…I'll just write to Mr Selway,' she concluded, turning her attention to the ragout. She understood Rob Inman's worry. Maybe it *was* best to keep Emery in the dark. The less he knew, the less likely Ugly Butler could worm anything out of him.

'What *is* that man's name?' Grace asked. 'We've been calling him Ugly Butler. You worked for Lord Thomson—surely you know his name, Emery?'

'Ugly Butler?' The former yardman came as close to mirth as Grace had even noticed. 'I believe he rejoices in the name of Nahum Smathers.'

The parolee winced. 'That's awful! I prefer Ugly Butler.' He grinned at Grace. 'Reminds me of New England names back home, which all come out of the Bible, or maybe some virtue.'

He sounded almost like himself again. It was too facile of her to think he could overlook her rude behaviour, but he seemed to want to try. 'What do you mean?' she asked, intrigued.

'Would you believe Elaine's sister was named Patience? Which she was not,' he added, under his breath. 'And one of my neighbours rejoices in the name of Tidal Wave, because his father had a dream about that just before his son was born.'

Grace burst out laughing. 'You're serious?'

'We call him Tidy, for short.' Rob grinned at Emery. 'So Nahum is nothing. I still prefer Ugly Butler.'

Emery dished up more ragout for Rob, who nodded his thanks and dug in again. 'Smathers walked up and down in front of the dower house a few times this morning,' he said. 'I thought he went to town, but I lost him.'

'Doesn't matter. Emery, you're a regular Bow Street Runner,' Rob exclaimed.

Emery lowered his eyes modestly, looking surprisingly coy for someone of advanced years. Grace turned her head so he would not see her smile.

'As to that, Captain, I'm becoming skilled at sidling along just out of sight, and blending into the foliage.'

If I don't leave right now, I'll embarrass him, Grace thought, her weary brain suddenly lively with visions of the cadaverous Emery, so ramshackle, turning into an elm. She got up. 'Goodnight!'

Grace braided her hair and got into bed, lying in the dark, her hands behind her head. Her worries returned as she stared at the ceiling, with its whorls of plaster applied during the reign of a much earlier George. Tomorrow she would write to Mr Selway and… 'Ask him what?' she said out loud to a plaster whorl that looked like a lopsided apple. 'Where he is? Tell him I'm worried about Ugly Butler? Demand some money?'

She punched her pillow, wishing it were less lumpy. *I could use more money, considering that I spent the last of it on our fruitless trip to Exeter,* she decided, then turned her face into the pillow, smothering a laugh. At least Emery was watching

Mr Smathers. *I would almost give a portion of my increasingly hard-earned legacy to see that,* she told herself.

Still aching with the needless pain she had caused Rob, she listened to the house grow quiet. Finally she heard the American's footsteps on the stair. *Don't pass my door,* she thought suddenly. *Knock and come in, please.*

She held her breath. He knocked.

'Come in,' she said, mystified at the ways of providence.

He had removed his shoes. He closed the door quietly behind him, stood a moment, uncertain, then sat cross-legged on the end of her bed. She watched him, unsure of herself, even though she had wished him here. The room was still light. She hadn't bothered to close her curtains and he was visible, down to the wry look on his face.

'I ate too much ragout,' he said. 'Never thought I'd ever say I ate too much, but I did. Do you have a remedy?'

'Peppermint tea,' she said, pulling back the sheet, relieved to think she could do something for him besides wound him. 'I'll get you some.'

He put his hand on her foot. 'Later.' He released her and she got under the covers again.

'I worry too much. Is there a remedy for that?'

'I do, too,' she admitted. 'No remedy.' *If you can overlook my rudeness, I can, too,* she told herself.

He leaned back against the footboard, making himself comfortable. 'Maybe Captain Duncan would have been less trouble to you than Rob Inman.' He smiled, his eyes reflecting an earlier memory. 'He was always more inclined to let matters take their own course. On the *Orontes*, I was more like you: worrying, testing the wind, wondering why no one else seemed as concerned as I was about the smallest things.'

'You sound like a captain.'

He looked at her seriously, then nodded. 'Before the old man died, Dan's stepfather told me to keep an eye on him and not fear to prod him into action when he needed it.'

'Did you?'

'Aye, often.'

Grace drew her knees up and rested her chin on them. 'I will allow you to worry about both Emery and Mr Smathers, if you want.' She hesitated a moment, wanted to hold out her hand to him, but was afraid to. 'Forgive me?'

'For what?' His expression turned to something close to chagrin. 'I have to confess, this afternoon when I said I was going to look for a broadside—anything with news about the war—I was planning to do a runner.'

'Rob! You assured me you wouldn't!'

'I know.' He sighed. 'I noticed two East India merchant vessels in the harbour. I could have been on one...'

'...going to India.'

'Out of here, at least,' he finished. 'Once I got

into a foreign port, it would be simple to jump ship for home.'

'I think you know I wouldn't have screamed for a constable. Why didn't you?'

He scratched his head; the wry look returned.

'I can have peppermint tea for you in a minute or two,' she offered again.

'That's not the matter. It's a delicate thing, Gracie.'

'You'd miss my Quimby Crèmes,' she teased, then threw up her hands. 'Rob, you baffle me.'

'I realised if I fled Exeter, I'd miss you.'

He said it so quietly she wondered if she had heard wrong. 'What did you say?'

'You heard me.' He put his hand on her ankle again. 'I think my sojourn, courtesy of Captain Duncan, has taken a strange turn.'

Chapter Sixteen

Good thing I'm sitting down, Grace thought, her mind a jumble. She moved her foot and he removed his hand, murmuring 'Sorry.'

'Poor man,' she told him gently, even as her heart hammered against her ribcage. 'You're missing your late wife. Do I remind you of her?'

'Not at all and that's the funny part,' he said, shaking his head. 'Elaine was calm and peaceful and never raised her voice. You're a worrywart and a manager and not precisely shy about ordering me around.' He grinned at her. 'You remind me of a little rat terrier Dan Duncan used to own. Tenacious little thing.'

'Oh, horrors, then, you've lost your mind,' she joked. 'Do I *look* like Elaine at least? I know you're homesick.'

He shook his head again. 'I can't imagine two more different people, in temperament *and* looks. She had curly blonde hair and was short and round. Sorry, Gracie, but kneading bread has given you quite a set of shoulders and we nearly see eye to eye. Of course, you have the trimmest waist I've ever seen.'

'And my hair is straighter than a market road and my eyes are brown,' she concluded, her face rosy. 'Rob Inman, you're just lonely for *women*!' Her face felt even hotter. 'Pardon my plain speaking.' *That's all it is,* she thought, relieved and sad at the same time.

'You're entitled to your plain speaking,' he said. 'It's what I expect from you, words with no bark on them. Since we're speaking plain, it's true I haven't enjoyed a woman since my wife died, and that was going on four years ago. That's not it, Grace. I've been trying to figure this out. Part—but only part—of your charm is that you seem to have no idea how lovely you are.'

She couldn't think of any quick remark. 'Mama said I was pretty,' she said cautiously, after a long silence between them.

'She was right. You're also lively and opinionated. I loved my wife, Grace, but she had no opinions of her own. Humour me here a minute.' He glanced at her. 'The way I see it, my dear, is that you and I have something in common. I've never noticed it in a woman before, but let's face it, a seagoing man isn't around a lot of females. Maybe women like you are a penny a dozen, but I seriously doubt it.'

She prodded him with her foot. 'You're stalling, Rob Inman, and I'm losing patience with you.' *That's right, Grace, just joke with him,* she thought.

'Elaine never, ever would have said that to me. She was patience personified, even if her sister wasn't.' He grabbed her ankle through the sheet and she laughed, covering her mouth, before remembering that Emery was in the servants' quarters off the kitchen.

He released her ankle and raised up on one elbow to look at her. 'Grace, you're an impresario.'

'A *what*?' she asked, amazed.

'You heard me and you know what it means,' he said. 'You can take an idea and turn it into a success.'

She moved closer to him so she could take him by the arm and shake him. 'Rob, you peabrain, I am an assistant in a bakery! If I can't raise the money to buy it, that is all I will ever be!' She waved her arms around. 'Ordinarily, I live behind an oven.'

She grasped him by both arms now, trying to make him understand, when the silliness of her situation struck her. 'I'm raising my voice, I'm frank and I am opinionated, which must make me well nigh irresistible to you right now,' she said as she started to laugh.

'Oh, Grace, you can't imagine,' he teased.

'But by God, if I owned that bakery, I would make some changes.'

'See there? I told you so,' he declared, triumphant.

'"See there" what?' she demanded.

'It's this way, Grace, some day, someone besides a prisoner of war from—horrors!—Nantucket will see that quality in you,' he explained. 'And he'll be a lucky man, because he'll never, ever have to worry if you could manage things, should their whole world fall apart.'

'I don't follow you,' she said. She moved closer, then stopped herself, wanting him with all her heart, even as her heart broke, because he had no idea.

'I'm an impresario, too, so I know one when I see one. So what if you live behind the ovens! If something ever happened to the man…the man you might love some day…you would carry on and prosper. That lucky man would never fear for his children.' He tugged her braid. 'Do you have any notion how seductive that knowledge is? I thought not.'

'You belong in Bedlam,' Grace said at last, but it sounded feeble.

'I've never been more serious. While you've been feeding me, worrying about me, giving me things to do to keep away boredom, I've been studying you. I did it first because I was too ill to move. Then I started to pay attention because you're interesting.'

Grace decided that was unexceptionable enough. 'And this will render me irresistible to some poor fellow some day?'

'Absolutely,' he agreed promptly.

'That's a relief,' she teased in turn, grateful for the light-hearted tone the conversation now took. 'But there are more important issues and you know it. We can't find Mr Selway and we don't trust anyone.'

'The Wilsons. I trust them,' he told her. 'I trust you.'

It would be better for my heart if you didn't, she thought. 'And you know that if Lord Thomson can, he will find a way to return you to Dartmoor.'

'I almost depend upon him to do that.'

She couldn't help the tears that welled in her eyes. He brushed them away with his fingers.

'Don't worry so much, Grace,' he said, his voice soft. 'Some day soon, God willing, I'll just be a memory. You'll own the bakery and find yourself a wonderful man.'

The tears spilled out of her eyes at that. *I don't want anyone but you,* she thought.

He kissed her cheek with a loud smack that made her laugh out loud through her tears. 'Tell me this, because I'm curious—why did you *choose* me?'

She was silent for a long time then, remembering Dartmoor, and the dying captain and the bearded skeletons grouped around their commander. *Why did I choose him?* she asked herself. 'I…I'm…'

'Think. You were kneeling by Captain Duncan. Did he say anything to you?'

'Be quiet! I'm thinking.'

She sat up suddenly, the event clear in her mind, even though she had hoped never to revisit that corner of her brain again: the dying man, the filth, the stench, the fear. There was something more. Funny she hadn't thought of it before.

She spoke slowly. 'I don't think you were aware of this, I barely was. Rob, when I looked around to choose someone, the other men moved slightly away from you. It was as though they *wanted* me to see you. That is what happened. I swear it.'

It was his turn for his eyes to fill with tears. Knowing she shouldn't, she put her hand on his face, because he seemed so bereft.

'The crew of the *Orontes* obviously held you in high esteem,' Grace said.

'Hold, not held,' he contradicted swiftly. 'Pray God they are still alive. There isn't anything I wouldn't do for them.'

'And they knew…know…it. Oh, Rob. What are we going to do?'

'"We", is it?'

'Yes, of course,' she replied, trying to sound brisk, even though she wanted Rob Inman more than she had ever wanted anything in her life. 'The war won't last for ever.'

She looked at him, a handsome, healthy man her own age. She thought of him in the stream, chewing on watercress with a singleness of purpose that told her volumes about his will to live. She knew he would take charge of his own life, if he could. Until that happened again, no matter what she felt, she would help him. 'I'll help you all I can, but no more escape attempts. Don't even think it.' She shuddered.

He nodded and she released his hand. He made a face and wiggled his fingers. 'Your grip must come from all that kneading.' He blew her a kiss from the safety of the doorway. 'Tomorrow, madam, it's doughnuts.'

'What?' she asked, taken off guard.

'Doughnuts. I plan to make the Wilsons' fortune with doughnuts. You are not the only impresario in the room.'

'Doughnuts?' Grace made no effort to hide her scepticism.

'Aye-yah, as my Nantucket neighbours would say, Gracie. And don't give me that prune face! If your face got stuck that way, no man would ever marry you!'

'You're right,' she whispered, after the door had closed behind him. 'How could I marry someone else, when I love you?'

'They're only doing this to humour me,' Rob whispered to Grace the next morning as he stood over the bread trough, blending the yeast into the flour with a paddle. 'I find that flattering.'

'They like you,' Grace whispered back, as she stirred another batch of Crèmes. 'You did ask for a lot of lard and Mr Wilson barely batted an eye. You've piqued his curiosity. And mine.'

'Just wait, Gracie. This'll be the best thing you ever ate.'

Whistling to himself, he added sugar. 'Hand me that nutmeg and grater,' he said. He grated a small mound of the fragrant spice into the bowl and added the milk Mrs Wilson had warmed just so. He covered the bowl and stood back. 'Now, it rises.'

An hour later, the risen dough was rolled out and resting on the table. 'At home, the bakers use a tin circle with a smaller circle inside it,' Rob said. He glanced at the lard Mr Wilson had put in an iron pot. 'Since I have no doughnut cutter, I'll pinch off a little dough, roll it into a rope, like this, and join the ends.'

He worked swiftly until he had a dozen doughnuts. Grace watched as he carefully lowered the doughnuts into the hot fat, which quickly sizzled and set off the smell of nutmeg. She handed him a long-handled fork, which Rob twirled about. He struck a fencing pose, which earned giggles from two boys waiting to select biscuits.

'Now I turn them over until this side is golden brown, too,' he told Mrs Wilson. 'Ma'am, would you put sugar in this bowl? Grace, spread out that cloth, will you?'

In another moment, the doughnuts, brown and sparkling from the grease, rested on the cloth. When they were still warm, Rob dipped each one in sugar, then set them on a plate. Everyone came closer to look at the doughnuts.

When the air almost hummed with suspense, Rob declared the doughnuts cool enough. He handed the plate around.

'My word,' Grace said, even before she swallowed. 'Ro…Captain Duncan!'

He was eating his own doughnut. He nodded. 'Yep,' was all he said, then, 'Well?'

Grace swallowed and took another bite, entranced by the crispy outside and warm, smooth interior, with a hint of nutmeg to tantalise. She closed her eyes, savouring the experience. Rob nudged her. 'Look at Mr Wilson,' he whispered.

She did and almost laughed at his beatific expression. 'I think your tenure here is secure until the war ends,' she whispered back, then finished her doughnut and eyed the ones remaining on the plate.

Mr Wilson beat her to a second helping. 'I disremember when I've had anything so tasty.'

'If you think this is good, trying dunking a doughnut in coffee, or even milk. I prefer coffee.' Rob came closer to Mr Wilson. 'You could sell a batch of these each morning to that coffee shop at the other end of the High Street. Give out free samples one day, and shazam, you'll have orders for the week.'

'Where did you learn to make doughnuts?' Grace asked. She reached for another doughnut and he whisked them out of reach.

'You have to kiss me first,' he teased.

Mrs Wilson marched to the parolee, grabbed him by the shirt front and kissed him full on the lips. 'Irma!' Mr Wilson said, even as he laughed.

Rob came around the counter, holding the plate high and out of reach of the little boys, and stood in the doorway, scanning the street. 'Grace, come here a moment.'

She stood beside him, enjoying the trailing odour of nutmeg.

'Isn't that Ugly Butler…what is his name… over there?'

'Nahum Smathers,' she told him and made a face. She looked down the street and sighed. 'And there is Emery.'

'I'm going to take them each a doughnut, so you'd better come along, my favourite jailer.'

'Only if I get half of that doughnut.'

'You still have to kiss me.'

She kissed his cheek. He divided one doughnut, put one half in her mouth and ate the other, crossing the street to the doorway of the candlemaker's, where Mr Smathers read the *London Times* and lurked.

'Have a doughnut, Mr Smathers,' Rob said

cheerfully. 'We went to Exeter yesterday. Should have invited you, I suppose, but you're not much fun.'

His face impassive, Ugly Butler took a dough-nut. Not taking his eyes from the captain, he ate it. 'I've had better.'

'Where?'

Perhaps Smathers hadn't meant to say that. Face red, he snapped the newspaper shut and went into the candlemaker's.

Rob nudged Grace again. 'Look there, it's Emery. He's watching Smathers for us.'

They walked three doors down to the green-grocer's. Rob held out the plate to Emery. 'Here you are,' he said with a smile. 'Mr Smathers wasn't too polite about his doughnut.'

Emery took the doughnut and ate it. 'Excel-lent! Did you make these?'

'It was my late wife's recipe,' Rob said mod-estly. 'Her mother was a Dutchwoman from New York City. You like it?'

'Very much, sir,' Emery replied, then lowered his voice. 'Grace, I was checking at the green-grocers for you.'

'I didn't ask…'

'I know,' he replied. 'I thought I would ask and he assured me that the invoice he sent to Mr Sel-way, care of that post office in Exeter, was an-swered and payment made.' He shook his head. 'I can only assume that Mr Selway has an ulterior motive in making himself scarce.'

'I mean to write to him anyway and ask for a little more expense money,' she said, and couldn't resist smiling at Rob. 'I think we will need more operating expenses to keep us in nutmeg and lard.'

'Then he will likely send you a sufficiency,' Emery replied.

'"A sufficiency"?' the parolee joked. 'Emery, you may claim to be a yardman, but you're sounding more and more like a butler!'

'I know it,' he replied modestly. 'Ain't it a wonderful thing?' He bowed as grandly as he could. 'Now I shall go back to watching Mr Smathers.'

They laughed and returned to the bakery, handing out the last doughnut to Lady Tutt and her mousy companion, who happened by. He smiled at Lady Tutt's cries of delight.

He stopped in front of the bakery, looking up. 'Do you know if there is a length of canvas in the bakery?'

'Probably.'

'Paint?'

'Yes. What do you have in mind?'

He took a stance and spread his hands out. 'A sign. How about Yankee Doodle Doughnuts?'

'You are destined for Bedlam. I know it now,' she said, trying to keep her voice stern and failing miserably, because she couldn't help the enthusiasm she felt, right down to her stockings. 'Quimby prides itself on being discreet, Captain Impresario!'

'I would rather the Wilsons were a little crass and much wealthier. This, my dear, is our first joint effort. Maybe others will follow.'

'Only if peace takes its sweet time being declared,' she assured him.

'That's true,' he agreed. He took her by her shoulders, his face close to hers. 'I dare you to tell me a time when you've had more fun than right now.'

'I'd be lying, if I did,' she said quietly. Whatever magic this was—call it love, call it fun—she felt that peculiar, persistent feeling somewhere in her stomach. Maybe it was heartburn—that doughnut was rich. It felt more like hope.

Chapter Seventeen

The sign was up by mid-morning the following day. Mr Wilson carried two dozen doughnuts to the coffee house. When he returned, he had an order for two dozen each day, except Sundays.

'And there I was, showing them how to dunk a doughnut in coffee,' he said. 'I feared for a moment that Squire Redd would burst into tears.'

'Why?' Rob asked.

'He served in New York City during that late unpleasantness when your country declared its independence,' Mr Wilson explained. 'He told me his whole regiment left the city with heavy hearts, because the Dutch cook wouldn't come along with them.'

Rob laughed, and Grace felt her heart turn over. *He is enjoying this,* she thought.

Was it the sign? The little boys from yesterday? Lady Tutt? The bakery soon filled up with

interested customers, ready to sample the wares.
Grace had always been intrigued how quickly
news could pass from house to house.

'It's that way in Nantucket,' Rob said to her as
he rolled a half-dozen of the nutmeg-flavoured
doughnuts in oiled paper and handed them to
the vicar's wife, who had condescended to visit
the bakery herself. 'Thankee, ma'am. Tell your
friends, if you please. If you have any,' he muttered under his breath after the vicar's wife
looked down her long nose at him and left the
shop. 'Aye, news travels just as fast back home.
Something happens at one end of Orange Street,
and before you can say Jack Robinson, the miller
on the hill has heard it!'

The doughnuts were just a memory before
noon. Rob mixed another batch and set the dough
to rise while he and Grace went to the tinsmith's
shop to request the fabrication of two doughnut
cutters. Rob perched on the edge of the smith's
workbench and sketched the cutter in the wood
with a piece of charcoal. He had brought along the
sole remaining doughnut for the smith, who ate it
in two bites and promised to have the doughnut
cutters ready in the morning.

The smith studied the simple diagram on his
bench. 'What do ye do with the little hole that's
left over?'

Rob ran his tongue over his lips. Grace laughed
inside to watch the tinsmith's expression. 'The

doughnut hole is probably the best part. A handful of those and a glass of milk, and I guarandamn-tee ye that nothing will go wrong for the rest of your day.'

The smith and the sailing master laughed together, all because of doughnuts. Grace beamed at both of them. The smile drained from her face when they left the smith's and saw Smathers across the street, his arms folded as he watched them.

'Now let us look for Emery,' Rob whispered to her, his eyes lively. 'Ah, there he is, trying to hide behind that elm. He'd be more successful if there were less Emery and more elm.'

He waved cheerfully at Nahum Smathers, who glowered back. 'Testy fellow,' he murmured. 'I wish I knew why my continuing presence at Quarle was such a burr under the saddle to Lord Thomson. If that's why he's here.' He started across the street. 'Let's ask him.'

Grace grabbed his arm. 'Rob In—' she looked around '—Captain Duncan, behave yourself!'

'You're a killjoy,' he protested, but not without a smile playing around his lips. He whispered to her and winked, 'You probably wouldn't let me have my way with you, if I said please, and now you won't let me twit Ugly Butler. Must you earn your thirty pounds per annum so relentlessly?'

Grace couldn't help her blush. 'Rob, how on earth did Elaine put up with you?'

His expression turned a little faraway. He

touched her shoulder—just a pat, but his hand on her shoulder felt so good. 'She just loved me, Gracie.'

So do I, she thought. 'Right now, you will not bait Ugly Butler.'

He sighed, but still waved to Smathers and gave Emery a thumbs up when they passed the elm tree. Grace closed her eyes and counted to ten.

Everyone in Wilsons' Bakery counted higher than ten that evening after Mr Wilson closed the shutters and locked the door. He rubbed his hands together and chortled as Mrs Wilson carefully emptied the cash box onto the counter. 'Wife, we are in the money!' he announced to the rest of them when Grace finished totalling the pennies and halfpennies, and occasional shilling.

Humming to himself, the portrait of contentment, Mr Wilson portioned out Grace's share into a small canvas bag. He portioned out another share and put it in front of Rob Inman. 'That's for you, lad,' he said. 'I should probably give you the lion's share.'

Rob shook his head. 'You're kind,' he said, fingering the small pile. He glanced at Grace. 'I was just the impresario. You're the man with the yeast and flour.' He turned to Mrs Wilson and blew her a kiss. 'And you're the better half.'

To Grace's surprise, the redoubtable Mrs Wilson smiled and actually blushed, something she never did, and so Grace told Rob on the walk home after dark.

'The first time she smiled at me like that, I knew that all would be well in my world,' she said. She gave him a little push. 'But it took me more than a year to earn such a smile! You're working some sort of Yankee magic on her, I vow.'

'Jealous, Gracie?' he teased back.

'No, just grateful,' she said honestly. 'Rob, I think you need all the allies you can find, especially if Smathers keeps hanging around like a bad smell.'

Dinner just naturally took place in the kitchen now, Grace laughing with Emery over his surveillance of Ugly Butler, as she stirred and braised and soon had a simple meal on the table.

'I tells myself, says I, "Just watch the old plug ugly",' Emery said. 'He thinks he can hide from me, but he can't.'

'It's cat and mouse,' Grace said. 'Today, Mrs Wilson even told me she wasn't sure if you were watching Smathers, or he was watching you!'

Emery laughed and shook his head. 'No one ever said Mrs W. was a genius.'

'That's a little small of you, Emery,' Rob said, frowning at him. 'I'm surprised.'

The yardman-turned-butler shook his head. 'It's regrettable—my tendency to weigh her in the balance.' He brightened. 'I know I was unfair. Didn't she think Yankee Doodle Doughnuts were a grand idea?'

'Precisely,' Rob said. He grinned at Emery. 'Confess it, you wish you had thought of it!'

'Guilty as charged,' Emery said. 'You'll turn us into Americans yet!'

For the first time in Grace's memory, there was a queue forming fifteen minutes before the bakery opened the next morning. She had just returned from posting a letter to Mr Selway—wondering if it was an exercise in futility—and could barely squeeze into the bakery without a stampede behind her.

'Look at them, checking their timepieces,' Mr Wilson said, when he glanced up from the oven he was tending. 'I fear that if Mrs Wilson is a few seconds late in opening the door, we will be stormed. Like the Bastille!'

'Aye, sir,' Rob said. 'There's the tinsmith with the cutters. Let the man through.'

'You're working a miracle there,' Grace told Rob hours later, as they sat in the back, shoes off, stockinged feet up on the same ottoman, resting from the rigours of an entire day spent making doughnuts. 'Things were sad here, after the Wilsons' son-in-law died in a battle on some lake called Erie. Did I pronounce that right?'

He nodded. 'That was a sharp engagement, so I was told, with blood everywhere on both

sides.' Rob offered her a doughnut and she shook
her head. 'I knew the Wilsons weren't too keen
on having me here.' He tipped his chair back, a
smile of tired contentment on his face. 'It must
be the force of my sparkling wit, character and
Yankee know-how.'

She knew he was joking, but it was true.
'You're not like us, and I think it's a good thing,'
she told him impulsively. 'I mean…' She stopped,
flustered. 'I don't know what I mean.'

'Try, Gracie,' he said quietly. 'Your government insists that once an Englishman, always an
Englishman. Do you feel that way?'

'I used to, but that was before I knew an American,' she said, then leaned closer to him. 'Even
if you were born English…and maybe that's the
point.' He was so close. She wanted to touch his
hand. 'You are an entirely new species—frank,
honest, casual and…'

'And?' he asked, that slow smile on his face,
the one that never failed to make her want to
hug him.

'…full of yourself and supremely confident,'
she concluded.

He gave her that slow look, watching her out
of the corner of his eye. She wished he would not
do that. 'That is how I seem to you?'

She nodded, unsure of herself. There was so
much she wanted to say. She wanted to ask him
how he could be so positive, him a paroled prisoner of war, a man from a background so decid-

edly beneath her own, someone she would have ignored in her better days. She stood up, fishing for her shoes again. 'I think democracy must be a great leveller,' she said, after more thought.

'Aye, Gracie. Once you know that, you can't go back.'

To Grace's delight, Quimby's residents discovered a profound liking for Rob Inman's doughnuts.

'Look at them,' Grace whispered, as Mrs Wilson handed out one and two doughnuts, and then a dozen at a time, as the addiction spread.

'I can be modest—' Rob began.

'No, you cannot,' Grace interjected. 'You knew these would be a success!'

He only grinned at her and returned his attention to the customers, his new best friends.

Grace watched him joking in his easy way to all and sundry. He had time for everyone.

You are wasting your time, pining for a quarterdeck again, Grace thought, as she stamped out more doughnuts. *With so much charm, you could own Nantucket.* She admired his shoulders. *You own me.*

When colder wind signalled the arrival of autumn, she helped him take down his improvised Yankee Doodle Doughnuts banner, which had caused a brief stir in Quimby. Fearing the removal of the sign meant the end of the doughnuts, the squire himself shouldered his way to the head of the usual line to ask what was going on.

'Never fear, sir,' Rob told him. 'Quimby's such a genteel village and perhaps my sign is crass.' He held up his hand. 'The doughnuts are here to stay.'

Grace had to turn away her head to hide her smiles at the collective sigh that rose from the small gathering. Satisfied, Quimby's citizens paid for their purchases and filed out.

Except for one man. Grace couldn't help taking a step back, even behind the counter. Nahum Smathers had never come into the bakery before. She had not stood so close to him until now.

Perhaps dubbing him Ugly Butler hadn't been entirely correct. True, he was bald and his complexion scarred with pockmarks, but he was as solid as a stone wall, with a certain lift to his shoulders that impressed Grace, in spite of herself. Maybe it was his eyes that made her step back involuntarily: they were as expressionless as the eyes of a great fish she had once seen tangled in a fisherman's net.

'May…may I help you?' she asked, wishing the words had come out cool and calm.He shook his head, his eyes on Rob Inman, who was watching him now from behind the table where he cut doughnuts. 'It's not just the doughnuts that aren't going anywhere.'

She jumped when he slapped a newspaper on the counter. The cat curling around her skirt hissed and moved away.

Smathers opened the paper and pointed to the article at the top of the fold. 'Burned your precious capitol, Duncan. You're an American? You're a citizen of nowhere.'

He turned on his heel and left the bakery as Rob, his face white, came around the table and snatched up the paper. Silent, seething, he read the article. Grace watched his expression travel rapidly through scepticism, shock, despair and then grief.

'They burned Washington,' he said finally. 'The damned British burned our capitol.' Maybe he hoped the words would change before his eyes, if he stared at them long enough. Remembering the reading of her father's will, Grace could have told him that bad news rarely improved on a second perusal.

She put her hand on his arm, but he shook it off. She had never seen such a wintry expression on anyone's face, not even her own when, that night, she stared into the mirror and told the woman looking back that Rob Inman, the man she chose, would leave as soon as he could and never choose her.

He straightened up as Ugly Butler, his back to them as he crossed the street, started to laugh.

'Damn him,' Rob said, his voice low and burning with anger. Then softer, but no less menacing, 'Damn you, British.'

She flinched at his anger, felt her own rise in response, then willed it to subside, unwilling to flay a man who had just received bad news and from a terrible source. She said nothing, but looked at Smathers's back, as he resumed his typical pose in front of the candlemaker's shop, watching them, always watching them.

She felt her own blood boil at the thought of Ugly Butler, except there had been something in his eyes that left her puzzled. She wished she could interpret his expression. She glanced at Rob and looked away, startled to see so much winter in his own eyes.

Chapter Eighteen

Rob said nothing on the walk back to Quarle, setting his face resolutely away from the manor house, where Smathers, home now, watched him from an upstairs window. When they reached the dower house, he walked slowly upstairs, his head down.

In the kitchen, Emery shook his head over the news. 'Maybe the United States are going to be a short-lived experiment.'

'Best not say anything so dismal to our parolee,' she advised.

'Maybe he needs to face facts.'

Gloom down here and gloom upstairs, Grace thought, feeling discouragement settle around her. 'I feel sorry for him,' she said, her words pointed.

'So do I, lass, but sometimes…' He shook his head again.

I should just leave Rob alone, she told herself, settling down in the kitchen with a basket of mending. *Maybe he'd rather not see a British face just now.* That line of reasoning lasted no longer than it took her to darn one of Rob's stockings. She thought of all the lonely hours she had spent behind the ovens, once the Wilsons were upstairs for the night. She had been alone then and she had never liked that kind of solitude. She doubted Rob Inman did, either, considering how gregarious he was. *Far more than I am,* she reminded herself.

That was all the resolution she needed. She prepared a bowl of still-warm stew and put it on a tray with a beaker of tea.

She stood outside his closed door before she knocked.

'Go away.'

'You're a sore trial,' she muttered, as she opened the door.

He lay on his back, staring at the ceiling. When she came into the room, he put his forearm over his eyes, which made her heart go out to him. *Poor man, you've been crying,* she thought.

'I told you to go away,' he said, his voice sulky.

'I chose to ignore you,' she replied, setting down the tray on the table next to the bed. He had wadded the newspaper and thrown it down beside the bed. She picked it up and sat down in the chair, making herself comfortable.

With a sinking heart, she read the article, which appeared to have been a dispatch from

General Ross, who had truly burned the country's capital, after routing the 'so-called army',
as he wrote, at a place called Bladensburg. 'We
were mainly impressed with how fleet of foot the
American army was,' she read silently. 'Let us be
generous to our defeated foe and call that battle
the Bladensburg Races.'

Increasingly agitated, she read of Ross and his
officers sitting down to dinner in 'Little Jemmy
Madison's house', the table spread for the country's president, who had fled. 'We shall have to
apologise someday for our rag manners, but we
left soon after dinner, since we had set the place
on fire. What thoughtless guests we were.' *Churl.
I don't like that man,* she thought, reading how
the whole region would soon be ablaze, now that
the army was going to march next on Baltimore.

She put down the paper, unable to read more
and understanding Rob's tears.

'Does it bother you, too?'

Grace nodded, deliberately balling up the
broadside again and tossing it toward the unlit
fireplace.

'It does,' she told him in a small voice. 'I
thought… Hadn't we heard earlier that your country and my country were meeting for treaty talks
in Belgium?'

'Aye, lass.' His arm was back across his face
and his words were muffled. 'And now Britain
bargains from a position of strength. Lord, this
chaps my hide.'

'They'll surrender?'

'Not flaming likely. The frontier's on fire, our seacoast is in ruins and who knows where the government is, but we won't yield. You can't give up on a good idea whose time has come. But it's all so painful. And the deuce of it is, this is six-week-old news! Do I even have a country now?'

He was crying again. He had tried to suppress his tears, pressing his fingers against the bridge of his nose, but nothing could have stopped his utter misery.

Grace watched him a moment, her eyes welling, too. He had been so cheerful this morning as they had walked into Quimby, telling her of his plans to return to the sea and maybe some day command his own brig, carrying American commerce around the world. He had joked and laughed with the people of her village, who had come to like him, maybe even trust him. And then Smathers, damn him, had slapped down that broadside on the counter and stood there long enough to gloat, if that was how she should interpret the man's expression. *I hate him,* she thought.

Her heart went out to Rob Inman as he sobbed. There was nothing he could do for his country, even though she knew every fibre in his body yearned to find a way.

'That's enough of that,' she murmured as she slipped her feet out of her shoes, removed her apron and lay down next to him on the bed.

She had no idea what he would do, but she

could no longer just sit there and watch his sorrow. After thinking through all the things she could have done and deciding this was perhaps the most foolish, Grace put her arms around Rob Inman and pulled him close to her.

She knew she had startled him, but in a very few moments, his arms went around her, too, and they clung together. She pillowed his head against her breast, murmuring words that weren't words until his tears stopped.

Rob must have realised she was hanging over the edge of the bed. He tugged her back to the centre, his arms still tight around her, and she made no objection. She stroked his back, enjoying the strength there, even though she knew he was at low tide. 'No need to suffer alone. You won't always feel so sad,' she whispered.

He pulled her closer. She said nothing more, just rubbed his back, then caressed his hair.

The room was dark now and growing chilly, testimony to the passage of the season from early autumn to the chill of coming winter. 'Rob, wouldn't it be a wonderful thing if you could get news from America the instant something happens, instead of waiting weeks and weeks?'

'Grace, you're a cloth head.'

'I know. Go to sleep.'

In a few minutes, he had relaxed and was breathing deeply, as though her simple grumble—he had heard that tone of voice from her before—had given him permission.

When she knew he slept, she sat up and unbuttoned his shirt, tugging it out of his trousers, after sliding out his belt. His shoes were already off. He stirred when she unbuttoned the fall front of his trousers, trapping her hand on his crotch until she felt her face flame. He muttered something fierce, then shifted onto his side, freeing her hand.

She tried to edge off the bed, but his fingers went around her wrist. 'Grace, don't leave me. Please.'

She lay down next to him again. 'Only because you said please,' she told him, content to lie beside him again. He returned to sleep. When she was certain he was deep under, she took a handkerchief from her sleeve and gently wiped around his eyes and the tear marks on his cheeks.

Rob Inman was more cheerful in the morning. She woke up to feel him tugging down her dress, which had ridden up around her thighs.

'You're supposed to still be asleep,' he said. 'I didn't want you to think I had been involved in anything naughty last night, while you were drooling on your—my—pillow.'

At some point he must have covered them both with his blankets and the room was just cool enough to make her reluctant to rise. Her head was pillowed on his arm. 'I don't drool. Your arm is probably asleep,' she said.

'Aye.'

'I should raise my head,' she told him, even as she made no effort to do that.

'I suppose you could,' he replied, 'but then you would expect me to move my arm, wouldn't you? I don't want to, Grace. I like the feel of a woman's hair on my arm.'

There was nothing to say to that, so she snuggled more firmly into the blankets. 'I don't mind working for my living, Rob. What I *don't* care for is getting up early.'

'Maybe you'll be a lady of leisure again some day.'

'When pigs have wings.'

'Grace, I am depending on you to make a brilliant match some day. You know, when you find your own impresario.'

'I repeat what I said about pigs.'

They lay close together. He sniffed her hair. 'I don't know how you do it, but you still smell of cinnamon.'

He growled suddenly and nipped at her neck. Grace shrieked and leaped out of bed, to stand laughing and barefoot by the door. He smiled back at her, then flopped on his back again and closed his eyes.

'I'm not going to the village today,' he told her, his voice firm. 'I can't bear the thought of the bakery customers smirking and gloating at my ill fortune.'

She came back to the bed and gave him a good shake. 'No one's going to gloat. *You're* the cloth head, if you think so. I'm going to the Wilsons' to make more doughnuts and I don't trust you here alone. You'll do a runner.'

'I might,' he said, sounding a little grim.

'You promised you wouldn't. I have my eye on you, Rob Inman. If that means I sleep in your room every night, too, I will.' She tried to sound firm, but felt only foolish. 'So there we are.'

'Grace, you're the damnedest,' he said, his tone admiring. 'What a fishwife! Elaine would have folded like a wet towel before crossing me.'

'I am not Elaine,' she said simply. 'I never will be.'

She hoped she hadn't hurt his feelings, not after the rude things she had flung at him after their trip to Exeter and which still bothered her. He sat up, his face serious. Silent, she watched his expression change from something close to exasperation to a thoughtful look. He seemed to be examining her from the inside out, taking her words to heart. For the smallest heartbeat, she wondered if he was deciding that very thing, that maybe not being Elaine was all right, too.

'I'll be in the kitchen getting breakfast,' she said quietly, not wanting to break his mood. She closed the door behind her and leaned against it for a moment. *I would follow you anywhere,* she thought. *No need for you to know it, though.*

Breakfast had been a quiet affair, full of porridge and silent contemplation. When they walked to Quimby, the air was cool. She smelled leaves burning on the Quarle estate. Lord Thomson's few remaining yardmen were raking the leaves into mounds. This was always her favourite time of year. 'Are…are there lots of elm trees on Nantucket?' she asked, shy about the question because it seemed to imply something between them. Surely he wouldn't take it that way.

'Aye, Grace. You'd never be homesick for elms,' he said, then amended hurriedly, 'If you lived there. But the maples! Oh, the maples, so red and glorious. There's a maple in our front yard.'

She was suddenly too shy to look at him, because he seemed to be implying the same thing. She stopped. 'Rob…'

She wasn't even sure what she was going to say, but it didn't matter. He looked around quickly, then took her in his arms. Without asking, he held her close and kissed her long.

He was better at kissing than she was, which came as no surprise. 'I'm not good at this,' she whispered, their lips barely parted.

'You're better than you know,' he replied, his voice as low as hers. 'Let's try it again, in case I was wrong.'

They did, but she pulled away first, which seemed to bring Rob to his senses. 'What was I thinking?' he said, letting go of her.

She wanted to tell him not to stop, but she knew better. 'I told you weeks ago that you miss women,' she said.

He gently pressed his forehead against hers, then stepped back. 'Too right.'

If that never happens again, at least it happened, she thought, as they resumed their slow walk into Quimby. *At least I'll never wonder what a kiss from the man I love feels like.*

Rob Inman tried to throw the doughnuts' banner away, but Mr Wilson overruled him, insisting that it be tacked to the inside of the back wall now.

'I see it this way, lad—Quimby isn't an ostentatious place,' he explained as he steadied the banner for Rob to tack up again. 'We know where the doughnuts are now. We'll just crow about it more discreetly.'

Rob was silent in the early hours before the shop opened for business, head down, his thoughts his own, as he rolled dough and stamped out doughnuts. 'I'm sure half the village will stop by to gloat,' he told her finally.

He couldn't have been more wrong. So indignant that the feathers on her ridiculous turban trembled, Lady Tutt was the first person in the shop, followed by her meek companion.

'Here it comes,' Rob whispered out of the side of his mouth.

Without a word to the Wilsons, Lady Tutt lifted up the barrier on the counter and stood in front of

Rob at the kneading table. She banged her parasol, then shook it at him.

'You just wait, Captain Duncan! Your upstart nation will come about!' She made an abrupt about-face and marched out of the shop again, not even stopping to pinch the fresh bread. Her mouth open, Grace stared after Lady Tutt, who marched across the street to the candlemaker's. The door to the bakery was closed and they couldn't hear, but from the startled look on his face, Nahum Smathers was getting an earful.

'Lord love her!' Rob exclaimed. 'I'm gut foundered and blowed.'

So it went all day—words of commiseration and comfort from everyone, as they came for their daily fix of doughnuts and left their sympathy, awkwardly spoken—he was the enemy, after all—but no less well meaning. A time or two, Rob came close to tears. By the end of the day, his smile was genuine.

'Sometimes it's nice to be wrong,' he admitted that night, as he stood in the doorway to his room, leaning against the frame. 'Are you going to watch over me again tonight to make sure I don't escape?'

'Is that a wise idea?' she asked, standing in her doorframe.

'Of course it isn't,' he said promptly. 'It comes

to this, Grace, I've never liked sleeping alone. What if I promise you no naughtiness?'

'*Can* you?' she asked, then could have bitten her tongue.

'Can *you*?' he countered, a twinkle in his eyes.

'Yes, absolutely,' she replied, her voice crisp, even if her face felt fiery. 'Since my speciality seems to be plain speaking, I would always shoulder the worst of the consequences, should we… um…succumb to naughtiness.'

'True. I give you my word,' he said simply. 'Lie down with me.'

She did without a qualm, slipping out of her dress after taking a deep breath. She resisted the urge to tug on her chemise and make it magically longer, but she allowed herself to sink into Rob Inman's gentle clasp. He settled his arms around her and rested his chin on her shoulder. 'If I get too warm, just push me off,' he told her. 'When Dan Duncan and I were boys together—he wasn't so much older than me—we shared a narrow bed. I got used to close quarters.' He kissed her neck.

'Don't do that!' she whispered. 'I doubt you kissed Captain Duncan.'

'He'd have thrashed me.' Rob sighed. When he spoke, his voice was drowsy. 'I think I won't run away tonight.'

Chapter Nineteen

Grace slept beside him all week, accustoming herself to his warmth and the feel of his body, so relaxed against hers. She wondered what her mother would have thought about this arrangement, but came to no conclusion.

At first, she wondered if her love for Rob Inman, and the delight of sleeping next to him, was some measure of her desperation to find a man of her own, when none had ever offered even his friendship before. She decided the answer was no, mainly because she had known with an unassailable conviction than no man would offer for her. She was either too high for some, or too low for the rest.

And then came Rob Inman, a paroled prisoner of war from a nation as foreign to her as Persia, but a place she came to identify with, as he told her of his home in Massachusetts, on an island much smaller than her own. Allowing for the embellishment she expected from one who was homesick and sorely missing his country, she knew she would like America.

As the week wore on, she lay awake in his arms late into the night, comparing his misfortune of birth, which had done nothing to stop his ambition, and her bad luck with parents who should have been wise enough to prevent the state to which she had slid, through no fault of her own. How ironic then, that Rob Inman's father, a thief, had done more for his son's future than Sir Henry Curtis had ever done for his more privileged offspring.

They had talked about it late into the night, finally. 'You're awake, aren't you?' he had whispered into her ear one night.

The kindness in his voice gave her permission to spill out all her disappointments and she did, finally dabbing her eyes on his sheets and begging his pardon for being such a whinger.

'You've done so much with so little,' she said, when her eyes were dry again.

'So have you,' he replied, with just a touch of humour in his voice. 'When you were at the counter one day, Mrs Wilson and I took our ease, feet up, in the back room. She told me how you came to the bakery, all calm as a May morning—Lord, I've never seen that side of you! Ow!'

She punched his arm again for good measure. 'I'll have you know I can be calm and biddable,' she insisted, as his smile increased. 'I vow you are bringing out the worst in me, you parolee!'

He laughed at that. 'Is that the worst thing you can think to call me?' he teased. 'Mrs Wilson told me how brave you were. "I have never heard her complain," she told me.'

'What good would that have done?' she asked.

'Spoken like a lady,' he told her, his voice drowsy now. 'But how would I know, since we both agree that I am not a gentleman.'

She winced at his words, grateful for the dark, and still ashamed of her intemperate words. But he was a gentleman. If keeping him company in this odd way brought some peace to his generous heart, she would make it do for the rest of her life without him. Grace closed her eyes, secure in her knowledge that he was more of a gentleman than he knew. *I wish I were less of a lady in his eyes,* she thought, as she slept, too.

Lady Adeliza Tutt *was* less of a lady, to Grace's relief and delight. Two weeks after the dismal news from America, the knight's widow came to the bakery and rapped on the door with her parasol. Grace looked up from the kneading table, where she was working over the bread dough. Rob had suggested they try raisin bread with cinnamon and walnuts, which was proving to be a steady seller.

Grace glanced at the clock. The bakery wasn't due to open for another half-hour, but there was

Lady Tutt and she wouldn't stop rapping. Her hands floury, Grace called to Rob in the back room, where he had taken to chin wagging with the Wilsons as they finished breakfast.

'I don't know what she wants, but I can't get the door,' she told Rob, when he came out of the backroom. 'Maybe her clock doesn't work.'

He smiled and gave Lady Tutt a good-natured salute from the other side of the door, then opened it, stepping back quickly as she threw herself into the room, the feather on her hat bobbing like a flag in a breeze.

'Lady Tutt?' he asked in surprise, as she took a newspaper from under her arm.

'Read it! Read it now!' she said, in her most declarative voice. 'Ladies aren't supposed to read newspapers, but, Captain Duncan, I have been following the news every morning for the past two weeks…' she paused dramatically '…all for you!'

'It couldn't wait?' he asked. His lips were already set in a tense line as he unfolded the paper.

Wiping her hands on her apron, Grace watched his face as he read the paper. Lady Tutt practically danced up and down like a child in her excitement. A slow grin worked its way across Rob's face. With a whoop that brought the Wilsons running into the room, he set down the paper and picked up Lady Tutt. He whirled her around the room as she blushed and made all kinds of dire threats. With a resounding smack, he planted a kiss on her lips.

Mystified, Grace picked up the paper he had dropped. She scanned the page, then took a deep breath of her own. 'Where's Baltimore?' she demanded, when Rob had set Lady Tutt back on her feet.

'In Maryland, not far from Washington City,' he said, his excitement almost palpable. 'Look you there, Mr Wilson—your armies couldn't take Baltimore and have left Chesapeake Bay!'

'Not my armies, lad,' Mr Wilson said mildly. 'Your Yankee Doodle Doughnuts have turned us all into flaming radicals.'

'I thought this was good news and knew you needed to know,' Lady Tutt said, her cheeks still rosy. She patted her chest. 'Captain, I haven't had that much kissing since my husband…' She paused and looked around, remembering herself. 'Captain, you are a rascal!'

Rob grabbed her by the waist, hauled her in and kissed her again, this time on her cheek and gentler. 'And one more for good measure, Lady Tutt. You've made me a happy man.'

Grace sighed with relief as she watched the joy on Rob's face as he read the entire article. They had quarrelled last night over some inconsequential business she couldn't even remember in the morning, all because his nerves were on edge at the news of the burning of Washington, and the constant daily appraisal of Nahum Smathers.

After their quarrel, she had retreated to her own room for the night. It had been a long night, spent tossing and turning and wishing Rob Inman to Hades, then worrying about his country, the men still in Dartmoor, the state of things in Nantucket, Emery skulking after Smathers—anything she could think of to worry about. By dawn she had had a headache and a frown. She had snapped his head off at breakfast when he had the temerity to run his finger gently down the frown line between her eyes. 'You know, it'll freeze that way,' he had said, which made her burst into tears and run from the room, something so missish that she was promptly ashamed of herself.

They had both apologised on the walk into town, but it had still been a silent progress, unlike their usual ambling stroll, full of far-ranging conversation. 'We'll know something good or bad, sooner or later,' he had said to her as they had arrived at the still-shuttered bakery.

Now they knew, thanks to Lady Tutt's speedy visit to the bakery. 'What else does it say?' she murmured, looking around his arm as he leaned on the counter.

He started to include her in his embrace, then remembered himself and did not. 'Says here that the fleet moved out of Chesapeake Bay and is heading south.'

She looked at him, a question in her eyes.

'I think they're making for the port of New Orleans,' he said. 'It's a grand place, if you don't mind a yearly plague of yellow fever, or air so heavy you feel like you're drinking it when you breathe. Great food.' He hesitated and shook his head.

'What?' she asked, ready to worry again.

He must have seen that in her eyes. He glanced at Lady Tutt, whose interests lay now with the raisin bread Mr Wilson had placed on the counter to cool. He touched Grace's hand. 'The army that controls New Orleans controls the Mississippi River. We'd be boxed in like clams in a bucket.'

'Does America have an army down there?'

He shrugged. 'It's mostly Creoles, slaves and pirates. I hope there will be an army, when the British arrive.' He looked at Mr Wilson. 'Sir, what day is it?'

'December 14, lad.' He wrapped up a loaf of the raisin bread for Lady Tutt and handed it to her. 'Here you are, dearie. Good news deserves a reward.'

'That's Lady Tutt to you, Adam Wilson,' she said crisply.

Mr Wilson just smiled. 'I knew ye when ye was Adeliza Jenkyns, your ladyship!'

She gave him a levelling stare. 'Adam Wilson, you are impertinent!'

He nodded. 'I know it.'

As they walked home that afternoon, Rob took her hand. 'As far as we know, the war goes on. Who knows what is hanging in the balance?'

Emery had already heard the news. 'Captain Duncan, have you forgotten that I am keeping an eye on Smathers for you?'

'How could I forget?' Rob asked. 'Was he unhappy?'

Emery nodded, his eyes serious for a moment. 'I followed him back to Quarle—'

'Lurking from beech to beech,' Grace interjected.

'Ah, yes. I have become somewhat of a woodlands expert,' he said mildly enough, enjoying the joke as much as they did.

Rob smiled. 'Emery, has this little dower house no smuggler's wine? We should lift a glass to Baltimore.' He grinned at Grace. 'Great crab cakes in Baltimore, by the way.'

'Captain Duncan, do you eat your way through the American seaboard?' Grace asked, relieved at how relaxed he sounded now. 'Beans in Boston, something I can't pronounce in New Orleans...'

'Étouffée,' he supplied.

'...crab cakes in Baltimore, and...'

'Brunswick stew in Georgia,' he concluded. 'After Elaine, I gave up wenching and concentrated on eating.'

'You are a rascal,' she said.

'I am a sailor.' He beamed at her. 'That's what we do.'

While Grace struggled to keep from laughing, Emery broke the sad news that there were no spirits of any sort in the dower house. 'I have looked,

Captain.' He paused, and his voice sounded almost prim. 'Besides, Captain, this is only one
victory. Best not celebrate too soon.'

Rob sat back, a frown on his face. 'Emery, if
I want gloom, I'll knock on Ugly Butler's door.'

There was no denying Emery had put a damper
on the discussion. Grace sat in the servants' hall
long after Emery had said goodnight and Rob
had gone upstairs, using the excuse of preparing
tomorrow's evening meal and then scrubbing out
the bean pot. The room was deep in shadows. The
elusive Mr Selway's money needed to stretch and
she had become a martinet about candles.

I worry too much, she told herself, as she
rested her head on her arms.

She must have slept. When she woke up, the
candle had guttered out and Rob Inman sat across
the table from her. He wore the nightshirt that
Emery had found for him and he was just looking at her.

'You gave me a start,' she said, her voice shaky.

He reached across the table and put his hand
on her arm. 'Are you planning to stay down here
all night and worry some more?'

'If I feel like it,' she said.

He stood up, but kept hold of her hand, so she
had to rise, too. 'Very well,' she grumbled.

Rob walked her to the end of the table, then released her hand to put his arm around her, when

they stood together. 'It's too much for me,' he said, his voice low, as they left the kitchen and climbed the stairs. 'Each day I wonder, is this the day the war is finally over? What about tomorrow? What if it never ends and I am stuck here? What if Lord Thomson revokes my parole and I am sent back to Dartmoor?'

She shuddered. His arm went around her then and they reached the top of the stairs, to just stand there.

'You chose me, Grace. Here I am,' he said simply.

She nodded. She moved out of his embrace and went to her door, angry with herself for not accepting his obvious invitation, but even more distressed with how lonely she would be when he left, a free man. 'Goodnight, Rob. Things aren't so bleak now, are they? I don't think you need me in your room now.'

The look he gave her was long and thoughtful. She felt her resolve slip away like water on a hot griddle.

Go away, only don't, she thought. 'Goodnight, Rob,' she repeated.

Without a word, he went into his room and closed the door. She was hours and hours getting to sleep that night.

Chapter Twenty

Something had changed with the good news from Baltimore. More likely, it was her rejection of him, if that's what it was. *Is it I?* Grace asked herself in the days leading up to Christmas. *Is it Rob?*

To call it euphoria would be no exaggeration, she decided. Rob even smiled at Nahum Smathers the next day and admitted to her later that he was just as surprised when Ugly Butler smiled back.

'It looks genuine,' he whispered, after Smathers left the bakery, where he had actually purchased a dozen doughnuts. 'Should I worry?'

Grace just rolled her eyes. She glanced at Rob as he popped another dozen doughnuts into an oiled paper twist, pleased to see him chatting so casually with Lady Tutt's mousy companion. She blushed when he teased her gently, and almost became pretty; Rob could do that.

* * *

He already sees himself back home on Nantucket, she thought that evening. Rob lounged on the sofa in the sitting room, shoes off, reading and then dozing like any normal man and not someone constantly on the edge. If that was what good news about Baltimore could do, she was grateful.

It took her most of the week to admit to herself that the prospect of peace had changed Rob Inman. He and Mr Wilson had spent a spirited hour in the back room, scooping flour into smaller bags and talking about commerce on the seas, once the war ended. Grace could almost see the wheels turning in Rob's agile brain as he told her of his plans, once he was back on Nantucket. She knew it was inevitable—she had tried to steel herself against it, after all—but the pain was lacerating, all the same.

And why shouldn't he be overjoyed? she asked herself. The time was coming when he wouldn't need her protection; he would be a free man. She nodded and smiled as he talked about his plans to captain his own ship some day, and hire all the men from the *Orontes* to crew it.

Grace hadn't meant to, but she said to Mrs Wilson mid-week, 'We'll be just a distant memory to him, won't we?'

She couldn't help blushing at the look that Mrs Wilson gave her then, harder to bear because it was such a kind look, almost as though Mrs Wilson could read her tangled thoughts.

She began to dread the nights. In the evenings, they still walked upstairs together and he usually blew her a playful kiss. There wasn't any talk of her returning to his bed to do nothing more than keep him company. Her virtue was in no danger, if it ever had been. After the terrible news of the burning of Washington, he had been a sorrowful man in need of comfort. Baltimore had changed things.

She decided she had been making mountains out of molehills by imagining for even one minute that Rob Inman actually needed her. It was not a comfortable reflection, but an honest one. She convinced herself that the less she thought about Nantucket, the better off she would be, when the war ended and Rob Inman left. If only he would not talk about the island's quiet streets, and the way the mist rolled in from the bay, and the sight of Quakers in grey, walking to Meeting on Sunday.

Thank God they were busy at the bakery, making the usual bread, rolls, biscuits and doughnuts now, plus the extra Christmas treats. There was barely time to talk. Grace found herself doing what she always did during the Yuletide season: watching Quimby's citizens—the mighty and the modest—shopping, planning parties, laughing with each other. When she'd lived at the bakery, she had fallen into the habit of walking around the village, hoping for glimpses of curtains left open so she could see into homes where families and friends gathered. She had never spied or pried; she hadn't been brought up to do that. She did no more than cast quick glances and hurry on, so no one would think she was gawking.

She was grateful, at least, to walk back to Quarle and the dower house each night with Rob Inman. He bubbled over with his plans and he didn't seem to notice her silence, or her glances at passing homes.

She was wrong; he had noticed. It was three days to Christmas and they had closed the bakery long hours after the usual time. Her back ached and she wanted nothing more than to take her shoes off and lie down. Still, she unconsciously slowed her pace as they passed the final row of houses before the copse and meadow that bordered Quarle.

She knew from years past that this was the night when Quimby's solicitors dined at the senior partner's house. The curtains were invariably left open. Once she had ventured into the garden to watch the couples chatting and laughing, punch in hand, mistletoe overhead.

Suddenly Rob took her hand and stopped in the road, looking where she looked. 'Do you imagine yourself inside?' he asked quietly.

She nodded, surprised that he had noticed.

'Every year. The squire's wife appears to be increasing again. And look, there are Mr and Mrs Holden. They were married only a month ago. Remember? Mrs Wilson and I made their wedding cake. Josiah Bramley—he of the garish waistcoat, do you see?—I think he must be unlucky in love, because he comes by himself every year.'

She stopped speaking, horrified with how wistful she sounded.

'He never buys more than two doughnuts at a time. It's downright unnatural,' Rob joked, taking up her narrative and not giving her a chance to feel foolish. 'And is that Melinda Caldwell, casting sheep's eyes at the justice of the peace's oldest son?'

She shivered. 'It's too cold to stand here, isn't it? On the outside looking in.'

He nodded and started walking again. 'If things had been different, Grace, would you have been in a gathering like that?'

'For a time, I was,' she said, unable to resist a final look at the entertainment she would never be part of again.

'And it hurts a bit,' he said, tightening his grip on her shoulder. 'When I was still an indentured servant, I used to lie on my stomach at the upstairs landing and watch the party below—sea captains and their madams, usually wearing some finery from China or India.' He kissed the top of her head. 'I was on the outside looking in, too.'

He stopped in the woods as snow began to fall.

'We have more snow on Nantucket. Grace, even when I was indentured and at everyone's beck and call, I decided *I* would give that party some day.'

'Elaine probably made a lovely hostess.'

'She did.' To her dismay, he gathered her close as they stood there, snow falling around them. 'I've been nattering on all week about *my* plans and *my* goals, and you've been patient to let me. Grace, rein me in when I do that. It smacks of the worst kind of pride, the kind Nantucket preachers really don't like.'

'It's your life,' she said, her voice muffled by his overcoat, the one Mr Wilson had found for him in the vicar's pile of cast-offs suitable for the deserving poor.

He was a long time silent. 'I think it would be an empty shell without you in it,' he replied, sounding tentative and unsure of himself, qualities she barely recognised in him. 'Let's have a party next year in Nantucket.'

She couldn't speak, not even daring to hope he was serious.

'It'll be a good party. Our party.' He was silent again. When he spoke, he sounded almost apologetic. 'I know I'm not the man of your dreams, but I can wish, too.'

She started to cry then, weary with Christmas baking for other people and tired of loneliness that warred against the little strands of optimism and tendrils of hope that wanted to believe every word Rob Inman said. She had lived so long without hope that she wasn't sure she even recognised it.

'Shh, shh, Grace,' he crooned into her hair. 'I was afraid of that.'

'You're an idiot!' she sobbed.

'I know.' He clapped his arm around her shoulder and started them both in motion again. 'Forget I said that. You already know what you want, don't you?'

She cried harder, too shy to speak her heart, too afraid to trust this man who meant the world to her.

Rob laughed and kissed her forehead. 'Oh, Gracie,' he said, his voice gruff, 'let's have a Merry Christmas anyway!'

And then it was Christmas Eve, with the shop closing at noon because the Wilsons were in a pelter to get to Plymouth and celebrate the season with their widowed daughter, and daughter and son-in-law, a ropemaker.

Nahum Smathers wasn't at his usual post across the road. Rob had commented on Ugly Butler's absence as he sold the last of the doughnuts to the proprietor of the coffee shop.

'Perhaps this means Lord Thomson has returned and is expecting a report from his minion,' he told Grace as she scraped down the kneading trough. 'We should take Lord T. a token of our genuine esteem. Stale bread? Pudding that I have spat in?'

'We should stay as far away from him as possible,' Grace insisted. She looked out the window. 'But there is Emery. Perhaps he doesn't know that Ugly Butler isn't watching you. Poor man, he will catch his death.'

When the floor was swept and the ovens carefully damped, the Wilsons took their leave. With a small sigh of relief, Grace locked the bakery door. Rob extended his arm to her and they strolled together at a sedate pace. Grace breathed deeply of the brisk air, glad to see daylight on their walk home, considering how many evenings they had trudged home in full dark, tired from the bakery. The light was already faintly turning lavender.

'Please God, let this be my last Christmas in England,' Rob said.

Grace swallowed the lump in her throat that had resided there all week, whenever she thought of Rob Inman and peace.

When they passed in front of Quarle, Grace was surprised to see the manor bright with many lamps, confirming Rob's suspicion that Lord Thomson had returned.

I refuse to let Lord Thomson ruin my holiday, she thought. *I'll think of something more pleasant.* She glanced at Rob Inman, wondering what it would be like to wake up beside him in Nantucket, to watch his animated face at rest. How close to heaven would it be to hear his even breathing and watch him sleep, relaxed and unencumbered with no cares beyond that of any normal husband earning a living and raising a family. She had trouble imagining that much peace.

'Penny for your thoughts, Gracie,' Rob asked as they entered the dower house.

She blushed and was glad dusk was too far advanced now for him to notice. 'I was imagining what peace must feel like,' she said and it was an honest answer.

'Maybe a little like this,' he said, as he opened the door for her. He stepped into the tiny foyer. 'We could be coming home from church.' He sniffed. 'I can almost smell the sea.'

To her heart's delight, he kept his arm around her until he heard Emery in the kitchen. 'I guess he got tired of watching out for me.' They laughed together.

I never will, Grace thought.

She held that thought through a simple supper—after so many hours in the bakery no one wanted to cook—and an evening in the sitting room, debating the merits of venturing out again to midnight church services and, rejecting them, being content to read aloud from Luke.

Finally, Rob stretched and yawned. 'We're old sticks in the mud,' he said. 'But we worked hard today, didn't we?'

Grace nodded. After she blew out the lamp in the sitting room, she noticed the flicker of a candle from the bookroom. Curious, she went inside and noticed the envelope on the rickety table. She opened it, pulling out several pound notes and a letter, with nothing more on it than 'Happy Christmas, S.'

Rob had followed her down the hall. Wordlessly, she handed him the note and money. He shook his head. 'Mr Selway strikes again. How did this get here?'

'I have no idea. I'll ask Emery in the morning.'

'He would have said something, if he knew about it,' Rob said. He made no attempt to hide his misgivings. 'Who else has a key to the dower house?'

'Lord Thomson? Maybe Ugly Butler.' Grace rubbed her arms, suddenly chilled.

'Oh, that's a laugh,' Rob said. He grinned at Grace. 'Maybe we should wish Smathers a Happy Christmas tomorrow and thank *him* for the money!'

'Tease all you want,' Grace scolded. 'I want to lay my eyes on Mr Selway again.'

Rob put the envelope and money on the desk, staring at them as though he wanted the paper to talk. 'You know, Grace, if you and I hadn't spent a day or two—or more in your case—with Mr Selway, I'd almost start suspecting he didn't exist.'

It was a disconcerting thought and not one she wanted to carry to bed with her. She went upstairs alone, troubled in her mind. Rob said he would come up later, after he had finished some business in the bookroom.

* * *

She sat up in bed a long time, not willing to sleep until she heard his footsteps on the stairs. She had become so used to keeping him constantly in her sight, that even a floor away from him in a small house seemed too far. She rested her chin on her updrawn knees, thinking that another year would turn soon. Before Rob, there had never been a reason to look ahead, because the years had stretched on with an unvarying sameness to them that she knew would not change. She sighed. That sameness would return, once he left. It was time to store up every tiny memory against the day word came about peace and the parole ended.

She heard Rob on the stairs and held her breath as he paused in front of her door. She hoped he would knock, but he just stood there and then crossed the narrow hall to his own room.

'It's not locked,' she said softly, but his door closed quietly. 'Happy Christmas, you dear man.'

Chapter Twenty-One

Christmas began with the luxury of waking up late. Eyes barely open, Grace heard a small sound and looked around. Rob was putting a final lump of coal on the cheerful blaze. He had already pulled open the curtains; snow was falling.

'Happy Christmas, Gracie,' he said, coming to the bed and sitting down.

She had not expected that. 'S…s…same to you,' she stammered.

He glanced around elaborately. 'Snakes in here.'

She laughed softly. He rubbed her cheek with his. 'I should shave today,' he said, 'even if there is no work and I don't have to impress anyone.'

'Not even me?' she teased.

'Especially not you,' he told her. He took a deep breath, as though worlds were ready to collide, and reached inside his jacket. 'Happy Christmas, Grace.' He kissed her lips this time, dropped the folded paper in her lap and left the room as quietly as he must have entered it.

'You could have waited until we were convened in the sitting room and my paltry present to you was on your lap,' she grumbled out loud, thinking of the socks she had knitted.

She opened the paper and sucked in her breath. He had been wise to give it to her now. She read his confident note, her eyes taking in the formal notary's public seal, wondering when he had been out of her sight long enough to do this thing of monumental proportions.

'Is there anyone on this planet as stupid as you have been, Grace?' she asked out loud, her voice foreign to her own ears.

With a sob, she threw back the covers and ran to the door, practically jerking it off the hinges. He was starting down the stairs, but he turned around, startled as she hurtled herself into his arms, sobbing, wrapping her legs around him when he lifted her up.

She clung to him, not caring that her nightgown was old and well ventilated, and that her hair was all over her face and not neat and tidy. Her nightgown had hiked up to her thighs and she just didn't care.

'I can't take this!' she cried into his shoulder as he held her close. 'Not your house!'

'Yes, you can, Grace,' he said, his lips on her ear. 'I want you to have it. If anything happens to me, I—'

'Nothing is going to happen to you!' she said, her voice fierce. She put her hand over his mouth. 'Don't say it!'

He was carrying her back to her room. 'I hope not, too, but this paper deeds the house to you. Grace, don't cry.'

He laid her on her bed, but she clung to him. He lay down next to her, holding her close. 'It's a fine house, Gracie, with three or four chambers upstairs—lots of room for children—and a very fine sitting room. The kitchen could be larger, but I think I can add on to the back of the house. It's the prettiest clapboard, with grey boards and red trim. I always wanted a red door, even if my Quaker neighbours think I am prideful. You'll like my neighbours.'

She grabbed him by his shirt front, startling herself with her own passion. 'Nothing is going to happen to you!' she repeated. 'Rob Inman, I love you!'

'I was hoping you might,' he told her, after another deep breath.

He seemed to know he was wasting his words. He held her close until her tears subsided to shuddering sobs. When she was sniffing, he pulled out his shirttail and wiped her face with it.

Grace took a deep breath and wrapped her arms around him. 'I'm a ninny,' she managed to say finally.

'I know,' he replied. 'You're still a baronet's daughter, though, and I—'

She put her hand over his mouth and he kissed her palm. 'Gracie, have you any idea how your eyes give you away with every look?'

She shook her head. 'I knew you couldn't possibly love me, after I was so rude.'

'Oh, now, which time was that?' he teased, holding her closer. 'I wanted you to have a house of your own, even if it is a long way from here.' He looked at her then, his eyes bright. 'You really do love me?'

'It's been my torment,' she told him simply. 'Please don't say another word about something happening to you!'

She tried to say more through her tears, but he took her chin in his hands. 'Grace, listen to me. Be the strong woman I know you are. Even if there is an ocean between you and your new home, I am convinced you will find a way to get there, should something happen to me. Don't disappoint me, Grace.'

'I won't,' she said, her voice small, scarcely audible to even her own ears. She held herself off from him to look into his eyes. 'But you had better propose to me, or I'll tear this up.'

'You're a hard one,' he chided gently, then pulled her to him again, so close she wasn't sure where she left off and he began. 'Very well, if that is your condition. I love you nearly beyond fathoming, even though I am far out of your league, a foreigner and a prisoner of war.' He shook his head. 'I can't believe I am even asking this, but will you marry me?'

'Certainly,' she said. 'I love you. I have a lot to say to you, as soon as I stop crying and get dressed.'

He put his finger to her lips. 'Let this be one time you don't scold me for being impractical. It's Christmas, after all.'

So it was. After a long look at Rob, which only made her whole body grow warm, Grace shooed him from her room. She sat for a long moment, just staring at the handwritten deed, wondering how much she had changed since she had chosen Rob Inman. She knew there was no more practical, logical, realistic person in Quimby, because her wrenching circumstances had made her so.

Since she had walked to Quimby to throw herself on the mercy of a baker and his wife, she had schooled herself to expect nothing, because it was the surest way to avoid disappointment. She had told herself there never would be a home and family for her because she belonged in no social sphere. She had set her sights low, because it was less painful than more disappointment.

Grace picked up the deed and couldn't help smiling. Rob Inman's handwriting was as confident as he was. This man she had chosen, had chosen her, in turn. In the middle of war, with its diabolical machinery that grinds down the notable and the unknown with equal impunity and shows no mercy whatsoever, she had fallen in love with a man who could be taken from her at any moment. Still, if she had never taken the bold step to choose, and then to love, hers would be a truly blighted life. No matter the outcome of these uncertain times, Grace Curtis knew that someone had chosen her and it was enough. There might be great pain ahead, or great bliss, but she would not go to her grave knowing that no one had ever singled her out and cared for her above all others.

She put the deed to her lips, wishing she knew what lay ahead, and then grateful that she did not. From somewhere in the back of her mind, she remembered something old Lord Thomson had told her. In one tiny, indiscreet moment, she had complained to him about her sterile life, where nothing happened and nothing would. He had only nodded and told her of a Spanish proverb: '"Patience, and shuffle the cards", my dear,' he had said. 'None of us knows what lies ahead.'

She stared at the ceiling, wondering what it was about her that had appealed to Rob Inman. He knew all her deficiencies and shortcomings. He had taken her scolds and nags in his stride, amused by them almost, as though he was humouring her. Maybe it was something only he could see. She would have to ask him some day.

Rob was standing in the sitting room, rocking back on his heels, watching the snow fall. He clasped and unclasped his hands, and she could imagine him standing just like that on a quarterdeck. She would have preferred a man who stayed at home and didn't require the world's oceans to earn his bread, but as inexplicable as choosing him had been, equally hard to understand was why people did what they did. She would love him no matter what.

'I love you,' she whispered.

The words came out of her mouth so softly that she could barely hear them, but he turned around and smiled.

'I told you I have the best hearing of anyone on the *Orontes*,' he reminded her. He held out his arms.

She would have walked into his embrace without a qualm, but a shadow stopped her: one shadow, then another through the storm.

Rob stepped back from the window, alert. 'Let Emery get the door, Gracie. It's just Lord Thomson coming to wish us a Happy Christmas.'

'That's a crock,' she muttered, angry at herself to look down and see her hands balled into fists.

Rob briefly covered her hands with his. 'You're more protective than a mother cat,' he told her. 'It's Christmas. We are here together—parolee and, um, parolee-keeper—obeying every jot and tittle of Lord Thomson's conditions.'

When Lord Thomson came into the sitting room, Rob stood up and held out his hand, which the marquis ignored. Standing right behind his employer, Nahum Smathers glowered at them both, which sent little armies of gooseflesh marching down Grace's back.

'Happy Christmas, Lord Thomson,' Rob said, withdrawing his hand. 'I truly hope it is a good season for you and Lady Thomson.'

It was quietly said. Lord Thomson pressed his lips tight. Grace couldn't overlook the red flush that rose from his neck, bloomed on his cheeks and passed on to his scalp, with its thinning hair. The marquis looked at her, or tried to. Rob deliberately stepped between her and Lord Thomson, as though he had the power to protect her. *You brave, foolish man,* she thought, taking heart from his own courage, which seemed almost second nature.

'I have a word for Grace Curtis,' the marquis said.

I can be brave, too, she thought. 'My lord?'

Some tiny spark within her was suddenly weary of men like the marquis, who thought themselves superior, simply because they were born with pedigrees they had not earned. Even Sir Barnabas Tutt, butcher and landowner, had worked hard for his title. In the short second while Lord Thomson tried to stare her down, Grace saw clearly Sir Barnabas's superiority over this fool.

'It is merely this,' the marquis said, slapping his gloves from one hand to the other. 'I have no intention of paying you one groat of that thirty pounds until that infamous will has been in effect for a year.'

'And Happy New Year to you,' Rob said, amused.

'I have sufficient for my needs, my lord,' Grace replied, feeling calm in that odious man's presence because she found herself looking at him through new eyes. *You, sir, are the toady,* she thought. *Rob Inman is worth ten of you and so am I. Why did I never see that before?*

Perhaps her face was too expressive; Rob had said as much. Never mind, though—Lord Thomson's gaze was directed over her shoulder, where a portrait—and not a good one—used to hang, before his spite landed it in some dark corner of Quarle's attic. What a small man he was.

Smathers was looking at her and she returned his gaze, determined not to let him frighten her. There was nothing in the curl of his lip to indicate anything but animosity. If she hadn't already weighed his character and found it wanting, she might have thought she saw a grudging admiration in his eyes. No matter—she was likely wrong. All she wanted now was for the two unwelcome guests in the dower house to quit it.

'Don't let us take any more of your valuable time on this most blessed of holidays, when people generally try to think well of each other,' Grace said, her voice as serene as she could make it, because she knew Rob Inman had her back. The reality of his love seemed to bloom before her with all its promise. She need never fear anyone, since Rob Inman had chosen her. 'In fact, let me show you out, my lord.'

What could he do but leave? She held out her hand graciously, indicating the door to the sitting room, imagining herself ushering out an unwelcome guest at her home—her home and Rob's home—on Orange Street in Nantucket. He had described it to her in detail, so she could almost see the highly polished floor of fir, the rag rug in front of the fireplace, and the high-backed chairs with cushions Elaine had made.

Lord Thomson looked her in the eyes then, and she took an involuntary step back. There was no disguising his dislike. *I pray I will never strain so hard over thirty pounds,* she told herself, as she refused to let him ruffle her new-found equanimity.

It gave her enough courage to put her hand briefly on Smathers's arm as he turned to follow his master into the snow.

'Mr Smathers, did you deliver a letter to the dower house yesterday, while we were all at the bakery?' She couldn't help herself. 'You must have given Emery the slip.'

'It's not a hard thing to do, Miss Curtis,' he replied, not giving her an inch. He turned to face her, his hand on the doorknob and Lord Thomson calling to him, demanding his presence. 'Yes, I took a letter into your bookroom.'

'It was money from Mr Selway, who—'

'The elusive Mr Selway, who dodged you in Exeter, a few months ago.'

She couldn't help her intake of breath. Had he followed them to Exeter? Was he that clever?

Smathers seemed to read her mind. 'Don't attempt a deep game with me,' he told her. 'You will lose.'

He looked over her shoulder and she knew Rob was behind her now. He executed a mocking bow. 'Happy Christmas to you both. May I give you some New Year's advice?'

'We can hardly wait,' Rob said.

'Captain Duncan, there is a Chinese saying, "If you are ignorant both of your enemy and yourself, you are certain to be in peril".' Smathers turned into the wind without another word.

'Bastard,' Rob said, settling his hand on her shoulder after she closed the door with more force than she should have.

Grace leaned against him, relishing the feeling of a man's strength to protect her from the Ugly Butlers of the world. 'He knows something about Mr Selway.'

'He just wants to frighten you,' Rob said.

He's doing a very good job then, Grace told herself as she turned the key in the lock.

Chapter Twenty-Two

Her world changed again four days later. Grace knew she would always remember the moment, because she was cutting gingerbread men and idly dreaming of doing precisely that in her own Nantucket bakery. She was beyond the point of scolding herself for her extravagant daydreaming. Things had changed.

She worked alone, content, because she found solitary biscuit-making soothing. Rob and Mrs Wilson were talking in the back room, and Mr Wilson had taken the day's supply of doughnuts to the coffee house. Apparently Quimby's usual bakery-shop patrons were still recovering from Christmas, because the shop was empty.

It was just as well. She couldn't hear what Mrs Wilson and Rob were talking about, but she heard him laugh from time to time, which pleased her. He had spent a good portion of the past few nights after work just standing at the sitting-room window, hands shoved deep in his pockets, staring into the darkness.

'I've been too long away from home,' was all he would say, when she asked him. Generally he ended up with his arms tight around her, but she couldn't reach that deep core of sadness inside him, a captive American yearning for liberty. No wonder her heart lifted to hear him joking with Mrs Wilson, whom no one ever accused of being a jolly sort. Even *she* was trying to lift his spirits.

She was considering the merits of blue versus red piping on the gingerbread men when Mr Wilson ran into the shop, out of breath and panting.

'Mr Wilson?'

Mr Wilson, who never hurried anywhere, bent over until he could breathe, then straightened up and held out the latest broadside from Exeter.

'Belgium,' he managed to gasp.

'Belgium?' she repeated, mystified, taking the paper he was waving at her. She scanned the article, which occupied most of the broadside's front. Her breath came more rapidly, too, as she understood what it all meant. The war was over. Diplomats from England and the United States had signed a peace treaty on Christmas Eve in Ghent, Belgium.

'Rob?' she called. 'Rob!'

He came into the room, concern in his eyes, and his hands balled into fists. 'Grace?'

She waved the newspaper in front of him,

much as Mr Wilson had done to her. Rob grasped her hand to stop the frantic motion and read the article, a slow smile crossing his lips. He read it over again, savouring it even more than she did. When Rob finished, he sighed, as though he had been holding his breath for two years, then took her in his arms.

Grace gladly held him close, eager to press against his chest and rest her head there. His heart was hammering at a rapid rate. 'It's over, Rob, it's over,' she murmured.

Mrs Wilson read the paper she had pried from Rob's grasp, devouring each word. Rob held Grace off for a long look, then kissed her.

Mrs Wilson observed them, something close to triumph in her eyes. 'High time,' was all she said. Whether she meant the peace or the kiss, Grace neither knew nor cared.

Mr Wilson managed a huge sigh of his own and looked at Grace. 'I suppose you will be giving me your notice soon and asking for a glowing character,' he said, trying to sound stern and failing. 'Taking your doughnut receipt with you, Captain?' he asked Rob.

The sailing master put his other arm around Mr Wilson. 'Sir, you will have the sole claim to Yankee Doodle Doughnuts in England. Let the imitators beat a path to *your* door.'

Rob looked out of the window then, a frown creasing his forehead when he saw Nahum Smathers standing in his usual place across the street. It had begun to rain, but he took the newspaper from Mrs Wilson and darted out of the door before Grace could stop him.

She watched him, a smile on her face, which froze when she realised he wasn't to so much as budge out of doors in Quimby without her accompanying him. 'Ro…Captain,' she said, following him. 'Wait!'

She saw Emery leave his spot several shops down by the elm tree, making for Rob, too, as though to stop him before he reached Smathers, whose expression of surprise turned to something she could not interpret. She ran as both Smathers and Emery moved towards Rob, bent on gloating over the news at the Ugly Butler's expense.

She wasn't sure what happened then. In his own excitement to collar Rob Inman, Smathers stepped in front of Emery, tripping the man. Both men went down, Smathers coming up swearing and Emery looking around in surprise, shaking his head to clear it.

'You're a brave man to trip an old fellow,' Grace said to Smathers, sitting in the middle of the street with a look of real distaste on his face to see her arm linked through Rob's now, tugging him back to the bakery.

Rob didn't go quietly, but waved the paper in front of Smathers's face as he sat there fuming. 'It's over, Smathers. Just a matter of time now before a bunch of us show a clean pair of heels to your puny island.'

'You think so?' Smathers said, every word bitten off and spit out. 'Think again, fool.'

Rob just smiled. As Grace helped Emery to his feet, Rob released the newspaper to let it float down into Smathers's lap.

'It's over,' he repeated. 'Get used to it and look for another job, Smathers. Someone besides Lord Thomson must need a skulker. You're eminently qualified.'

He turned on his heel.

'If he was an enemy before, he is a bigger one now,' Grace whispered, watching Smathers. 'You shouldn't have done that.'

He shrugged. 'What's the difference? He'll be a mere memory soon.' He looked over his shoulder and held out his hand to Emery. 'Are you all right, old fellow?'

'Just my dignity,' Emery muttered. 'Will Smathers go away now, do you think?'

'We can hope.'

Once the news was out, everyone in Quimby seemed to find an excuse to visit the bakery. Lady Tutt even came by with her own copy of the paper, ready to explain to anyone who would listen that the terms of the treaty—*status quo ante bellum*—meant that any land or property acquired during the course of the struggle would revert to its respective side, restoring all to life before the war.

Rob could be generous, even with Lady Tutt,

which warmed Grace's heart. He listened to her officious explanation, nodding gravely. 'That's a load off my mind.'

'Perhaps you can advise your president not to attack Canada again. It's for his own good, mind.'

'Next time I see him, Lady Tutt,' Rob said, which satisfied the woman.

Dinner was a quiet affair. Emery had a limp, so Grace made him bathe his foot in warm water and Epsom salts while she prepared the simple meal. 'Your little contretemps with that odious Smathers was a timely reminder to Captain Duncan of the danger of attempting anything rash before we hear from Mr Selway,' she told the former yardman, as she peeled carrots. 'We cannot be too careful.'

'I dare say we cannot,' Emery agreed, wiggling his foot and wincing. 'I shouldn't leave my foot in Epsom salts during dinner, Grace,' he said.

Grace laughed. 'Lady Tutt would not approve, but we are a little more ramshackle here at Chez Dower House!'

Rob's exuberance had turned introspective by nightfall. He continued his perusal of the darkness outside the sitting-room window as Grace knitted. He stopped his pacing and looked at her. 'Everything as it was before the war, eh? Then Captain Duncan would be alive and the *Orontes* would be sailing to the Caribbean for sugar cane.'

He shook his head. 'I wonder, my love, if everyone—winners and losers—feels this way when a war is over. I feel so sad.'

Grace put down her knitting . He sat beside her and took her in his arms. He kissed her, then nuzzled her neck, which made her sigh and raise her chin so he could do a more thorough exploration.

'There's a hawthorn tree outside my bedroom window on Nantucket,' he murmured, his hand on her breast now. 'In the spring, blossoms cover the bed, if the wind blows.'

'And this is apropos of what?' she managed to say, as she unbuttoned her dress, suddenly glad this morning that she had decided to wear the dress that buttoned down the front.

'Nothing. I just thought of it,' he said as his hand went inside her dress and he caressed her breast with gentle fingers, then with his lips. 'Gracie, you're so soft.'

'Very glad to know that,' she said. Nothing but her own desire made her arch her back then, giving him more room to explore both breasts. Warmth and heaviness seemed to be gathering between her legs now in a way that was pleasant and frustrating at the same time. He wasn't even touching her there yet, but she wanted him to. *Grace, the man has only two hands*, she thought, and it made her smile.

He looked at her, his eyes bright. 'What's so funny?'

Somehow, her dress had been pushed up to her

hips and she was lying on the sofa now. 'I was thinking of those Indian statues—you know, the ones with four hands.'

He laughed. 'You're a rascal.'

'Who knew?'

'I did. You're irresistible.' He was unbuttoning his trousers now. 'Gracie, my love and my wife— as soon as possible—prepare to be impressed.' He laughed softly. 'Or not. Does it matter?'

He stopped, alert. 'Damn. Emery.' He stood up, buttoning his trousers, as her hands went to her own buttons. 'I'll just stand at the fire-place with my back to the door and gaze into the flames. Men in high blood aren't too subtle.'

She felt her face flame red, grateful, at least, that his nuzzling had been confined to her breast, and not her face, where whisker burn would be hard to ignore. She stood up and shook down her dress, then reached for her knitting, which had ended up halfway across the room. She put on her calmest face as Emery entered, even though her heart pounded in her recently explored chest.

'Grace—oh, Captain, I didn't know you were still up.'

She held her breath, hoping he wouldn't require Rob's full attention.

Rob nodded, from his position in front of the fireplace. 'Just winding the clock,' he said. 'D'ye need me for something?'

'Not at the moment.' Emery held out a letter

to her. 'I found this just inside the front door.' He winked at her. 'Maybe a secret admirer?'

Grace took the letter. 'You know I have no secret admirers, Emery.' She put her hand to her cheek. 'My blushes!'

He stood there, probably wanting to know what the letter contained. Grace decided to satisfy his curiosity, considering how little she had shared with him. She opened the note, which was sealed with a dab of wax. With a start, she felt the warmth from the wax, newly applied. She couldn't help the chill that ran down her back.

'"Do nothing foolish",' she read out loud, then held it out to Emery. 'And see there? It's signed with an S.'

'Mr Selway, I don't doubt,' Emery said. 'What do you suppose he means?' he asked Rob.

Rob joined them by the sofa, holding out his hand for the note. 'Maybe the elusive Mr Selway watched us this afternoon, when I so foolishly ran across the street without my ever-present shadow.'

'Then why does he not show himself?' Grace asked, practical as always.

The three of them looked at each other. Rob tapped the note against his wrist. 'I have heard older seamen tell about the revolution. They say the most dangerous time is when a war is just beginning, or almost over.' He looked Emery in the eye. 'There are no rules.'

He took the note back to the fireplace and flicked it into the flames. 'We've been warned, I suppose. I'm depending on you to keep your eye on Ugly Butler, Emery.'

'I always do,' was Emery's quiet reply. He nodded to them both. 'And now, me for bed.' He smiled faintly. 'A peace treaty is excitement enough for one day.'

Emery closed the door behind him. 'Emery is right.' Rob put his arm around Grace's waist, the gesture belying his words, his face so close to hers. 'I shan't mince words, my dearest. These are truly dangerous times.' He couldn't quite meet her eyes and she knew she was not misreading the disappointment in his voice. 'We had better wait.'

'I don't want to,' she whispered

'Nor do I,' he told her as he released her, 'but needs must when the devil drives.'

He closed the sitting-room door behind him. Grace rested her cheek against it. 'Why should we wait? The war is over,' she whispered.

Chapter Twenty-Three

It wasn't the answer she wanted, but as she undressed for bed, Grace had to agree that Rob was right. She stood barefoot and naked in her room until she felt the winter's chill, wondering how it would be when they finally made connection in that way of men and women.

She knew it must be pleasurable. Once or twice, not recently—maybe they were getting old—she had heard Mrs Wilson moan in their room upstairs from the bakery. Now and then the bed upstairs made a squeaking rhythm that had intrigued Grace. She sometimes explored her own body, enjoying the feeling of release, but wondering how much better it could be with someone to share the pleasure.

She pulled her nightgown over her head, crawled into bed and tried to sleep. Nothing.

'The war is over, and I love that man,' she said out loud, finally.

She sat up. *I am twenty-eight,* she thought—as if she needed reminding—as she pulled back the covers. She sat for a long while, weighing the merit of her decision. She had been restless before, but an urge deep inside her told her that the only remedy for Rob was Rob. She thought of the deed to his house, and his near-desperation that she have it, should something happen to him.

The thought chilled her. 'Needs must, indeed,' she said. What if something were to happen and she was destined never to know the love of the man she adored? She knew she could never survive such a sterile life, not now, not after knowing her heart for the first time.

Grace took a deep breath, opened the door to her room and stood there in surprise.

'Rob?'

There he stood, his eyes lively, even in the gloom of the hallway, with just the moon giving pale light.

'You can't sleep either?'

She shook her head.

'Look at you,' he said, his voice low. 'You're going to get cold feet.'

'I already have cold feet,' she assured him and he smiled.

'If it's any consolation, I do, too,' he told her. 'Take my hand, Gracie. I suppose two bigger fools never lived.'

Then they were in his room, with the door closed against Emery and Smathers, a whole village of busybodies, Lord Thomson, horrible Dartmoor and every slight she had endured in the past ten years.

Rob led her to his bed and sat there, watching in silence, his face serious, as she unbuttoned her nightgown and let it slide down her body. She stood naked before him, resisting the instinct to cover her breasts and private parts from the steady gaze of the man she loved, but never dreamed she would be loving so soon.

'Are we celebrating the peace treaty?' he asked, his gaze so steady, so honest.

'I'm celebrating you,' she whispered, blushing.

He sighed audibly, a contented sound, if ever she had heard one. He slowly unbuttoned his own nightshirt, not taking his eyes from her.

Naked, he stood up and came to her, pulling her body close to his. She closed her eyes as his arms went tight around her. Heat and weight rushed to her loins, the feeling not unpleasant, but not comfortable, because she felt such an urge to press closer.

Rob was in no hurry. When she felt brave enough to look at his face, he was looking at her, his expression hard to interpret. She put a hand to the pronounced frown line between his eyes and rubbed it gently.

'Why so serious?' she asked.

'This is a serious business, Grace,' he replied.

He took her hand and kissed the palm. 'I want you in my bed, but you know there are risks.'

He didn't need to spell it out. She nodded. 'I know that. Rob Inman, my door didn't fly open by itself,' she told him, wondering if she was destined to be for ever more practical than he.

He chuckled at that, led her to his bed and held the coverlets up, his hand caressing her hip. 'Slide in, Gracie.'

She did as he said, then carefully rested her head on his chest. She closed her eyes as his fingers cupped her breast. 'The maid was right, you know. You are 'andsome.'

She felt his chuckle as he ran his other hand along her hip, stopping at the fleshiest spot and patting her. In another moment, she slid onto her back, pulling his head down to rest on her breasts.

'I used to dream about this in Dartmoor, until I started forgetting what a woman felt like,' he whispered into her breasts. 'That was a bad day.'

It was her turn to chuckle. She realised he was trying to put her at ease, even while he probably wanted to move much faster, considering his personal drought, brought about by Elaine's death, war and prison. And he was thinking of her.

Her fingers found his growing organ with no difficulty and curled gently around him. He spread his legs slightly, his breath coming faster.

She stroked him. His sigh suggested it was the right thing to do, so she continued.'I hope I'm doing the right thing,' she whispered.

He didn't answer. When he rested his hand on her private parts, she opened her legs, too.

He raised up on one elbow, his fingers probing her, as she raised her hips. She closed her eyes as he kissed her inner thigh. His lips searched higher and his breathing became ragged. No, it was her breathing.

'Open your eyes, Gracie,' he murmured as he fitted himself on top of her. Her arms went around him, but it wasn't enough; she wanted him closer.

'How does anyone survive this?' she asked. His face was too close to see, so she kissed him instead of worrying about anything else.

'Grace, you amaze me,' he whispered back, his lips just above hers. 'Steady as you go now.'

And then he was inside her. Her hands tightened across his back. She didn't want to talk then, but to concentrate instead on what he was doing and how liquid she felt, how different. 'What is it we do?' she asked finally, when she felt the strongest urge for more.

'Exactly this,' he whispered into her neck, as he began to move rhythmically.

The fact that she understood Rob completely made her suspect that instinct had a delicious way of trampling all over inexperience. Eager now, she relaxed as much as she could, her hands gentle on his back and buttocks. He didn't have to suggest she put her legs around him, because she could think of no better thing to do.

The only sound then was their breathing, which fell into its own rhythm. She felt the deepest pleasure she had ever known when he sighed, pulled her closer and released himself inside her. She clung to him, kissing his shoulder, knowing in her very soul that he needed her—not just any woman, not just any body, but her. He said so, over and over. 'Grace, oh, Grace,' he whispered in her ear.

She touched his face, surprised to feel tears. 'Don't cry, Rob,' she whispered back. 'You're going to be home soon.'

'I am now,' he told her, still holding her close, but raising up on his elbows to give her more room to breathe. 'I don't want to weigh you down, but I can't leave you yet.'

She kissed his shoulder again, and then his lips, her body relaxing now, even as his did. 'Rob, can we do this again? Fairly soon? I want to get the knack.'

He chuckled in her ear. 'I think we can find occasion in our busy schedules, Grace. I, um, plan to give you a more thorough effort, because you're entitled to some pleasure of your own.'

'Now?'

He laughed and turned over, pulling her on top of him now. 'You're going to lead me a merry dance, aren't you?'

'If I can,' she told him, resting her head on his chest now, surprised a little that they were still joined together and pleased with her own dexterity. And here she had always thought herself so awkward.

'I know you can, but my dear, it takes men a little time to regroup.'

'Oh?'

'Aye, lass, even a sailor! There now. At the risk of sounding mundane beyond belief, if you dismount carefully, you can probably find a cloth by my washbasin.'

She blushed in the dark, but he was right: time for a wash. When she finished, he came to the basin, too, and accepted the wrung-out cloth from her.

'It's not the world's tidiest business, Grace,' he told her when he finished. He picked her up and tossed her back in the bed, which made her shriek, then cover her mouth with her hand.

He took her hand away. 'No fears, love. Emery is sleeping a warm and peaceful sleep two floors below. It's just me and I'm no critic.'

Grace thought about returning to her own bed, but the door was miles away and Rob was warm against her back. He lay on his side, one leg thrown over her, his arm under her head, his breathing slow and steady.

She closed her eyes and thought through their mating, savouring each moment because she'd never had any hopes that she would ever dance to Cupid's tune. The long war was over. The world was at peace; so was she.

She turned over carefully, hoping not to disturb her man. There was just enough moonlight to show her the relief on his face, his hands open and relaxed. She touched his hair, which had grown long again, and traced the brand on his neck. She wondered again how civilised people could condone stamping a man with a hot iron, even if he was their enemy. *I'll never understand governments*, she thought, kissing the scar. *Who does?*

Sleep had come softly then, until early in the morning, when she woke to feel Rob's hand on her breast. She stirred and moved onto her back, relishing the way he stroked her. She felt the now-familiar heat gathering again in her loins.

The room was cold, but he threw off the blankets and worked his way down her body, kissing her from her breastbone to that calm, soft place no longer calm, but even more soft. This time he let her guide him into her body with no flinch and no hesitation.

'Told you it didn't take long,' he murmured as he settled himself on her again.

Grace gave him no argument on that score. Now that the newness of their connection had mellowed her mind, she eagerly wrapped her arms and legs around him and gave herself to his rhythm, savouring his weight, the way he murmured in her ear, the beating of his heart against hers, the odd security he gave her, even though she knew they were both so vulnerable. The years of aching loneliness fell away like scales as she realised, to her utter joy, that she was finally close enough to another human being, the man she loved. It was a gift and a blessing greater than any she could think of.

He climaxed, which lifted her on until she was moaning, tossing her head from side to side and gripping him ever more fiercely as her turn came. If she could have turned herself inside out, she would have, so intense was the ebb and flow of the waves that left her spent and sweating.

'My goodness, Rob,' she said finally, when her breathing returning to normal, or what would pass for normal, if she hadn't been still caught in the rhythm.

As he smoothed back her hair and kissed her forehead, continuing his efforts inside her, she felt the climax grab her again, this time more subdued, but no less potent. She was nipping his shoulder now, which made him laugh softly and press his forehead against hers.

'Gracie, you're a wonder,' he whispered. 'I believe you're as strong as I am.'

She hugged him even tighter. 'You did say once that kneading bread had given me wonderful shoulders.'

He laughed again. 'This is the world's oddest conversation,' he said, as he left her body and flopped onto his back. He slapped his stomach. 'It's a good thing I am a fit man now and not the skeleton you rescued from Dartmoor.' He turned sideways then and rested his head on her breast.

'I believe I will reconsider a seafaring career. I'd rather own a bakery in Nantucket and come home to you every night! I'd be a fool if I did otherwise.' He lay back again and took her hand in his.

She brought his hand to her lips and kissed it. 'I suppose I truly am no lady,' she said, thinking there must be some way to explain her total delight in the pleasures of the flesh. Maybe she had slid further than she had thought.

Rob raised up and kissed her. 'The two issues are not compatible,' he told her. 'Grace, you were born a lady, raised a lady and you remain a lady. What you and I do with our bodies is our business alone.'

Grace digested his comment. She found it entirely to her liking, so much so that after a brief nap, and just after the sun rose, it was her turn to wake him as her hand explored his tender parts. He had no objection, beyond teasing her to be gentle with him.

Chapter Twenty-Four

It struck Grace as strange that no one seemed to have any inkling that she had travelled from spinster to lover in less than twelve hours. When she dressed in the privacy of her own room, she hardly dared to sneak a peek at her face in the little mirror, convinced that she would find some evidence of her tumultuous night emblazoned on her forehead.

When she did finally look, the same Grace Curtis stared, then smiled, back at her: the Grace with a few freckles, a nicely curved mouth, blue eyes and nose that just escaped—thank goodness—being called 'full of character'. She looked the same as always, right down to her small waist and capable shoulders, which seemed to amuse Rob, or perhaps excite him. The only one who could possibly have any inkling of the currents inside her was the man who had started the whole commotion: the lover she adored and the man she would marry, if God was good, now that the war was over. Her life had changed monumentally and no one knew.

The first test was Emery, who greeted her kindly when she came into the kitchen and asked her opinion about the eggs he was baking. She observed them, hoping he would think her cheeks were extra rosy because of the cooking heat. Grace chided herself for being so missish. She prepared bread to toast. When it was done, Rob had still not appeared. Emery looked at the clock.

'He's lazy in the new year. Too much celebrating in a dower house over the signing of a treaty!' He laughed. 'Gracie, d'ye suppose the captain celebrated by counting the flowers on the wallpaper in his room?'

Not precisely, Grace thought. *He did celebrate, though.* 'That must be it,' she said.

When breakfast was on the table, Rob still had not arrived. Grace and Emery ate, the butler with his eyes on the clock again.

You dear man. You're too old to be watching Ugly Butler so closely in all weather, she told herself as she poured more tea for both of them. She set down the teapot. 'Emery, the war is over now,' she reminded him. 'You've been a prince to watch over Captain Duncan and make sure Mr Smathers kept his distance. You can probably rest now. It's over.'

Emery nodded. 'Maybe it won't be necessary for you to stick so close to Captain Duncan's side, either. It must be tedious for you.'

Far from it, she thought. 'We'll see.'

She nodded to Emery, then took her way into the sitting room. She heard Rob's footsteps on the stairs, but she felt suddenly shy to look at him, not after a night of so much passion in one small dower house. A dower house, where old relics and relicts went to dwindle, not blossom!

She stood, gazing idly out of the window, where a few flakes of snow drifted down. Something caught her eye; she glanced at the mantelpiece and sucked in her breath. A letter with her name on it was propped against one of the ugly vases Lord Thomson had so grudgingly returned, after he had swept the place clean last spring.

Even from across the room, she recognised Mr Selway's bold script. *How can he be getting messages into this house?* she asked herself, as a chill went through her. *Does he have a key?* She retrieved the note, unnerved.

It was a short message; Mr Selway was not one to waste words, or for that matter to grant them a personal appearance, she reminded herself. The message did nothing to soothe her nerves.

Trust no one, she read silently. *When a war winds down, no one is in charge.*

She frowned at his scrawled S., then read the note again, wishing irrationally that it would expand and tell her what to do.

* * *

Theirs was a quiet walk to Quimby, ambling along, both of them too shy to look at each other. Rob stopped finally and turned to face her, his expression serious.

She looked around to make sure they were alone and touched his face. 'Rob, what is the matter?'

He kissed the palm of her hand before she withdrew it. 'Grace, what if…what if I get you with child?'

She had thought about it last night, long and hard and decidedly after the fact. 'The war is over,' she reminded him. 'How…how long does it take to get to Nantucket from here?'

'Nine to twelve weeks,' he said promptly. He shook his head, his expression rueful.

'Did Elaine…?'

He shook his head again. 'She had several miscarriages. It was our sorrow,' he said simply.

'Don't worry about something we have no control over,' she told him.

He gave her a wry look. 'We can, too, control this!' he assured her, blushing. 'Just lock your door.' He interpreted her expression correctly and smiled, in spite of himself. 'Or I'll lock mine.'

Men, she thought. *Are they all so dense?* 'You mean you'd make me lean a ladder against your window?' she teased.

'You like to live dangerously?'

'No woman does,' she said frankly. She kissed

his hand. 'But I am not afraid, as long as you are close by. And the war *is* over.'

He was silent then, a slight smile on his face. 'And I thought I understood women,' he said.

As they neared the village, Grace told him about the note from Mr Selway. 'I am not certain if I am more disturbed that Mr Selway, whom I like, has access to the dower house, to come and go as he pleases, or if someone else is playing us and biding his time,' she told Rob.

'For what purpose? Captain Duncan, your intended parolee, was nothing but an ordinary man. Believe me, I know.'

'His father was a marquis,' she pointed out.

'This was a subject that never came up, on land or sea,' he told her. He looked around and took both her hands. 'Write to Mr Selway.'

She did as he suggested that afternoon, warming her feet on the stove's fender and writing on Mrs Wilson's lap desk, because the day was raw. Through the open door, she watched Rob chatting with the customers. He had been surprised that morning with the continuing rush of good wishes Quimby's residents showered on him, now that the war was concluded.

'Why should that surprise you?' she asked softly, admiring the set of his shoulders under his checked shirt, knowing now how good his naked skin felt to her touch. 'You have made friends in this village who will miss you.'

* * *

On their return to the dower house, after she left the letter in the hands of the postmaster, who assured her—to Rob's amusement—that he knew what to do with a letter, Grace felt her unease grow. 'Now would be a good time for Mr Selway to show himself,' she grumbled to Rob.

'You are a worrywart. Calm down.'

He found a way to calm her down after the dower house was quiet. He came to her bed this time, clad for only a brief moment in his nightshirt before they were naked and twined together. She had left the curtains open by design, just enough to satisfy her curiosity, but not so much that she felt shy. She wanted to see his body this time, and hers, joined together. The lightly falling snow gave the room a lustre that lent an almost magic glow to his skin. There was no stress or tightness this time, only huge anticipation bordering on frustration, that crowned, spread and left her drowsy with relief. Her conviction grew that making love with the man she had chosen in Dartmoor could only become more pleasant, as he became more familiar to her hands, her lips, the eager space between her legs.

'There now,' he said when they were rational beings again and she had pillowed her head on his chest. 'No fears, Gracie.'

His hand was gentle on her head. He laughed when she took his hand and placed it on her breast. He obliged her by kneading it in much easier fashion than he kneaded bread dough. 'Maybe we have hit upon something, my love,' he told her a few minutes later, as his hand went lower, still busy, but more gentle. 'Maybe bakers are the best lovers of all.'

She took him at his word, considering that her experience went no further than the man lying next to her.

By the end of the week, Grace felt sure enough to leave a light on as they made love.

Always before dawn, Rob returned to his own bed, or she to hers. Only when she was alone now did she lie there and worry, willing Mr Selway to appear in the bakery and reassure her. She knew Rob needed the reassurance, too, even though he said nothing. More than once during that first week in January she had opened her eyes to see him standing by the window, his face serious.

She had gone to him, wrapping her arms around his waist, leaning her head against his back. 'You want to go home.' She whispered it into the smooth area between his shoulder blades.

He said nothing, but he turned around and hoisted her into his arms, holding her as she twined her legs around him now. In another moment, they were back in bed, blotting out everything except each other. He had stayed all night in her bed that time.

Mostly they were silent, words unnecessary. Sometimes he liked to talk about their future, which she almost came to crave as much as his body.

'You know, my love, the more I think about a bakery at home, the more I like the idea,' he told her, when she was tucked up close to him, her legs over his. 'I haven't told you this, but there will be prize money waiting for me when I get to Boston.'

'Prize money?'

'Aye, lass.' He chuckled. 'The *Orontes* was a grand ship for diddling British cargo. From the Baltic to Malta, we all took turns running captured vessels into neutral ports.' He patted her hip. 'It's a tidy sum and will buy a bakery.' He sighed and his hand began to caress. 'You've ruined me from ever wanting to go to sea again.'

Every morning Grace had come downstairs before him, wondering if there would be a letter in the sitting room. She considered asking Emery to be alert for a message, but decided the responsibility was hers alone. Mr Selway's missives had all been addressed to no one but her. And hadn't she alone promised to watch over Captain Duncan?

The letter was there finally, as bleak January grew more stormy. The letter rested against the same ugly vase. The sight of it made her heart beat faster. She opened it and went to the window, where feeble dawn tried to cast a light on an otherwise dismal daybreak.

She had to stifle her disappointment that the letter was not a long one, especially since she

wanted to know, chapter and verse, what lay
ahead, and why nearly a month had passed since
she had written to Mr Selway, care of a Post Office box in Exeter that seemed to have no owner.

*Do nothing rash and keep Captain Duncan
in your sight,* she read. 'We have been nothing
but rash. Mr Selway, you are too late,' she whispered to the lines in front of her. She continued.
*Understand, please, that the treaty is on its way
to Washington, where it must be ratified by Con-
gress and returned to Whitehall. Tell Captain
Duncan to be patient. It could be many months
before freedom. The British are not people who
submit easily to directives. S.*

'No, they are not,' she said to the letter, then
paused as she grasped the enormity of what she
had just said. 'They are not,' she repeated. It
wasn't *we are not,* but *they are not.* She went to
the window and held the letter close to her, wondering at what moment she had begun to think
of herself as an American.

*You have never even seen the country! How
can you be an American?* she chided herself silently. She remembered last summer, when Rob
had asked her what England had ever done for
her. The question had shocked her then, but it did
not shock her now. She knew the answer; she had
probably known it then.

Rob swore with some fervour when Grace
handed him the letter on their cold walk to

Quimby. 'Months!' he raged, slapping the note. 'I wish I could speak to an American!'

Speak to me, Grace thought. She dismissed the idea immediately because it was still an infant thought, too tender to share, even with the man she loved.

'Is there not anyone to plead the American cause here?' she asked tentatively. He seemed so angry.

He allowed his anger to diminish. 'Aye, there is, a miserable excuse of a man, name of Reuben Beasley. He is our agent here, sent by President Madison himself.' His voice was heavy with scorn. 'He is supposed to make sure we are treated well enough at Dartmoor. God damn the man.'

'Did he ever go to Dartmoor?'

'Once? Twice? I suppose he is spending taxpayer money in London.' His voice was bitter. 'Maybe he dines at the best restaurants.'

'Can I write to him?'

'Save your ink and paper.'

He had nothing much to say that day. Soon even Mr and Mrs Wilson were tiptoeing around, looking at him with worried expressions.

'It's just so hard for him to wait and wait,' she said to the Wilsons before they closed the shop that evening.

Grace tried to engage him in conversation as they walked home, but Rob would have none of it, jamming his hands deep in the pockets of his coat and ignoring her. She walked along beside him, determined not to make matters worse by scolding him, holding her tongue for once. Then it was too much and her indignation boiled to the surface.

The snow was mostly gone now, except in the shady side of the copse. As he stormed ahead, she held back, scooped up a generous helping of snow, pressed it firmly together, took aim and fired at his head.

She was no ballistics expert, but to her astonishment, and then glee, the snowball crashed into the back of his head.

'You little devil!' he roared, reaching down for his own snowball.

Grace crouched down and covered her ears as the snowball slammed into her hip. She mounded another snowball and threw it at him. It went wide of the target and he laughed, grabbing her by the neck and dropping bits of snow down her dress. She gasped as the snow slid between her breasts, then punched him in the arm, which made him pick her up and toss her on his shoulder as if she weighed nothing.

She thought to protest, but he was laughing so hard that she didn't bother. As he stalked past a snow-laden bush, she grabbed another handful of snow, reached under his coat and pushed it down his trousers.

He set her on her feet quickly enough, reaching around behind him to try to remove the snow.

'Grace, you look like such a lady, too,' he said, as he laughed.

'I told you I have slid,' she retorted, wiping the snow off her face.

She was in his arms in another moment, swaying side to side with Rob as he just held her, his face in her neck.

'I'm sorry, my dear,' he said, his voice muffled. 'It's hard to wait, when all I want to do is get us home.'

When he finally released her, Rob took her hand and kissed it. 'You're a patient woman,' he commented, as they walked past the manor house now. She could see the welcoming lights of the dower house, where Emery was probably finishing supper. 'Teach me how to be patient.'

Before she could say anything, he stood still, staring at the manor. 'Look there. Do I see another carriage? Perhaps Lord Thomson is holding a convention of ugly butlers.'

She looked at the window in sudden panic. 'I don't like this,' she whispered, tugging at Rob's hand. 'Let's hurry past.'

'You're a goose, Gracie,' Rob teased, but offered no objection as she hurried him into the dower house. He draped his pea coat over a bust of some Quarle progenitor and went up the stairs, whistling now.

'You were a trial today,' she called up the stairs.

He paused halfway up, leaning over the banister. He opened his mouth to make some rejoinder, when he stopped and looked further up the stairs.

'Grace, get out of the house,' he said quietly. 'Now.'

She stared at him, then put a hand to her mouth as a man started down the stairs towards him. He backed down a step or two, looking at her now, his face filled with alarm.

Grace started towards him as the front door slammed open. She shrieked and tried to run to the stairs as Lord Thomson and Mr Smathers took her by her arms.

'Grace!' Rob shouted, just as the man on the stairs grabbed his arms and pinioned them behind his back.

She held still, looking from the butler to the marquis, who seemed to find the whole scenario entirely to his liking.

'Miss Curtis, you've done such an excellent job of sticking like glue to Captain Duncan,' he said. 'Precisely as my uncle's will dictated.'

He released her arm and she backed closer to Nahum Smathers, simply because the look of triumph on Lord Thomson's face frightened her more than Ugly Butler. She jumped when Smathers rested his hand on her shoulder, his grip not strong, but firm enough to stop her.

The man on the stairs walked Rob Inman the rest of the way down the steps. His face white, Rob looked at Grace, then turned his head at the sound of footsteps from the kitchen.

'Emery!' Grace said. 'Help us!'

She felt like a fool for pleading for aid from a man older than all of them. His face as blank as Rob's, Emery looked at them and shook his head, sinking down onto a chair in the foyer. He put his hand to his heart.

Lord Thomson stepped forward. He regarded them all, his mouth prissy as usual, but his eyes alert, his expression bordering on the predatory. Grace edged even closer to Nahum Smathers, even though she wanted to break free and throw herself into Rob's arms. The practical side of her nature, always strong, promptly dismissed that idea. No need for anyone to know how intimate their connection was. *I will not cry*, she told herself.

Lord Thomson cleared his throat. 'We have a dilemma. My butler was going through some of old Lord Thomson's papers and he found a curious thing. It affects you, Grace. I fear I cannot give you that thirty pounds per annum. Not this year, not ever.'

'I never expected it,' she said quietly, her head high.

'Wise of you,' he replied. He took a miniature from his coat and held it out to her.

A young man, probably in his teenage years, gazed back at her. He had dark brown hair and a deep dimple in one cheek. She leaned closer. His eyes were brown, too.

'Am I supposed to know him?' she asked.

'Hard to say,' Lord Thomson said. He turned over the miniature. 'It says here, in case you cannot read the small print, that *this* is Daniel Duncan.'

There was nothing pleasant on Lord Thomson's face. 'We seem to have a difficulty, Miss Curtis.' He looked at Rob, his face set and wary. 'Who, sir, are *you*?'

Chapter Twenty-Five

'Rob Inman, sailing master on the *Orontes*,' Rob said proudly. 'Let Gracie go, Smathers. She knew nothing of this.'

Smathers's grip on her shoulder loosened, then tightened again, making her cry out, when Lord Thomson snarled at him. 'She's a drab and I don't trust her!' Lord Thomson exclaimed.

'You two are bastards!' Rob raged, struggling against his confinement. 'Captain Duncan was dying and he chose me for parole in his place. Let her go!'

Everyone was shouting now. Grace wrenched herself from Smathers's grasp and stood toe to toe with Lord Thomson. She guessed right. A natural coward, he stepped back.

'Lord Thomson, I knelt by Captain Daniel Duncan in a filthy stall in Dartmoor. He was near death from ill treatment, but he had the strength to ask *me*, not Rob, to choose someone else in his place.'

'What nobility from an American bastard,' Lord Thomson murmured, making no effort to disguise his contempt.

'You're the bastard,' Rob said. The man holding his arms cuffed the side of his head.

'I chose Rob Inman,' Grace said, suddenly feeling proud of Captain Duncan, of Rob Inman, of herself, even.

'If that is not a felony, it is at least a misdemeanor,' the marquis said. 'What do you think, Smathers?'

'The matter is small beer, my lord,' Smathers replied, his unpleasant voice assuming a wheedling quality. 'Not worthy of you to prosecute. She's a bakery assistant. That's all she will ever be.'

Grace turned to look at Smathers. His eyes were as hard as ever, bits of flint in a face marked by the ravages of smallpox. It was a face of no compromise. She looked at Rob again, thinking of the deed to his house in Nantucket. *You are wrong, Mr Smathers,* she thought. *I own a home in America.*

The mere thought gave her heart. She stared at Lord Thomson, who, to her gratification, bore the scrutiny only a moment before lowering his gaze. 'Lord Thomson, even you would have done the same thing, rather than leave a man in Dartmoor.'

He stared at her in disbelief. 'Not I. Never I.

What else do they deserve, these…these mongrels who had the audacity to form a nation?'

He returned his attention to Rob Inman. The man twining his arms together had forced the sailing master to kneel at the foot of the stairs. Lord Thomson stood in front of him, idly slapping his cane in his hand. Quicker than thought, he brought it crashing down on Rob's back.

Rob groaned, but said nothing.

Grace could not help the sob that rose in her throat. She tried to go to him, but Smather's grip was iron now. 'What are you going to do with him?' she demanded.

'Return him to Dartmoor tonight.' He looked at the man who held Rob. 'Reilly, make him walk every step of the way. Don't bother with his coat.'

'Please, no…'

Lord Thomson whirled around and raised his cane over her. Rob, hands tied now, roared out his disapproval and tried to step forwards. Grace closed her eyes, ready for the pain.

It never came. Smathers grabbed the stick as it descended. 'Lord Thomson, you know that's not a good idea,' he said, his voice calm and coaxing, as if he spoke to an ill-natured child. 'Miserable as she may be, Grace has friends in this stupid village. Just throw her out of the dower house. It's enough.'

'You are a killjoy, Smathers,' Lord Thomson declared.

'Please don't return him to Dartmoor,' she pleaded.

He smirked at her. 'Ask me nicely.'

'I'm begging you,' she said softly as she sank to her knees. 'I'm on my knees. Put him in the gaol in Exeter, if you must. Peace has been declared! How long can it be? But don't send him back to Dartmoor.'

She was speaking to Lord Thomson's back now. He laughed, but did not turn around.

'What makes you think for even one second that I care what happens to this prisoner, who has been impersonating my bastard cousin? For that matter, that I care what happens to *you*?'

He did look at her then and she recoiled from the unkindness in his eyes. 'All you are to me is an unnecessary expense, thirty pounds per annum of annoyance and money that is rightly mine.'

'Thirty pounds? Judas money,' Rob said, his voice filled with contempt.

Lord Thomson brought his cane down on Rob's shoulder again and again. Grace shrieked at him to stop, looking around for help. Emery sat like a stump. She twisted around to see Smathers's face, so inscrutable.

'Stop him, stop him,' she whispered. In ten years of feeling powerless, she had never felt as helpless as right now, with the marquis's blows raining down on the man she loved, a man she could not defend.

With what seemed like incredible slowness, Smathers sauntered to Lord Thomson, who continued to beat Rob Inman, lying on his side now, his eyes closed. Smathers grabbed the cane.

'Temper, temper, my lord,' he said, his voice light and teasing.

Or was it? Grace raised her head to look at Ugly Butler. For the smallest moment, she thought she saw great contempt of his own. The moment passed; all she saw was Lord Thomson's thug, the butler who had found the damning miniature in the first place.

Gently, so gently, Smathers tugged the marquis away. In a moment, the cane was in his hand and Lord Thomson was breathing heavily, but sitting down by Emery, who leaned away from him. She rushed to Rob's side, helping him upright as he shook his head to clear it. The cane had opened a cut above his ear. Grace bunched up her apron and dabbed at it, stopping the blood.

Whatever you do, don't let on how much you care, she told herself, letting pragmatism trump emotion. *It would be infinitely worse for him.*

She offered no objection when Smathers hauled her to her feet, as if she were of no more consequence than ashes in a dustbin. She was no fool. There was every possibility that Rob would never survive the march to Dartmoor, not in the cold and the dark, and in pain. Any further protestation on her part would only bring down more torment on Rob's head.

Smathers gave her a push towards the stairs. 'Gather your belongings and go back to the bakery. Do it now.'

Grace looked at Smathers, searching his face for some kindness. Nothing. She started for the stairs, after the smallest brush of her hand against Rob's face. She hoped the marquis hadn't noticed; she didn't care what Smathers thought.

What happened next happened fast. Grace was halfway up the stairs when she heard a shout. Every nerve tingling, she whirled around to see Rob suddenly jerk away from the black-coated man, shove his wounded shoulder at Emery, who appeared to be trying to grab him, and bolt for the open front door.

But there was Smathers, still holding Lord Thomson's cane, but as a club now. 'No!' she screamed, as Rob Inman, wounded but on his feet, staggered towards the door, Ugly Butler behind him, with Reilly close on his heels.

Mouth open, she watched Smathers swing the cane over his head, managing to clip Reilly and send him crashing to the floor. Unaware of the damage he was doing, Smathers blundered forwards, knocking down Emery again, who also seemed intent on reaching Rob. Shrieking like a girl, Lord Thomson backed into a corner.

Grace stared at the carnage in front of her, the result of Smathers's spectacular mismanagement, then at the door. She held up her hand as Rob stumbled through it, took a last look at her and vanished into the blackness. She sank down on the step and put her head in her hands, even as Lord Thomson came to life and screamed at her to do something for Reilly, bleeding and unconscious.

'You told me to leave,' she said. Calmly, she got to her feet and continued up the stairs. She stuffed her few possessions into a bag. The only thing of value in her room was the deed to Rob's Nantucket home. Rob had nothing of value.

On second thought, she pushed the deed down the front of her dress. Her apron was bloody where she had bunched it to staunch the wound on Rob's head. The gory streaks would probably not deter Smathers from searching her, but she did not think Lord Thomson, unstable man that he was, would be inclined to touch her.

She took a deep breath and went down the stairs. Smathers was sitting by the wounded man, holding a cloth to his head. Emery was speaking to Lord Thomson. He glanced at her and frowned, shaking his head. Her heart went out to Emery. He had tried so hard to keep Rob Inman safe. She sighed and looked away. No one had reckoned on a miniature of the real Captain Duncan.

The still-open door looked far away. Grace forced herself to walk slowly towards it. In one of his rare moments of concern for others, Papa had told her once never to run from menacing dogs. 'They will consider you fair game,' he had said. 'Walk slowly.'

She did that now, passing Lord Thomson, who said filthy things at her, and Smathers, who narrowed his eyes and stared at her. Her heart thudded in her breast, but she moved gracefully through the foyer, slippery now with Reilly's blood. She calmly plucked Rob's pea coat from the statue and made for the open door.

Grace was almost there when Smathers grabbed her arm. She jumped in terror, but knew better than to struggle.

At first he did nothing more than look at her, his dark, expressionless eyes reminding her of that big fish. The sight had provided her with a summer's worth of nightmares when she was younger.

'If you have any inkling where he is, tell me.'

He almost seemed to care; she felt only scorn. 'You are the last person I would tell,' she said matching him calm for calm, '*if* I knew, and I don't.'

'It will go bad for him,' he told her, his eyes never leaving hers. 'He is subject now to being shot on sight.'

'Not if he can get to Plymouth and ship out,' she said.

'Not in his condition. You're a fool if you think Lord Thomson or his butler will not block that avenue of escape!'

Her contempt overflowed. The despicable man was speaking of himself in the third person, much like royalty. *Good Lord,* she thought, disgusted and finally beyond fear. What a bumbler he was.

'Mr Smathers, I will hate you until I die,' she said.

'That's a damned long time,' he said. 'Better rethink it, if you ever hope to see Rob Inman again—oh, God, Rob Inman, a sailing master! You two have diddled me and I don't like it.'

'I don't care what you like or don't like,' she told him, standing outside the door now. Snow was falling more heavily now. She felt tears start in her eyes, thinking of Rob stumbling about in the snow, wounded, with nowhere to go. 'Mr Selway told me to trust no one.'

'Selway, eh? Is he that solicitor you thought to find in Exeter when I followed you?'

'You did not!' she declared, chilled at his abilities, if it was true.

'Of course I did. Didn't find Selway, did you? I doubt he exists.'

'Of course he does and he's a far better man than you,' she snapped back.

He only shrugged. 'What fools we are.'

She slammed the door, but she heard his laughter through it. Grace put her hands over her ears.

Chapter Twenty-Six

Upstairs in the Wilsons' rooms, Grace cried in Mrs Wilson's arms. When she could speak, she told the Wilsons everything.

'I have no idea where he is!' she lamented. 'How far can he go? Lord Thomson struck him so many times.' She pounded the pea coat in her lap in her frustration. 'He will freeze!'

'Now, Gracie,' Mr Wilson said, obviously mulling over the matter, 'you would think Lord Thomson would be glad to know that Captain Duncan is long dead. Why does it matter to him if Rob Inman is captured or not? The captain is dead and the war is over. The Americans will leave soon. Why?'

Why indeed? Grace wondered, as she came downstairs into the dark bakery, still carrying Rob's coat and her bag. She took out Rob's handwritten deed of sale to his Nantucket house.

Looking around, Grace lifted the day-old bread bin from its compartment and slid the deed underneath.

'You tell me to trust no one, Mr Selway,' she said quietly. 'I believe you, but that is all I believe of you now, because you have been no help to me.'

The deed was between her and Rob Inman, a tangible link to a better life. She got up once to retrieve it—just to hold it again—then changed her mind and left it there. She couldn't help herself, sobbing out loud as she remembered Christmas morning and his calm desire to give her a home, even if something happened to him. And now it had.

Grace finally slept, but woke with a start at the sound of banging on the front door and angry voices. Heart in her throat, she listened as Mr Wilson lumbered down the stairs and unlocked the door.

Grace shrieked when the door to her room crashed open. It was Reilly, the black-coated man, followed by Mr Smathers.

'Turn out now!' Reilly shouted. 'We're searching the premises. Outside!'

He used his cudgel to raise the blankets, as Grace glared at him and tugged on her chemise. The man grabbed Grace and pulled her from the bed.

'Just a minute!' Mr Wilson roared. Reilly whirled around and raised his cudgel as Grace threw herself in front of him, pushing against his arms.

'I am moving as fast as I can!' she implored. 'Please don't hurt these good people.'

He lowered the weapon as Grace dragged on her dress. Not looking at the Runner, Grace buttoned her dress, tied on her apron and scuffed her bare feet into her shoes. She reached for Rob's pea coat, but he stopped her.

'Leave it here. That bag, too. We're going through everything you took away from the house.' He leered at her. 'And if I feel like it, I might search you, too.' He started to reach under her dress and she backed away, to come up against Mr Smathers, who stood in the doorway.

'You watched her get dressed!' Smathers roared. 'That's enough! Grace, why did you get mixed up with an imposter?'

There was no point in appealing to his better nature; he had none. 'I chose him, Mr Smathers,' she said, her voice brittle. 'I doubt you would understand.'

Smathers shrugged. He glared at the Runner, then spoke in a lower voice to Grace. 'Reilly's tightly wound.'

She left her room, flinching as she heard the sound of a knife ripping into her mattress. She turned around, surprised to find Ugly Butler right behind her, his face as set as hers. Furious, she gave him a shove with both hands.

'Why destroy my room?' she raged, shoving him again. 'I didn't sew Rob into the mattress!'

Lips tight, she waited for Smathers to strike her. Instead, he grabbed her wrists and held them, backing her towards the outside door, where the Wilsons stood in the snow.

'Behave yourself, Grace Curtis, if you can.' Smathers held her until she looked away, then gave her a little push towards Mrs Wilson, who enveloped her in her cloak.

'I despise him,' Grace said, when Smathers re-entered the bakery. 'He has spied on us at every turn.' She turned bleak eyes on the Wilsons. 'I pray he has not harmed Emery.'

Silent, they stood in the snow, listening, as Reilly and Smathers, joined by the town's less-than-enthusiastic constable, worked their way through the bakery. Lights came on all along the road and others in their nightclothes came to stand beside them and watch.

'I thought an Englishman's home was his castle,' the tinsmith said, loud enough to be heard by Reilly and Smathers, when they finally left the store as dawn approached.

'Not in Quimby, apparently,' Lady Tutt offered. She was dressed in her nightclothes, but had taken the time to attach a purple turban to her head.

'The show is over,' Reilly said, waving his cudgel in a shooing motion as the sun began to rise. 'Anybody with news of the fugitive had better let me know. He's a danger to the community.'

'So's my pet rabbit,' someone yelled. Everybody laughed as they straggled away.

'Miss?'

Grace turned around to see Bobby Gentry, the little boy whose coin and dignity Rob had rescued from the mud last summer. He had wrapped a thin blanket around his nightshirt.

'Bobby, it's too cold!'

He plucked at her sleeve. 'Please miss, will you have the day-old bread out soon?'

'Soon as we clean up the bakery,' she told him. 'Cross my heart. Are you hungry?'

He nodded. 'There's something more, miss.'

'Yes, my dear?' she asked, wishing him indoors.

Bobby leaned closer. 'He's with us.'

She hoped Smathers, his back to her, had not heard her sudden intake of breath. She took Bobby's hand and led him towards the bakery. It gave her considerable satisfaction to close the door on Smathers and Reilly, who started arguing with each other right there on the High Street.

Grace crouched by Bobby again. 'Is he all right? He was hurt.'

Bobby nodded. 'Mama fixed him. She fixes a lot of stuff with vinegar.'

Grace laughed, more out of relief than anything else. She went to the pastry keeper, taking out all of yesterday's remaining sticky buns. Bobby's eyes widened.

'Miss, I don't have…'

'Doesn't matter,' she said, putting the pastries in a box. 'They're a day old. No arguments, young man.' Grace knelt by him again. 'Tell Rob Inman I will find a way to get to your place.'

Bobby shook his head. 'He said you would say that and told me to tell you not to take a chance.' He glanced at the two men in the street, alone now because Quimby's residents had returned to their homes. Even the constable had vanished. 'Gor, miss!' he whispered. 'That bald man has been standing in front of the candlemaker's for months now! How can you get up the stairs?'

'I'll think of something,' she whispered back, with no idea at all. She opened the door and gave him a gentle smack on the seat of his trousers. 'Go on home, Bobby. I'll have the day-old bread soon. Just come at your usual time.'

After the boy left, Grace just stood in the centre of the room and let out a huge sigh, closing her eyes in relief that at least she knew where Rob was. She had heard Reilly trying to convince the sceptical constable to organise a house-by-house search of Quimby, to find one prisoner of war from a war that was over, and who wasn't even the man they thought. It made no sense to her.

When she opened her eyes, Nahum Smathers was standing in front of her. She couldn't help her involuntary step backwards, which made him narrow his eyes.

'Between you and me, Rob Inman would be better served if I returned him to Dartmoor.'

Smathers held up his hand when she started to
speak. 'Patience, Grace! Hear me out. Better I
find him than Lord Thomson or Reilly. He's a
Bow Street Runner and I can tell you they have
no compunctions.'

'I can't see a particle of difference between
you and the Runner,' Grace replied. 'Didn't Lord
Thomson look right at you and say his butler had
found the incriminating miniature?'

He had a temper no longer than hers. Smathers
took her by the shoulders, but seemed just to want
her attention and not her fear.

'You're so certain he was looking at me?' was
all Smathers said. He turned on his heel and left
her alone.

Smathers watched all day from his custom-
ary post across the street and Grace knew he was
watching her this time. Grace went about her
business, trying not to look at the candlemaker's
shop, trying to keep her eyes from the dusty windows upstairs that constituted the Gentrys' two
rooms over the shop. Once, during the afternoon
that seemed to stretch on for ever, she thought she
saw Rob standing at one of the windows.

'I swear I will smack you, if you do that again,'
she grumbled under her breath.

'I beg your pardon!' Lady Tutt exclaimed, as
she yanked her hand back from the loaf of bread
she was pinching.

'Not you, my lady,' Grace said, hard put to

keep the exhaustion from her voice. She was tired of worry, weary of wondering if the constable would make good Lord Thomson's threat to turn out the whole village. She glanced at Smathers across the street. Did the dratted man not blink? Did he honestly think she would lead him to Rob? Why was Lord Thomson so determined to trip up first Captain Duncan, and now Rob Inman? Was this much turmoil worth thirty pounds a year?

She had no answers; neither did the Wilsons. To make it worse, the Runner had taken up his own post inside the bakery. He sat by the door, watching everyone who came and went. *Leave! Leave!* Grace wanted to scream at him, but she remained silent, thinking instead of Mr Smathers's own admonition that she remain patient.

To her relief, Emery strolled into Quimby later, making none of his attempts to skulk around and hide from Mr Smathers. He winked at her and took up his usual post under the elm tree, so bare in winter.

Even an endless day comes to an end and it came to a quicker one for the Runner. As the shadows started to lengthen, Mrs Wilson came out of the back room with a pan of biscuits. Surprised, Grace watched her. Why had Mrs Wilson baked at the end of the day?

Mrs Wilson held the pan in the centre of the room, her only audience the Bow Street Runner. Mystified at Mrs Wilson, Grace watched him sniff and then swallow.

'Grace, what was I thinking?' she said finally. 'I waited too long to bake these and now there is no one in the store! They'll be day-old tomorrow.' Mrs Wilson pressed one hand against her chest. 'What folly!'

'I couldn't say,' Grace replied, wondering what strange creature had suddenly invaded Mrs Wilson's practical body.

'It's too late,' Mrs Wilson insisted with a sigh, her eyes raised in despair. She went to Reilly, his eyes on the chocolate biscuits. 'You have them. I'll not be able to save them.'

He gave her no argument, grabbing up a handful and returning to his stool, where he munched and swallowed, his eyes closed with satisfaction.

With another theatrical sigh, Mrs Wilson put the remaining biscuits in the day-old bin and returned to the back room, but not before giving Grace a slow wink.

Intrigued, Grace followed her. 'What are you doing, Mrs Wilson?' she whispered, her eyes still on the Runner in the other room.

Mrs Wilson spoke softly. 'Remember my black draught? And have you any idea what a nice addition that, plus jalap, make to my biscuits?'

Grace could barely stifle her laughter. 'Jalap *and* black draught? He will…' She couldn't speak.

'Indeed he will.' Mrs Wilson glanced into the shop, where the Runner was fishing out the rest of the laxative-loaded biscuits from the bin. 'I give him twenty minutes.'

'Mrs Wilson, you are a better actress than Siddons,' Grace whispered. 'I really thought you were agitated with yourself.'

'Agitated that I didn't think of it sooner,' she whispered back. 'I'm hoping Mr Smathers will follow him.'

Fifteen minutes was closer. Ignoring the Runner, Grace swept out of the shop. She had just put covers on the remaining pastries when she heard a strangled sound. She turned to see the Runner on his feet, clutching his stomach.

'Open the door!' he demanded.

He tried to walk to the door, but seconds later was bent over and scrambling fast.

Grace watched him stumble into the street, digging at his trouser buttons. Mr Smathers ran to him and led him between two buildings down the street.

Grace threw down the broom and dashed across the street, looking once in the direction where the men had gone. She hurried to the candlemaker, who stood in his open doorway. Smoothly, he stepped aside and pushed her towards the stairs. She took them two at a time. Rob opened the door, grabbing her in his arms after he had closed the door behind him.

She held herself off for an anxious moment, looking at his black eye and the gash by his ear from Lord Thomson's cane. She sniffed. Mrs Gentry had doused his shoulder with vinegar, just as Bobby had said. The widow and her son stood close together, watching them.

'Thank you, Mrs Gentry,' Grace said and put her arms carefully around Rob, who buried his face in her neck, holding her so close her feet came off the floor. 'Rob, you'll hurt yourself,' she scolded.

'Nay, lass. Lord Thomson already did that for me,' he said, but released her. He beamed at the Gentrys. 'I was running down the street, desperate to hide, and there was Mrs Gentry, sweeping in front of her uncle's shop.'

Rob sounded like he still could not believe his good fortune. 'Calm as a summer day, she was, Gracie. She just yanked me inside.' He gave Gracie another hug. 'And here I didn't think I had friends, this side of the Atlantic.'

Mrs Gentry blushed. 'D'ye think I've forgotten how you rescued my Bobby and found that penny in the mud?'

'Anyone would have done that.'

'Fact is, *you're* the one who did. I don't forget a kindness,' she said, with all the dignity of a lady, and a sailor's widow, who depended on day-old bread and the kindness of Quimby. She gestured towards the table. 'Sit down for some tea and we'll talk.'

Rob was too restless to settle for long. 'I daren't stay here,' he said, setting down his cup. 'I daren't put the Gentrys in such danger, not with Ugly Butler so close.' He rubbed his shoulder. 'I doubt I can make it to Plymouth. I need to find a safer place to hide. It can't be long until we're released from captivity.' He slammed his hand on the table then. 'I've been saying that for weeks now!'

Grace put her finger to his lips. 'Please, Rob.'

He kissed her finger, then glanced at Mrs Gentry, embarrassed. 'Please, ma'am, I'm not a bounder. I've proposed to Grace and she's accepted.'

Mrs Gentry nodded, as though something of this nature transpired in her rented room daily. 'You'll do. Grace always shows good sense.' She went to the window, then put her hand to her mouth. 'Oh, my!'

Rob stood up, but Grace tugged him down. 'You can't go to the window!'

Mrs Gentry returned to the table. 'Something of a bowel disorder must have happened to that horrible man who's been in the bakery. He's barely in the alley, his trousers down around his ankles.' She laughed. 'Mr Smathers is trying not to watch.'

'Gracie, what did you do?' Rob asked.

'Nothing,' she said, biting her lip to keep from smiling. 'Our Mrs Wilson fortified some biscuits with jalap and that black draught of hers you might remember.'

'Great God Almighty,' Rob exclaimed. 'Remind me to avoid her bad side.'

Bobby ran to the window and peered out. He whooped, then scurried back to the table. 'Mama, you would thrash me if I ever did that in public!'

'Indeed I would,' she scolded. 'Let us hope someone tells the constable. I would like to see that man declared a public nuisance!'

It was just a matter of time; they had no other resource except time. After a few minutes, they heard a whistle. Mrs Gentry sidled to the window, careful not to be seen. 'It's the constable,' she said from her vantage point. 'And wouldn't you know it, he is taking…what is his name…'

'Reilly,' Grace and Rob said together.

'…by the arm and leading him to the magistrate's, I shouldn't doubt.' She turned away in silent amusement. 'He didn't even give him time to pull up his trousers! Oh, he'll trip! And there is Mr Smathers right behind.' She glanced out the window, then covered her eyes. 'Oh, dear! Mr Reilly is in no shape to be walking down a street.' She turned to Rob quickly. 'You could leave now while all this is going on, if you had somewhere to go, Rob.' She looked at Grace, her eyes kind. 'He told me his whole story, Grace. I know who he is.'

Rob was on his feet now, pulling Grace up with him. 'Gracie, d'ye have any ideas? I can't endanger the Gentrys one more minute.'

'No, you can't. And, yes, I do have an idea. We'll know soon enough if it's a good one.'

Chapter Twenty-Seven

It was a good idea; even Lady Tutt thought so, when they arrived at Tutt Manor after dark, out of breath from running.

Getting away had been almost too simple. Rob had acted immediately, kissing Bobby and Mrs Gentry, then grabbing Grace's hand and pulling her down the stairs with him. When she started out of the front door, he pulled her back.

'No, Gracie.'

'But they're not in sight.'

He pointed toward the centre of town, where Emery still stood.

'That's just Emery,' she whispered back.

'What did that note from Mr Selway say? The one you found on the mantelpiece?' he reminded her.

'Trust no one,' she repeated, turning to the candlemaker. 'Do you have a back door?'

'I have better than that,' he told them. 'Come along.'

What he had was a tunnel. The candlemaker pulled aside a rug in the back room where rows and rows of candle moulds stood at attention and revealed the trapdoor. He pulled on the ring with a flourish and pointed down.

'It'll take you to the bank of the river,' he told them, as he handed Grace a candle.

Rob nodded his thanks to the proprietor. Grace looked down dubiously, then at the candlemaker. 'And here I thought yours was such a prosaic business,' she told him, which made him smile.

'You'd be amazed what went on in Quimby two hundred years ago, when candle tariffs were outrageous.' He winked at her. 'Come to think of it, if you see any French brandy down there, that's our little secret.'

Grace handed the candle to Rob and followed him into the gloom. He held out his hand when she reached the bottom step, then pulled her close and kissed her. She clung to him, trying not to hurt his shoulder, but eager for his touch.

'Lady Tutt? You're certain?' was all he asked, when they could talk again. He held the candle as they crouched and walked into the musty darkness.

'Everyone in the village had probably heard her opinion of the United States, which attacked the poor, outnumbered Royal Navy. What better place, Rob?'

She heard his chuckle in the semi-gloom. 'Ah, yes. She pretty well has decided that Yankee Doodle is a monster, compared to John Bull.'

'What is more important, she is still convinced you saved her life,' Grace reminded him.

'Dearest, I did,' he replied. 'Ow, that's my sore shoulder!'

Lady Tutt did think it was a good idea, when her butler opened the door, blanched and actually ran down the hall to fetch her. She came on the trot, too, at least as much of a trot as she could manage.

'Lady Tutt,' Rob said, holding out both hands in a gesture of surrender. 'I am throwing myself on your mercy.'

'It's about time,' she replied. 'Chimesby, lock that door.'

Over a light supper so overwhelming that even Rob, the bottomless pit since Dartmoor, finally yielded, Lady Tutt proved to be a fountain of information.

'I have sources,' was all she would say, as she told them on good authority that the constable had indeed arranged a search of the entire village and environs. 'It will begin in the wee hours.'

'Then I am no safer here than anywhere in Devon,' Rob said. Grace took his hand.

Lady Tutt poured herself another cup of tea. 'Actually, Rob, you are…ahem…safe as houses here.' She cleared her throat and Grace smiled, thinking of the times she had heard Lady Tutt do that precisely when she had extraordinary news. Her smile faded quickly, considering the gravity of their situation. What could the widow of Quimby's most encroaching mushroom do?

'We owe this all to my late husband, Sir Barnabas Tutt. I'll show you. Chimesby, give us a light.'

Purple feather bobbing on her turban, Lady Tutt told Grace to take a lamp. She led them upstairs behind the butler. 'Grace, you will probably remember when this house was built.'

'I think I was twelve.'

Rob stopped on the stairs. 'You're pulling my leg, Gracie. This house is at least two hundred years old!'

Grace and Lady Tutt laughed together, and she felt the tiniest bit of hope. 'Rob, Lady Tutt's husband was elevated to a knighthood and he built this house—'

'Mansion,' Lady Tutt corrected.

'…mansion in the Tudor style.'

'Never let it be said that Sir Barnabas would have a knighthood without a proper manor,' Lady Tutt said.

'He did a good job,' Rob replied. 'You fooled me.'

Chimesby stopped in front of the second bedchamber past the landing. With a flourish, he opened the door and ushered them in. Eyes wide,

Grace took in the canopied bed, such as Queen Elizabeth might have enjoyed on a stately progress about her realm, the elaborately carved clothespress and chairs.

'It's magnificent,' Rob said, but the frown remained between his eyes. 'Lady Tutt, I don't see how brocaded curtains, as authentic-looking as they are, will save me in a search.'

'Oh, ye of little faith,' Lady Tutt chided. 'Chimesby, lead on!'

'Lead where?' Grace asked, puzzled.

'Here.' Chimesby stood in front of the elaborate bell pull by the fireplace and tugged on a much smaller, scarcely visible cord behind it. Grace jumped back when a portion of the panelled wall slid aside.

'I'll be damned,' Rob said. He ducked his head through the opening and gestured to Grace. 'Gracie, it's a little room. Look, a bed and bookshelf.'

Grace stepped inside. She set her lamp on the bookshelf and looked around. 'Rob, with enough food, you could probably hide here until the treaty is ratified.'

He nodded, then ducked out of the room. Grace joined him in the main chamber again.

'What *is* this?' Rob asked Lady Tutt.

'It's a priest's hole, of course,' she said, obviously pleased with herself. 'Sir Barnabas spared no expense to be authentic.' She looked inside, then turned a kindly eye on Rob. 'You, sir, will take up residence in here. We can bring you food later. There is a ventilation shaft that runs next to the main chimney. I hope you have no fears of tight spaces.'

'Ma'am, I'm a sailing master on a privateer,' he said. 'This hole looks almost luxurious.'

The old woman pinked up like a maiden. 'I wish Barnabas were alive to see his priest's hole in use!'

'I wish he were, too,' Grace said, putting her hand on the woman's sleeve. 'Lady Tutt, you're a wonder.'

Lady Tutt grew serious then. 'Rob Inman saved my life.' She hesitated, then looked Rob in the eye. 'And I might, just might, have been slightly wrong about your navy.'

'Aye, Lady Tutt, after all, we *are* the injured par—'

Never let it be said there wasn't a sentence Lady Tutt couldn't ride over. She patted Rob's arm. 'I am certain that your United States of America didn't *intend* to cause all that trouble with the shipping lanes. That's what I mean.'

Bless Rob's heart. He gave a slight bow and smiled at Lady Tutt. 'I am convinced you are right, and, yes, I will tell President Madison, the next time I see him, that he shouldn't pick on a little island like this one.'

Lady Tutt seemed unsure what to say to that, but there wasn't time to say anything, anyway. Standing closest to the door, Grace heard someone pounding up the stairs. She stepped aside as

Lady Tutt's mousy companion, dressed in night-gown and cap, threw herself into the room, her eyes wide.

'Lady Tutt! The constable is here! And he has the effrontery to think he and his minions can search the manor!'

The companion's indignation brought a glitter to her eyes, similar to the one in Lady Tutt's eyes. *This is the most excitement you dears have had in eons,* Grace thought, touched at their willingness to court danger on an enemy's behalf.

'He's come sooner than I thought,' Rob murmured. 'Maybe they're crossing off the outlying manors first.' He stepped inside the priest's hole again and held out his hand for Grace. 'Maybe you had better disappear, too. You're as out of place at Chez Tutt as I am. How could you explain yourself here at nearly midnight?'

Lady Tutt's companion nodded vigorously. 'That would mean needles under your fingernails, or the rack, to ferret out information!'

'I shouldn't think Quimby's constable would stoop to that,' Rob said. He smiled his thanks to both women. 'My dears, you're nonpareil.' He blew them a kiss as the door closed. 'I'll tell President Madison that, too.'

Her ear to the sliding panel, Grace listened as the outer door closed. She could feel her heart pounding in her breast. 'I wonder if this is how those priests felt, two hundred years ago,' she whispered, her voice shaky.

Rob patted the space beside him. 'I doubt any of them had a lovely companion to share their confinement with,' he told her. 'Grace, it's a new house. No old ghosts.'

'I forgot.' She sat down.

He lay back with a yawn, tugging her down beside him. She needed no urging. His arm tightened around her shoulder as she rested her head on his chest.

'What a day this has been,' he whispered, as heavier footsteps even than Lady Tutt pounded up the stairs. 'Grace, you're trembling.'

'I'm afraid,' she whispered.

'You? Tough-as-nails Grace Curtis? The woman who has shouldered all her burdens alone for so many years? Great shoulders, I might add.'

'Yes, that one,' she told him. 'Life was simpler before I chose you.'

He hugged her closer. 'But not nearly as fun, eh?'

She put up a shaking hand to stifle her tears as the bedroom door opened. 'I'm afraid,' she repeated.

'Me, too,' he whispered in her ear. 'I'd give anything for a boring watch in the mid-Atlantic about now.'

The search of the bedchamber ended almost as soon as it had begun. Grace began to relax as the sounds retreated down the hall and eventually down the stairs. She strained her ears to hear other sounds of search, but Sir Barnabas had built a strong house.

* * *

An hour at least, after the last searcher must have left, they heard Lady Tutt outside the hidden panel.

'Yoo hoo! Yoo hoo!'

Rob got up and spoke through the secret panel. 'Lady Tutt, even if it's all clear, we're staying in here until closer to dawn. I won't have Grace traipsing about with Lord Thomson's thugs on the loose.'

'My sentiments exactly,' came her voice through the substantial panelling. 'Goodnight, dearies.'

He lay down again. 'I thought she might insist you come out,' he told her, as he unbuttoned her dress. 'Maybe she's a bit of a rascal, too.' His hand went inside her bodice, his fingers familiar to her.

Words seemed superfluous to Grace as she helped with her buttons, then sat up and removed it, and her chemise, too.

'I might have agreed with you earlier, dearest,' she said. She started on Rob's buttons as he gently massaged her breast. 'I think—no, I am certain—that Lady Tutt is a shrewd customer. Practical, too,' she added with a sigh, as she tugged off Rob's trousers so that he wouldn't hurt his shoulder. 'Let me know if this pains you.'

He was made of sterner stuff, apparently, but Grace should have known that already. After almost two months spent celebrating the signing

of the Treaty of Ghent nearly every night, Grace
had a pretty firm idea how Rob Inman felt about
special occasions, or no occasion at all. She knew
what pleased him: how much he enjoyed the way
she ran her tongue around his ear; the soft sighs
and their increasing urgency she never held back
when she climaxed; the way she enveloped him
in her arms and legs, holding him tight, keeping
away his own demons, as he exorcised hers.

'Grace, I've missed you the past few nights,'
he whispered when he still lay on top of her, unwilling to leave. 'I wish I could marry you tomorrow. Tonight, even.'

'I know you do,' she said, her arms posses-
sively around his waist, just as unwilling to let
him go.

He went to sleep almost immediately after they
separated, holding her as close in sleep as he had
in love. She watched his dear face by the flick-
ering light of the single lamp, relaxed now, with
that frown line gone between his eyes. She knew
she would want him again before morning and
she knew he would give himself to her with no
more encouragement than the slight touch of her
hand on his chest, or her foot running down his
leg. Maybe this time she would mount him. He
had wanted her to, but she had felt shy about that.
Maybe early morning in a priest's hole in Lady
Tutt's surprising manor would be a good time.

I know you well, she thought, as she closed

her eyes, relaxing her hand on his thigh. *No one will fault me if I pretend we are married and in Nantucket, with no sound louder than seagulls. I can dream now.*

Chapter Twenty-Eight

After a kiss and an embrace that lasted so long that Lady Tutt cleared her throat with some impatience, Grace waved Rob back into the priest's hole. She left the manor before dawn, walking arm in arm with Lady Tutt down the front steps, assuring her that she would have a letter that morning for the baroness to take to Mr Selway's Exeter Post Office box.

'It's no trouble,' Lady Tutt had assured her. 'I'll be in the bakery just after you open. I'll tell my coachman to spring 'um.'

Grace smiled at that, thinking of the geriatrics Lady Tutt employed and how much they seemed to be enjoying the cloak and dagger. 'I think that is a sound idea, my lady,' she said. 'In a day or two, I know we will hear from Mr Selway. He will surely tell us what to do.'

* * *

She made it back to the bakery as dawn was breaking, bleak and cold, even though it was early March, when the buds should have been shouldering aside the frost on bare limbs. She was grateful for the mist and fog, which hid her as she walked the alleys behind Quimby's High Street.

To her consternation, Nahum Smathers was already standing in front of the candlemaker's shop, which was shuttered and dark. His head was tucked down into his coat. She thought he slept, but then he stomped his feet. Grace felt a certain triumph to see him there so cold, knowing he had not found Rob. She found the extra key by the bakery's back door and let herself in quietly.

She went into the back room, lit a lamp and wrote a hurried letter to Mr Selway, telling him what had happened, describing Rob Inman's location so he could spirit him away to safety and asking for help. She wrote quickly, concluding with a plea: 'Mr Selway, I know you must be busy, but I am afraid Lord Thomson will do terrible mischief if he finds Rob Inman. I know Rob is not Captain Duncan, but the late captain's only thought was for his crew, when he asked me to choose another. Yours sincerely, Grace Curtis.'

She read it through twice, and saw no way to improve it, except to send it fast with Lady Tutt to Exeter. Where the note went from there, she had no idea. Hopefully, Mr Selway had a suggestion to end this tension and spare Rob from capture and death. She picked up her pen again and dipped it in the ink. 'Mr Selway, I have already agreed to go to Nantucket with Rob, when he is freed. You are helping not only an American, but a future countrywoman as well. G.C.'

Lady Tutt was as good as her word, looking around discreetly before stashing Grace's letter in her reticule. Waiting until only her companion remained in the bakery, she leaned forwards across the counter and spoke in her best stage whisper.

'Grace, when I return from Exeter this afternoon, the password will be "Evensong", if I have carried out our intentions.'

Grace leaned forwards, too, because Lady Tutt seemed to want a co-conspirator. 'I think all you need to do is tell me that the letter was safely delivered.'

'Never!' the woman declared in shocked tones. She glanced around again. 'At least that nasty Bow Street Runner is gone. I wonder what could have happened to him.'

Too much jalap and a charge of indecent exposure, I am sure, Grace thought, but that was probably more than even Lady Tutt needed to know. 'He is likely up to no good somewhere, ma'am,' she said, trying not to smile at the memory of the man squatting so desperately in the alley.

There was nothing to do but wait now.

* * *

Grace breathed a sigh of relief when Lady Tutt returned in the late afternoon, sidled up to the counter and murmured, 'Evensong.' Grace thought about attempting to see Rob, but decided she would be wiser to remain at the bakery, especially since Smathers glowered at her from across the road and Emery was equally observant.

She thought of the other letters she had written to the elusive Mr Selway. Perhaps Mr Selway would suggest Rob remain in his priest's hole. She didn't want to consider what the solicitor would do if the sailing master was not worth a worry, since he wasn't Captain Duncan. She had made it amply clear in her note that Lord Thomson had vowed to shoot him on sight.

Two days passed, long days with her usual bakery duties performed by rote, because her mind and heart were on Rob Inman. The nights seemed even longer. After two nights spent tossing and turning, Grace decided she was a bit of a rascal. It was hard to imagine a real lady feeling so empty without Rob close by, a man—her man—who required very little encouragement to refresh her. Maybe all men were that way; she didn't know. Maybe she truly had slid, as everyone in Quimby knew. Maybe it was normal for healthy women to crave healthy men; she had no one to ask. Rob would tell her, even if she blushed.

She did know the whole business was oc-

cupying her to distraction, so she concentrated
on making Yankee Doodle Doughnuts in Rob's
place, which only made her cry, because he was
gone and she was worried.

The Wilsons bore up admirably, Mrs Wilson
keeping her too busy in the shop to spend time
in fruitless thoughts and Mr Wilson going to the
coffee shop every morning without fail, to glean
any news about the treaty situation. All he came
away with by March was the news that the British Army, under the command of no less a general
than Wellington's brother-in-law, had been soundly
thrashed by pirates, Acadians, free black men and
a crusty General Jackson near New Orleans.

'This all happened *after* the treaty was signed,'
Mr Wilson told her. He shook his head. 'If news
ever travels at the speed of light, we won't know
what to do with ourselves.'

Still Mr Smathers watched the bakery, watched
her, thinking she would lead him to Rob. Angry
at his persistence, Grace took him a dozen doughnuts, thinking it might embarrass him. All he
did was thank her and bare his teeth in what he
probably considered a smile. No shame there, she
told herself, feeling foolish. *Well, they are good
doughnuts,* she scolded herself. *I am an idiot.*

On the third morning after she had given the
letter to Lady Tutt, Grace discovered what was
worse than having Smathers watch her: having
him not there at all.

Mrs Wilson noticed his absence first. She had
been stocking the day-old bin when she called

Grace's attention to it. 'The nasty man? He's gone,' she said.

Grace went to the door and peered up and down the street. The candlemaker must have noticed her, because he came to his own door, hands out, shoulders up.

She looked down the street, but there was no Emery, pacing back and forth by the elm tree that was slowly beginning to leaf again. No Emery. No Smathers. She turned to go into the bakery again but stopped, as her heart leaped into her throat.

Casting all dignity aside, Lady Tutt's companion ran down the High Street, bonnet gone, dress hiked up. *Oh, please, no,* Grace thought, her mind in a tangle, as she felt her whole life unravelling.

It was a few moments before the woman could speak. Grace led her inside the bakery and sat her down, calling for Mrs Wilson to bring some spirits of ammonia.

The lady waved away any ministrations. She grasped Grace by her apron front. 'Mr Smathers has him!'

Grace didn't wait for another word; she ran. She looked back once to see Mr Wilson gamely puffing along behind her. He waved her on and she redoubled her efforts.

A black-curtained carriage was just coming out of the long lane leading up to Lady Tutt's wonderful, foolish mock-Elizabethan manor. Grace ran to the vehicle, pounding on the door. She didn't think the carriage would stop, but it did. When the wheels were still rolling, she leaped between them, frantic hands on the door latch as she screamed Rob's name over and over.

His own face set, Mr Smathers opened the door and grabbed her wrists before she could scramble into the vehicle. Tears streaking her face, she looked around his shoulder to see Rob Inman, bound hand and foot and staring at her with a bleak expression, tears running down his face, too.

She didn't know if she spoke any words; she may have cursed Mr Smathers. She sobbed and begged the man to let Rob go. She might have tried to reason with a statue. With a grip far stronger than any he had laid on her before, he held her off from him and gave her a shake.

'Grace, don't,' was all he said. She heard nothing harsh in his voice now, but a steely determination to see the business through. He had captured Rob Inman.

'He's going to Dartmoor,' Mr Smathers said when she stopped to draw breath, confirming her worst fears. He shook her again. 'You two have caused me no end of trouble.'

She gasped at his monumental self-interest and tried to slap him: anything to wipe that unsettling calm off his face. 'They'll put him in the dark hole, the *cachot*! Mr Smathers, they will kill him!'

Her pride gone, Grace knelt in the road, pleading with Smathers, her tightly held hands clasped together now. 'You're a murderer!'

That must have been Smathers's last straw. With an oath so vile it made her flinch, Smathers dragged her to her feet as Rob tried to move closer. One terrified glance in his direction told her that not only was Rob bound hand and foot, but tethered by a chain bolted in the floor. Rob struggled to free himself as Smathers put his face close to hers, his eyes boring into hers until he commanded her attention.

'You fool! The only place he is *safe* is Dartmoor!'

With another oath, he flung her away, scrambled with no dignity into the carriage again and growled to the coachman to move off.

Grace ran after the carriage, screaming, until she could not breathe. She sank onto the empty highway and was still there when Mr Wilson found her. She looked at him and began to sob again, just when she thought she could not have cried another tear.

Gently, he helped her to her feet. 'Gracie, let's go home,' was all he said.

Hours later, she was still sitting in the back room of the bakery. The front of the shop had finally cleared of villagers, most silent and as shocked as Grace was. Maybe because she understood heartache, Mrs Gentry had taken over in the back room, helping Mrs Wilson finish the day's orders, her quiet comments restoring some tattered order to a day gone badly wrong.

Her eyes shocked, Lady Tutt had held Grace's

hand, dabbing at her eyes, as she described what had happened—how Rob had been safe in the priest's hole, panel closed, when Mr Smathers and two Bow Street Runners had burst into the manor, raced up the stairs and pulled the nearly invisible cord to open the panel.

'They didn't even hesitate,' Lady Tutt said. 'They went right to the spot and there was nothing I could do!' She dabbed her eyes again and the guilt was there in rich abundance. 'I delivered that letter to the Post Office in Exeter. We never said a word to anyone!'

Lady Tutt's heartfelt anguish finally pried Grace loose from her own terrible recriminations. Grace took the handkerchief twisted in her own hands, and touched it to the widow's eyes, ready to console now, because there was nothing else she could do.

'It's not your fault,' Grace said. 'Something happened in Exeter.'

Lady Tutt turned piteous eyes on her. 'We never said a word.'

'I know. In the letter, I told Mr Selway precisely where to find Rob,' Grace replied quietly. 'The guilt is mine. The only way we will know what happened is if Mr Smathers…' she could barely say his name '…if Mr Smathers tells us.' She tried to smile, to soothe Lady Tutt's profound misery, but found she could not. 'I doubt he will oblige us with answers.'

She was wrong.

Chapter Twenty-Nine

After two sleepless nights, Grace looked into her mirror and didn't like what gazed back.

No one else was up. She crept into the laundry room, pumped water, heated it and poured herself a bath. She washed her hair and scrubbed her face, maybe harder than usual. Maybe she thought she could erase the sadness there.

What Mrs Wilson had done last night had tipped the scales for living again. The woman had done nothing more than take Grace's hand, sit down and pull her on her lap, as though she were a child in desperate need of comfort and not a woman grown.

When an hour had passed in silence, she had kissed Grace's cheek. 'There now,' she said. 'What else can we do?'

It was a good question. Grace had stared at the ceiling most of the night, then rose in the morning to resume the business of living, if she could call it that.

By unspoken consent, no one suggested making Yankee Doodle Doughnuts. Silent, thoughtful, Grace kneaded bread dough, keeping her mind a deliberate blank. There it would have remained all that day, if Mr Smathers had not walked into the bakery.

'Grace.'

Her back was to the door. For a moment, the voice reminded her of Rob. She turned around, almost afraid to look. When she did, her eyes narrowed and she pointed her finger at the door. 'I never want to see you again.'

She didn't think she had raised her voice, but she must have, because the Wilsons tried to shoulder through the door from the backroom at the same time. Holding his baker's peel like a weapon, Mr Wilson glowered at Ugly Butler.

Mr Smathers held up his hand and levelled a look at the baker that could have stripped paint from wood. 'Don't think I won't haul you up on assault-and-battery charges,' he said. 'I must speak to Grace.'

Grace turned back to the bread dough. 'I have nothing to say to you.'

'I said it before,' he replied. 'I swear before God that I took Rob Inman back to Dartmoor to keep him alive.'

The words hung on the air like a bad smell. Grace felt the tears start in her eyes again. 'Please don't torment me, Mr Smathers,' she managed to say. 'Go away.'

'No.' He said it softly, and something in the saying of it compelled her to turn around. 'In God's name, hear me out.' Smathers looked around at all of them.

Mr Wilson snorted in disgust. 'Grace, take him upstairs. Listen to him. When he's done, send him out the back door and that will be all. Do you understand me, Smathers?'

'I ask no more,' Smathers said.

He followed Grace up the stairs to the Wilsons' rooms. He sat in a straight-backed chair. She sat down opposite him, but not too close.

'You have a village full of champions,' he began.

She finally noticed what was different about him. He *did* sound like Rob Inman. 'Mr Smathers, what has happened to your accent?'

'Gone, never to return,' he told her. 'My name is definitely Nahum Smathers. Who would lie about a thing like that? I own a farm near Braintree, Massachusetts. This may or may not interest you, my nearest neighbour is John Adams, second president of the United States.' He cleared his throat. 'His apple orchard is much better than mine.'

Grace felt the blood drain from her face. It must have been obvious to Mr Smathers because he took her hand. She shook it off, but he moved his chair closer.

'Who *are* you?' It was a simple question. It struck her for the first time that she had been asking it of so many people since spring—Emery, Rob himself, Mr Selway. She had never thought to ask it of Nahum Smathers.

He gave her a question instead of an answer. 'Did Rob ever mention Reuben Beasley?'

'That's no answer!'

'No,' he agreed, 'but I'm asking. Did he mention Beasley?'

'He did and not in a favourable light.' She couldn't keep the contempt from her voice. 'Mr Smathers, you are stalling.'

'I am not,' he declared firmly. 'Reuben Beasley is the American agent assigned by my government—Rob's government, too—as liaison with prisoners of war in Britain. He was—and still is—serving as American consul to Britain.'

'Rob said he has done nothing to ease their sufferings.'

Smathers nodded. 'He is nearly correct. After the treaty was signed in Belgium, Reuben visited Dartmoor.' He managed a sour smile. 'I've heard that after he left, the POWs made an effigy, labelled it Beasley and burned it.'

He paused, thinking she might have a question. She shook her head wearily. She wanted him to finish, then leave her to her misery.

'I am also an agent, working at the consulate in London. My role was to oversee the paroling of prisoners.'

'You've picked a strange way to ruin your own countrymen!' she burst out, leaping to her feet.

His sharp reply reminded her of the Smathers she knew too well. 'On the contrary, I am good at my job!' he retorted, standing, too. 'My task— until I was specifically assigned to Captain Duncan—was to visit the parolees, assess conditions and write reports. I am a mere pencil pusher. Eager to return to Braintree, I might add.'

'It couldn't be soon enough for me,' she murmured, daring him to placate her.

He sat down again, observing her in silence, as if wondering how she would react to what he said. When he spoke, she could tell he was picking his words carefully.

'Captain Duncan was a special case and Philip Selway assigned him to me.'

'Mr Selway! Where is Mr Selway? He has done me no good!' she declared, then burst into tears.

Grace had left her handkerchief by the bread trough. Mr Smathers took his own and pressed it into her hand. She put it to her face, wishing he would go away. 'I suppose you will tell me that Mr Selway is a…a…Red Indian from the forests of…of…wherever they live in America!'

Smathers smiled at that and she had to agree that she sounded ridiculous.

'No, Grace, he is a member of *your* government, also assigned, as I am, to parolees. We work

together, representing our governments. By now,
I would call him a friend.'

She thought about the letters she had written
to Mr Selway, sent to an anonymous postal box
in Exeter, and how swiftly they were answered.
She considered the implication and felt her face
grow hot with guilt.

'The letter I sent to Mr Selway betrayed Rob,
didn't it?'

He nodded and this time she saw nothing but
sympathy in his eyes. 'I'll take it one step further, Grace, and you won't care for this: *I* am the
one who checks that postal box at least twice a
week. *I* am the person who paid the tradesmen
and sent you funds to keep things going at the
dower house. *I* am the one who wrote you notes
saying "Trust no one", signed with an S.'

'S for Selway, S for Smathers,' she whispered.

'Yes, as it happened. I received that last letter
meant, as all the others were, for Mr Selway. *You*
told me where to locate Rob and I found him.'

Grace slapped Mr Smathers as hard as she
could. He made no resistance as she pummelled
him again and again until she was blinded by
tears and leaning against his chest. When she
felt herself sag, he picked her up and deposited
her on the sofa.

She turned on her side and sobbed into
Mrs Wilson's embroidered cushion, which Mr
Smathers had put under her head. She cried
until there was nothing left except a whimper,

aware that his hand remained on her shoulder the whole time.

He waited until she was silent before he spoke. 'Grace, you don't know who your enemies are. I do.'

He was kneeling beside the sofa, his hand still on her shoulder. 'You are Lord Thomson's butler!' she said. 'You cannot deny that he said his butler had found that miniature of the real Captain Duncan. I remember it. He looked right at you!'

Smathers shook his head. 'Grace, who was standing behind me?'

She thought and sucked in her breath. 'No! You are lying.'

'Who was it?' His voice was intense, relentless as always.

Grace closed her eyes, recalling as clearly as if the matter had unfolded just an hour ago. There was Lord Thomson, looking smug and satisfied, Rob standing close to her, and Emery.

'Emery,' she whispered.

'Emery,' he repeated.

Grace sat up and pressed both hands to her head. 'No! He is one of Lord Thomson's groundsmen, turned off when that penny pincher reduced his staff. He's been watching you!'

Smathers sat beside her on the sofa. 'Before the parole, had you ever seen him on Lord Thomson's estate?'

Grace considered the question. She shook her head, remembering that her few visits to the estate had only taken place when old Lord Thomson was too feeble to make his daily visit to the bakery. Come to think of it, Emery had not been present for the reading of the will, when other staff members were.

'I never saw him,' she said finally. 'I just believed him.' She frowned. 'As for him watching you…' She gasped, her hand to her mouth. 'Once Mrs Wilson told Rob and me that she thought you were watching Emery and not the other way around. We all laughed!'

'She was absolutely right. Young Lord Thomson is a petty and spiteful man. He wanted very much to separate you from, well, from whom I thought was Captain Duncan, so he could have him killed. It's one of those terms in a parole that all prisoners must beware of, death if they stray.'

'But why?' she whispered. 'Why is he so vindictive? He never knew Captain Duncan. There was never any possibility that the captain would claim or receive any part of the estate.'

'True.' Mr Smathers stared straight ahead, silent. He finally looked at her again. 'I wish I knew. Are some men that small and mean?'

Grace pressed Mr Smathers's sodden handkerchief to her forehead. 'I thought you were the small and mean one.' She couldn't help the way her eyes narrowed. 'Maybe you still are. How did you manage to get into Lord Thomson's house as his butler?'

'You still don't believe me, do you?'

He asked it calmly and she answered the same way. 'Why should I? Why did Mr Selway take such an interest in Captain Duncan that he would plant you—if that's the right word…'

'It seems to fit,' he agreed.

'…plant you in Lord Thomson's house? You obviously haven't done this for other parolees, have you?'

'I have not, Grace. There wasn't the urgency.'

'What was different about Captain Duncan?'

When he smiled, she decided maybe she had been wrong to think he had shark eyes. They were deep brown, but not shark eyes, because she saw the expression in them now. Maybe she had never looked for it before.

'You've hit on it. There *was* something different about Captain Duncan.' He took her hand and she did not pull away.

'Couldn't you just have left him alone? Surely it is only a matter of weeks until this war is officially over?'

'I am not as trusting as you are, Grace. I do know this, it is devilish hard for secrets like that to be kept, even among people with the best of intentions. I couldn't risk Lord Thomson's thugs finding Rob Inman. Lord Thomson knows he isn't Captain Duncan now, of course, but as I said earlier, he is a mean excuse for a man.'

She nodded and tightened her grip on Mr Smathers's hand. 'I'm sorry I hit you.' She felt her face go rosy.

He released her hand and stood up, pulling her up. 'You need to hear the whole story.'

'From Mr Selway?'

He nodded. 'Partly. And someone else, someone who might be able to explain Lord Thomson. Gracie, pack your best dress. We're going to London.'

She hung back, weary to the marrow in her bones. 'Why should I trust you, Mr Smathers?'

'I can't think of a single reason,' he said finally. 'Grace, do you trust anyone?'

'Only Rob.'

'Trust me, too.'

Chapter Thirty

'We called you Ugly Butler.'

Nahum Smathers threw back his head and laughed. 'Was it my bald head? My pock marks? My surly demeanour?'

'All that and more,' Grace said, looking out the chaise window at the scenery. 'It's greener in Quimby than here.'

'Don't change the subject!'

'I think I should. You already know me as a crabby, contentious person. Why should I give you more ammunition?'

He only smiled, put his reading spectacles higher on his nose again and returned his attention to the papers on his lap desk. Grace continued her perusal of the landscape. She had not been to London in her life, but she had never thought to make a rapid journey like this one. They had decided it would be better to get there as fast as possible and avoid stopping at an inn. Last night they had slept shoulder to shoulder in the post-chaise.

She woke up once in the night, thinking for just a moment that it was Rob's head lolling on her shoulder. Her heart thudded in her chest, then sank as she remembered it was Nahum Smathers, the man she had vowed to hate until she died. For a long time, she stared out of the window, hoping she was right to trust him, wanting to believe him, even as she doubted.

'You still doubt me,' he stated, looking up from his papers, reading her mind.

'I can't help it. You're playing a deep game.'

'A very deep game,' he agreed, mincing no words—very much the man he had always been, she realised. 'We are going to Half Moon Street, where I am going to ask to speak to Lord Thomson's butler, Emery. You will stay in the post-chaise across the street, because *I* trust no one.'

'What a pair we are,' she murmured. He merely shrugged and returned to his work.

Miles later, he looked up. 'Then we're going to Teddington. It's not far from London and there is someone you have to meet.'

'Please tell me it is Rob!' she burst out.

'He's in Dartmoor, as I told you. Pray for swift winds to guide the treaty ship to England. And pray it arrives ratified,' he concluded, under his breath.

* * *

They arrived at Half Moon Street after dark. Smathers directed the coachman to stop directly across the street from an imposing town house. He took a small box from his greatcoat.

'I will ask the footman to produce Emery, because I promised Lord Thomson I would return that miniature of Captain Duncan, the one Emery found.'

'So you say,' she couldn't help murmuring.

He gave her a sour look. *The Ugly Butler I know and despise,* Grace thought, returning his sour look with one of her own.

'Grace, you have to trust someone!' he declared. He shrugged his shoulders. 'Or not, I suppose. When Emery comes to the door, you will see him.'

She nodded, embarrassed at her shortcomings.

'Then we will depart immediately. When Emery opens the box, he'll find nothing but a stone in it and a rude note from me. I had better make myself scarce.'

'Do you have the miniature?'

He patted his inside pocket. 'Aye, and it's going to Teddington to the man who should have it.'

'I don't understand,' Grace said. 'The real man who should have it is Lord Thomson—well, *my* Lord Thomson.'

'No. We're going to spend a few moments with the Duke of Clarence.' He eyed her. 'That's why I asked you to wear your best dress.' He chuckled. 'Close your mouth, Grace. You're catching flies!'

She did as he said, full of questions that she kept to herself, because he was already out of the post-chaise. Grace leaned back, making her profile as small as possible as she watched Ugly Butler lift the knocker.

After a moment the door was opened by a footman. Smathers shook his head and waited outside, the box in his hand. Grace sucked in her breath when Emery appeared next, dressed much grander than she remembered, but Emery, all the same.

'Damn you,' Grace muttered. 'What fools you made of us.'

She watched Smathers take his casual time, chatting with Emery, then handing over the box. When the door closed, he wasted not a minute getting back into the chaise, after a quick word with the coachman.

'Maybe I shouldn't have written that note,' Smathers commented as they tore through London's streets as fast as was possible without attracting unwanted attention. 'I couldn't resist telling him what I thought. Rather like you, Grace.'

She nodded, staring into the dark. 'Why the Duke of Clarence?'

'I think his Grace would rather tell you himself. He's expecting us, by the way.'

* * *

Gradually the city fell away, as homes turned into manors, and then elegant estates. Finally they paused at one gate, which opened quickly when Smathers held out a sheet of paper stamped with an impressive seal.

Grace looked down at her best dress. Like her other dress, it was practical, tidy and oceans away from the pastel muslins and silk she remembered as the daughter of an over-extended baronet with no money, but miles of pretension. She brushed at the dress, suddenly proud of her own efforts that had kept her alive and productive, even though the bottom had fallen out of her world of privilege. She sat taller, calm and not ashamed. This was who she was now and it was enough.

She followed Mr Smathers into Bushy House's opulent foyer. She vowed not to gawk and stare like a misplaced milkmaid, but it took all her strength. What she had no resistance against was the appearance of Mr Selway, who came toward her with both hands outstretched. He seemed to know she would fold herself into his embrace without a word. Unable to help herself, she sobbed into his handsome suit, then reached out blindly for a handkerchief from the tall man standing next to him.

'Blow your nose, dearie,' he advised, sounding like a man with much female experience, or possibly many children of his own.

She did as he said, then took a good look. She gulped, then dropped a deep curtsy.

'Your Grace,' she murmured, 'I didn't mean to weep all over your handkerchief.'

The Duke chuckled. 'Miss…Miss Curtis, is it?'

'Yes, your Grace.'

'I have five daughters. Five! I learned years ago to be amply handkerchiefed.'

Grace wanted to smile, but found she could not. She blew her nose and glanced again at Mr Selway, also dressed impeccably in black and looking more elegant than a mere solicitor. This was no place to speak what was in her heart, not here in the Duke of Clarence's residence. Then she thought of Rob, suffering in Dartmoor, and could not help herself.

'Mr Selway, we needed you!' She hadn't meant it to come out so loud.

There was no denying the sorrow in Mr Selway's eyes. 'And we failed you both,' he said. 'More shame to us.'

She was silent then, embarrassed at her outburst. The Duke of Clarence led her to a sofa. 'I have daughters,' he said again and this time his voice was almost fatherly.

Grace swallowed down her tears. 'Oh, please, your Grace, we didn't mean to deceive anyone! When I knelt by Captain Duncan, he was dying! He asked me to choose someone else. I did, not thinking it would hurt.'

The duke said a strange thing then; she knew she would never forget it.

'Did he die bravely?'

Grace put the handkerchief to her mouth, remembering the filthy prison, the stench, the seamen crowded around their dying captain. Without a word of complaint, Daniel Duncan, bastard son of Lord Thomson, had begged her to choose life for someone else.

'If he had been *your* son, your Grace, you would have had no reason to be ashamed of him.'

She knew she was presumptuous. To her amazement, the duke bowed his head and swallowed hard, his hand to his eyes. She put her hand on his elegant sleeve and he covered it with his own. They sat together, heads nearly touching, until she wanted to put her other hand on his cheek and console him for a sorrow she did not understand.

No one in the room said anything. All she heard was the ticking of a clock. He raised his eyes to hers finally.

'Miss Curtis, he *was* my son.'

'My God,' she whispered, then did touch his cheek briefly. 'I am so sorry.'

The Duke of Clarence took a long moment to collect himself. Grace glanced at the others: Mr Selway, impeccable and inscrutable as a good lawyer; Mr Smathers's lips tight together in the grip of his own emotion. She returned her gaze to the duke, watching him gather himself together.

When he was in control, he returned his gaze to her. They might have been the only people in the room. 'Miss Curtis, you are probably wondering what the devil I am saying.'

He smiled, but there was no overlooking the pain in his eyes. 'Of all people, you deserve an explanation.'

'Mr…Mr Smathers did tell me he had been assigned to watch over Captain Duncan, but he would not tell me why.'

The duke nodded. 'That is rightfully my office.' He stood up, motioning the rest of them to remain seated and walked to the fireplace, where he stared for a long moment into the flames. When he looked at her again, he was himself once more. 'My dear, I suppose you know that my nickname is "Sailor Billy".'

She nodded. 'Did you not join the Royal Navy at a tender age, your Grace?'

'Thirteen. At the age of fifteen—nearly sixteen—I participated in the occupation of New York City, during the American War. Lord Thomson—a great friend of my poor, mad father—was billeted there, too. My father asked him to keep an eye on me.'

'*My* Lord Thomson?' she asked, startled.

The duke smiled at that. 'Ah, yes. Mr Selway said you took him Quimby Crèmes, when he could no longer totter to the village.'

'He was a crotchety old fellow, but I liked him.' Grace blushed when everyone laughed. 'Well, he was! But, your Grace, Lord Thomson was Captain Duncan's father.'

The duke waggled his hand. 'While it is true we both had our eyes on Mollie Duncan—lovely minx!—he gave me, uh, prior claim.' He coughed discreetly. '*Droit de seigneur* and all that.'

'Oh,' she said, not sure where to look.

The Duke was obviously made of sterner stuff. 'Come now! We know what kind of man I am! I have ten children by Mrs Jordan and I love them all. I rather believe I was Daniel Duncan's father.'

So did Grace suddenly. She thought of the miniature and looked at the Duke of Clarence, imagining him much younger. The resemblance was there, although the deep dimple must have come from Mollie Duncan.

He sat down again beside her. 'My dear, perhaps you can appreciate the moment. I was just sixteen, and we were preparing to pull out of New York City. Mollie had come to me, expecting some sort of help for her…er…dilemma. That was when Lord Thomson stepped in and settled the matter by assuring her that he would do the right thing. What could she say?' He sighed. 'As always, politics reared its ugly head, and I was… er…rather precocious in the begetting game.'

Grace couldn't help smiling.

'What kind of scandal would my sins have caused my father during this delicate time?' The Duke glared at Mr Smathers for a moment. 'And, sir, *your* General Washington had just got wind that I was in New York City and put a bounty on my head! The streets were suddenly not safe for Sailor Billy.'

Nonplussed, Mr Smathers returned a calm gaze of his own. 'All's fair in war, sir.'

The Duke looked at Grace again. 'So, my dear, your crotchety old marquis paid Mollie a small sum annually for the boy's upkeep and kept me informed of his progress. When we learned he was imprisoned in Dartmoor, I enlisted Mr Selway—my personal barrister, not a mere solicitor—to have the captain paroled to Quarle.'

'But, your Grace, how—why—did I come into the picture?' Grace asked.

'Lord Thomson knew he was dying. He wanted someone to watch over Captain Duncan. I believe he allocated the princely sum of thirty pounds per annum to you, both for your help with my son, and to reward you for your kindness to him, when no one else was kind.'

'Your Grace, if I may,' Mr Selway interjected. 'Lord Thomson had had no information about Captain Duncan for several years and he hoped that the captain and Grace would fall in love. So he told me.'

Grace felt tears prickle her eyes again. *I did, but it was the wrong Captain Duncan,* she thought. 'Rob said the captain's wife and children would have been surprised at such a turn of events,' she said. She turned to Mr Selway. 'Sir, why did you install Mr Smathers in Quarle?'

'A fair question, Grace,' the barrister replied. 'Let us just say that after observing the new marquis's pettiness and irritation when your paltry thirty pounds per annum was announced at the reading of his uncle's will, I began to worry. I really worried when I learned that Lord Thomson had insinuated his own butler into the dower house. I knew the captain needed someone else to watch over him.'

Grace nodded. 'Lord Thomson would have shot Captain Duncan on sight—or Rob Inman, take your pick—if ever he had wandered from the estate or left my oversight.' She looked at each man in turn. 'Why are some men so petty and vindictive?'

The Duke frowned. 'What I suspect about young Lord Thomson I learned from one of my sons, who knew him at Eton. As boys will, they got into some sort of contretemps. It seems that Lord Thomson is one of those petty fellows who never relinquish a hatred. I think he wanted to kill Captain Duncan to get back at me somehow.'

'He is certainly small enough,' Grace said. She sighed. 'And I suppose if Captain Duncan was dead, anyone else would do, too.'

'Why are some men so vindictive? That, my dear, is the question of the ages,' the duke said finally. He seemed to struggle within himself again. 'And why, my dear, are other men so brave?'

Grace regarded the Duke of Clarence in the silence that followed. *Perhaps I can give you comfort, even though I already know how removed I feel from this realm of yours.* 'I had such a brief time with…with your son, your Grace, but I know this, in thinking of others as he lay dying, he was a son and leader worthy of Sailor Billy.'

Grace could have gasped at her own frankness, but when the duke, tears welling in his eyes, gazed for such a long moment at her, she knew she had said the right thing.

Overcome with emotion, he would have left the room then, except Mr Smathers stopped him. 'Your Grace, one moment.'

'Ah, so I am "your Grace", you rascal American,' the Duke said, striving for a light touch, and almost succeeding.

Mr Smathers reached inside his coat and pulled out a miniature. 'Lord Thomson's butler Emery found this and used it to ruin Rob Inman. I'm certain old Lord Thomson wanted you to have it.'

The duke cupped the miniature of Captain Duncan gently in his hands, as a father might clasp an infant. 'Just like his lovely mother,' he said, his voice soft. He looked at Grace, tapping the miniature with his finger. 'Lord Thomson kept this miniature for himself. Tell me, my dear—do you think that through all these years of deception on my behalf, Lord Thomson felt a little fatherly toward this American?'

'He probably did, your Grace,' she said. 'I wish

he could have lived long enough to meet Rob Inman, who made a fine substitute.'

After the duke left, the rest of them sat in silence. Finally, Grace could not bear the quiet. 'Mr Selway, is there *nothing* we can do for Rob Inman? Can his Grace help?'

The barrister shook his head. 'My dear, the wheels of war grind everything in their path. I fear that sympathy to a prisoner in Dartmoor would be seen as great political weakness, especially when this ratified treaty is due on our shores. Times are touchy.'

Grace nodded, thinking of Mr Smathers's comment about the particular danger in the beginning and end of a war, when everyone was a little crazy.

Mr Selway helped her to her feet. 'It is nearly April, just a matter of days before we can expect a ship's arrival. What is another week or two, in the greater scheme of things?'

'But…'

'I agree with Nahum Smathers, Rob Inman is probably safer in Dartmoor right now.'

Chapter Thirty-One

Grace spent the night at Mr Selway's London house, but not before saying goodbye to Nahum Smathers, who would not tell her where he was going.

'Let me say that after leaving a stone and an angry note at Lord Thomson's, I had better go to ground.'

She didn't want him to leave, which surprised her, and so she told him. He laughed, and touched her cheek, much as Rob would have done, and which only brought on tears she didn't quite understand.

She took his arm. 'Sir, why did you not simply tell us who you were?'

'Would you have believed me?' he asked in turn.

'Certainly not!'

He laughed. 'Admit it, Grace, you know you're

glad to see the back of me!' He grew serious again. 'I'll find a way to keep an eye on your Rob Inman. Trust me now.'

'I do, actually,' she told him as he put on his overcoat, checked outside the front door, then came back in.

'If you need me, write to Exeter, as you have always done.' He tipped his hat to her. 'Chin up, Gracie.'

Over breakfast with Mr Selway, she received a small package from Bushy House. Her fingers trembled as she untied the strings binding it together. She felt her lips tremble when she opened the box and counted thirty pounds. She knew she would keep the note for ever.

My Dear Miss Grace Curtis, she read. *I'll see you get thirty pounds per annum, just as Lord Thomson's will stipulated. This will be our little secret, much as Captain Duncan is, and must remain, for the good of relations between my country, and what I suspect soon will be your country, if I am a good interpreter of daughters. Sincerely, William Hanover.*

She showed it to Mr Selway, who nodded.

Courtesy of Mr Selway, she went back to Quimby at a more sedate pace, pausing for a night at an inn. Mr Selway had told her to speak for a private parlour, but she decided against such an extravagance, choosing instead to sharing a dining table with a farmer's wife.

Yes, Father, I have slid, she thought as she ate, and appreciated the other woman's stories of children and crops. But it did not follow that sliding was a bad thing, considering how much she liked her circumstances. *Had I been as high in the instep as you, Papa, I would never have met Rob Inman.*

He was on her mind every minute of every mile that took her closer to Quimby. It was late in the afternoon and the streets were empty, but they filled up soon enough as the post-chaise pulled up to the bakery and discharged her into the waiting arms of Mrs Wilson. Soon the Gentrys came running from the candlemaker's shop, eager for news.

By the time Grace was seated on a stool in the bakery, Lady Tutt came puffing in, having exerted herself enough to trot, if not gallop. The tinsmith fanned her with his leather apron and even the constable stayed.

She told them what she could without mentioning the Duke of Clarence, glossing over Captain Duncan's illustrious parentage and hinting that he was a man somewhat powerful in English leadership and she could say no more. It seemed a durable lie.

To her heart's delight, her friends were more concerned about Rob Inman. 'He must stay where he is, I fear,' she concluded, forcing back her own tears at their long faces. 'I have it on good authority that the war will soon be over and he will be a free man.'

Lady Tutt's bobbing feathers indicated her own agitation. 'That is not good enough!' she declared. 'I will write immediately to the regent himself. He will listen to me!'

Grace thought of the years when her late father had labelled the Tutts encroaching mushrooms. She remembered Lady Tutt's utter willingness to hide Rob, without any thoughts to her own safety. *You were so wrong, Papa,* she told herself as she touched the woman's arm. 'Lady Tutt, I believe that is an excellent idea,' she said. 'I fear though, the matter will remain as it is. Even if *you* are not, the rest of us are very small cogs in the machinery of government.'

'I can try, though.'

'Please do.'

So it went, as the rest of March passed slowly, livened briefly by the news that the treaty had arrived at Whitehall and the war was officially over. Grace's heart had soared at the news, then returned to reality when she received a scrawled note from Mr Smathers a week later, telling her that still the prisoners remained in Dartmoor. 'There they will stay, I fear, until American ships arrive in English waters to take them off,' he wrote. 'Captain Shortland is not budging in his insistence on incarceration.'

He had worse news, too, of a smallpox epidemic in the prison, brought by a shipload of sailors captured by the Royal Navy off Africa. 'The prison now houses nearly six thousand Americans,' he added in a postscript. 'Would to God it were less crowded and the men strong enough to resist such insults to their bodies. But we know the truth of that.'

She shared the note with the Wilsons, who looked at her with solemn faces, but said nothing. Grace stared a long time into the dark that night. Even Mr Smathers's presence would have been comforting.

There was something else, too, so private that she waited a long time before telling the Wilsons. 'I should be ashamed that we went so far, but I am not,' she said, when she finished. 'If it's a boy, I will name him Robert. We two will have a home in Nantucket.'

She was almost afraid to look at the Wilsons. When she did, all she saw was love and concern on their faces. 'I hope you are not disappointed in me,' she said.

'Nay, lass,' Mr Wilson said, while his wife dabbed at her tears. 'War makes life hard to bear. If…if you never see Rob again, you'll have his son or daughter. It'll have to do.'

Bobby Gentry gave her the strength to make Yankee Doodle Doughnuts again. One day as he came with his penny for day-old bread, he had whispered, 'I don't think Rob would like us to do without doughnuts.' He stood on tiptoe and spoke in her ear. 'I think he would *deplore* it.'

He made her laugh, which drew her from the shell she thought she had left behind, and which she now rejected completely. 'You are right, Bobby,' she had declared. 'Doughnuts tomorrow. Spread the word.'

Every night, after she had finished sweeping the store, Grace took out the Nantucket deed from its hiding place under the day-old bread bin. She read its few words, remembering Rob's gift to her and his love when they celebrated the Treaty of Ghent, and celebrated, and celebrated. She took comfort that he had got her with child, as humiliating as such an experience might prove, if he did not return to marry her. The Duke of Clarence would understand, even if no one else did. Perhaps she would send him a note.

Even as each long day with no news, good or bad, seemed to make her stronger, no one was prepared for the news in April that Mr Smathers brought in person.

She was already in bed and nearly asleep, when she heard tapping at the back door. Nerves tingling, she crept from bed and threw a shawl around her nightdress. 'Please, God, let it be Rob,' she whispered as she opened the door.

She swallowed her disappointment to see Mr Smathers leaning against the doorjamb, looking exhausted. Without a word, she took him by the arm and pulled him inside. She turned to get him a drink of water, but he took her hand and pulled her close.

'Sit down, Grace.'

She shook her head. There was some horror in his eyes that suddenly made her want to flee the room and burrow under her covers in her own bed. She knew she was irrational, but some imp told her that if she did not see him, whatever he had to tell her couldn't be true.

Smathers did not release her hand. He pulled her closer and covered her hand with his other one. She had no choice but to sit beside him. His eyes bored into hers.

'Grace, I came as soon as I could, because I want you to hear this from me first. There has been a massacre at Dartmoor.'

She gasped and tried to tug her hand away. He would not release her. 'That is what they are calling it in Princetown, that village close to Dartmoor. I have been staying there.'

He passed a hand in front of his eyes and she saw how tired he was. She reached for his shoulder then, suddenly aware that as much as he cared about Rob Inman, there were six thousand prisoners Smathers cared about.

'The news is jumbled. Some say eight men are dead, some say fifty, others a thousand, with tales of many more wounded, crawling to get away.' He muttered a curse that made her flinch. 'God, how I hate rumours!'

'How did it happen?'

He released her hand, so she stood up again and brought him a glass of water. He drank it down without stopping and handed it back, asking if she had any bread and butter.

'I have not eaten in two days,' he said.

She went into the store and returned with a handful of doughnuts. 'We're making Yankee Doodle Doughnuts again,' she told him, distressed that her lips were quivering. She wondered if he could even understand her.

He took the doughnuts and looked at them with a half-smile. 'Your man has a flair for theatrics. He would be—he will be—an excellent impresario. A Yankee himself.'

'Do you know anything else? Please tell me.'

He ate a doughnut, not looking her in the eye. 'Nothing more. Some say that Captain Shortland has already buried the dead in a mass grave behind the prison, but I do not know.' He sighed. 'Apparently it started during a ball game. The ball went over a fence and the prisoners tried to get it back. The guards refused and the men broke a hole in the fence.' He shook his head. 'That's when the shooting started, apparently. I do know this, the prison is locked down.'

He stood then and paced the room, hands behind his back, biting off his words. 'I've written to Reuben Beasley, begging him to do his duty and find out more.' He swore again. 'I might as well write to a stone. Damn him, too!'

Grace closed her eyes, thinking of Lady Tutt's letters to Whitehall. 'Mr Smathers, as Rob would say, we are small potatoes, indeed.'

'He's right.' Smathers stopped pacing. 'There it stands, Grace. I must return to Princetown now.' He managed a guilty smile. 'I…uh…borrowed a farmer's cart and he'd probably like it back.'

She stopped him before he left and took him by the hand, pulling him into the store. She took the Nantucket deed from its hiding place and held it out to him. A variety of emotions crossed his face as he read it by the light of a full moon. The last expression was the one she was most familiar with—steely resolve.

'Know this, Grace, no matter what happens, I will get you to Nantucket. You have my word on it.'

She nodded, too full of tears to speak and reluctant to show this strong man how weak she really felt.

He took her hand again and this time his touch was gentle. 'Gracie, you must realise you might be a stranger alone in a strange land.'

She took a deep breath. 'I know, Nahum. I can bake and I can find work, if I have a home. I imagine many have come to America with less.'

He nodded. 'My own grandfather was an indentured servant.'

'So was Rob,' she said softly.

To her surprise, he kissed her forehead, then left as quietly as he came. Silently, Grace replaced the deed and made herself comfortable in the back room on a softer chair. She knew she would not sleep any more that night.

In the morning, Grace told the Wilsons what she had learned, begging them to tell others, as she had not the energy to talk about the massacre. In the days that followed, more news tumbled about, describing a small riot, easily contained, all the way up to a massive prisoner uprising that had led to the slaughter of every American in Dartmoor. Eyes dry, shoulders squared, Grace cut and fried doughnuts and made bread and Quimby Crèmes, wishing for more news from Mr Smathers.

She took heart as she heard nothing from him, deciding that no news was good news. She suggested to Mrs Wilson that she train Mrs Gentry to take her place. 'She's a good worker and she will never disappoint,' Grace told Mrs Wilson.

'What about you?' Mrs Wilson asked.

Grace saw how events had worn down her well-loved employer. 'My dear, I am going to America as soon as Mr Smathers makes arrangement,' she said.

'You won't see him again!' Mrs Wilson scoffed.

'I will. He gave me his word.' She smiled. 'And do you know, I trust him.'

Grace finally began to doubt, as April turned into as beautiful a May as she had ever seen before. Even the meadows, blooming trees and blossoming flowers seemed to conspire to fling their loveliness at her and mock her foolishness to think Nantucket was the answer to her troubles. Even Rob had told her it was not, considering that people were small and kind, mean and magnanimous everywhere. True, she would be alone until their baby was born, and that would be a trial. She strengthened her resolve, thinking of that small boy crawling across a slanting deck to wipe the shoes of an American sea captain, and how well he was repaid for his courage.

We can do no less, she told herself, including her unborn child.

Her resolve nearly failed her, as news came of Americans—former prisoners now—being carted daily down to Plymouth and waiting American ships. She was thankful that the main road to Plymouth did not cut through Quimby. She knew she could not bear the Americans' jubilation at freedom, when she had no word from Rob Inman.

She toyed with the idea that he might have left without her, then rejected it. He would never do that. Then she finally faced it—he must be dead. The pain of that bent her double and caused her to cry out like an animal, but it was late and she was sweeping up, and Quimby slept. Better to bear her grief in silence; too much sympathy would be harder to handle.

She was almost ready to tear up the deed and resign herself to England. It was a particularly beautiful May morning and she had promised Bobby Gentry they would take a walk in spring's loveliness.

Grace had finished rolling out a batch of doughnuts and was reaching for the cutter when the bell tinkled in the store. She turned around and dropped the cutter.

Mr Smathers stood there, his face calm now, all exhaustion gone. He smiled at her.

'Have you come to take me with you?' she asked, wiping her hands on her apron. 'I still want to go, even if I go alone.'

'Actually, this pencil pusher comes as an emissary, dear Grace Curtis. There is a man outside who wants to know if you could love him one-legged.'

Grace felt the blood draining from her face, and grasped the corner of the pastry case to steady herself. 'He's alive,' she whispered.

'Aye, quite alive. He's been in hospital in Bristol. Damn Captain Shortland! He sent the wounded everywhere and would not tell me anything. I had to search every hospital and physician's office in Cornwall and Devon.'

'Bless you,' she murmured, edging for the door.

She saw the emotion in his eyes then and her heart went out to him. 'I found him in Bristol.' He smiled at her. 'He wants me to find out your answer, before he either comes inside or continues down to Plymouth.'

Grace didn't try to stop her tears; she knew they would flow anyway, no matter how determined she was to be calm about the matter. 'You may tell him for me that I think he is a blithering idiot to even consider I could not love a one-legged man.'

'"Blithering idiot". I like that,' Mr Smathers replied. 'Any other embellishments? You always were prone to speak your mind.'

'That will do,' she said crisply, going to the bread bin for the deed as he left the shop. She turned to Mrs Gentry, who stood transfixed in the door to the back room. 'My dear, would you gather up my clothing into a bundle? Put in the Bible, but you may have the other books.'

She stood in the centre of the shop, hands clasped calmly in front of her. When the door opened again, Rob Inman stood there. He shouldered his way in, coming toward her on crutches. She sighed to see where his pant leg was pinned back below one knee, then put any doubts behind her. He was her man and she would cleave to him until she died.

'Rob Inman, it seems I own a home in Nantucket. I'll share it with you.'

Then he was in her arms, the crutches clattering to the floor. She held him up and she held him close, kissing his thin face and murmuring all endearments that came to her mind.

'Beloved, I have missed you from the day Ugly Butler took me away,' he said into her ear.

'He's not so ugly,' she said, shivering a little at the power of his breath on her ear and knowing quite well where it could lead. Where it *had* led, she amended. That bit of news could wait for a more private moment.

'Aye, lass. He's not so ugly. He assures me that we can find an American preacher on board an American ship who will marry us. Are you game, Gracie? It's time to celebrate some freedom, even if we have to share a tiny berth.'

She blushed, which only made him laugh. Mr Smathers had retrieved the crutches and Rob tucked them in his armpits again. 'I know there will be a carpenter on board who can whittle me a peg leg. D'ye mind, really?'

This was said seriously, so she answered as seriously.

'Not a bit, Rob.' She held herself off from him for a good look. 'I didn't love just that half a leg that's missing. I have no doubt that you could tread any slanting deck again, if that is your choice. And if it is, then it is mine, too.'

Rob looked around the room. She noticed his glance lingered longest on the now-fading Yankee Doodle Doughnuts sign. 'I have a better idea. There is my prize money, long overdue. Mr Smathers tells me that there is someone rather high up on this little island who wants to be a silent partner in a Nantucket bakery. He tells me you can fill in the details later.'

Grace clapped her hands in delight and smiled

at Mr Smathers this time, who bowed in answer. She kissed Rob's cheek. 'My love, running a bakery isn't nearly as exciting as…as visiting Jamaica, or maybe the Barbary Coast.'

'Thank God for that,' Rob replied. 'You may be right, but I'd rather wake up every morning from now on and see your face sharing my pillow.'

She was wiping her eyes again, close in the circle of Rob's arms, when Mrs Wilson came into the store, carrying her bundled clothes. She took the bundle and clung to Mrs Wilson for a long moment. 'You did so much for me,' she whispered. Mr Wilson tried not to cry and failed, too. Mrs Gentry kissed her and took over at the table, cutting doughnuts.

Grace went outside, where a wagon nearly full of Dartmoor's former prisoners waited. Mr Smathers handed up her bundle and accepted his own duffel.

'You're not coming, too?' Grace asked, after he helped Rob Inman back into the wagon.

'Not yet,' he told her. 'I have some more men to locate.'

'Your own family must miss you, Nahum.'

He shook his head. 'For a two-year war, it's been a long one. My wife and child died of a fever a year ago, so I have learned. No one is waiting for me, but I will go home to Braintree eventually.'

'I am so sorry, Nahum,' she said.

He flicked at her tears, then impulsively kissed

her. The look he gave Rob was a close cousin to the glower she knew well. He still held her hand and he pressed it now.

'As I said, I'll see to it in person that you receive your thirty pounds per annum.' He turned to stare at Rob, seated now in the wagon and holding out his hands for Grace. 'If I find that you are dead, or not treating this excellent woman well, I intend to court and marry her. Be on your best behavior, Sailing Master Inman.'

'Make that Baker Inman,' Rob said. His face was serious. 'I always knew I'd have to watch my back around you, Smathers.'

'Damn straight, you do,' Nahum said, giving Grace a hand up. He looked her in the eye with the kinder expression she had come to know, in her time of great need. 'Change your mind, Gracie?' he asked.

She shook her head. 'You're a good man, Nahum Smathers.' Her glance went to the man she loved. 'But I still choose Rob Inman.'

* * * * *

In Closing

The infamous Dartmoor massacre of American prisoners of war, nearly four months after the signing of the treaty to end the War of 1812, remains shrouded in mystery.

Some historians believe the Americans were trying to retrieve a ball that went over one of the interior walls. When the guards would not return it, the POWs broke a hole in the wall to get it back. Others think the Americans were angry about their continued imprisonment and reduction of the bread ration, and tried to break out.

Whatever the reason, prison guards were ordered—perhaps by prison governor Captain Thomas Shortland—to fire on the milling prisoners. Seven or eight men were killed, six POWs lost arms or legs because of injuries and another fifty-three were more lightly injured.

The dead were buried in what has become

known as the American Cemetery. In all, the cemetery contains the remains of 271 Americans who died in prison between 1812 and 1815.

Through the years, various American societies erected monuments and markers. Neglected for years, the cemetery recently received a needed facelift by U.S. Navy personnel stationed in the United Kingdom. At this time, serious effort was made to learn the names of all the American dead. These names are now memorialised by two new plaques at Dartmoor Prison. There may be others still unaccounted for; old records are sometimes vague. As Nahum Smathers wisely pointed out, that time when a war is ending is the most confusing time of all.

But many care. The new memorial plaques contain the following words: *Dedicated to the memory of those who died at Dartmoor Prison during the War of 1812. You have not been forgotten.*

A sneaky peek at next month...

HISTORICAL

IGNITE YOUR IMAGINATION, STEP INTO THE PAST...

My wish list for next month's titles...

In stores from 6th July 2012:

❑ An Escapade and an Engagement – Annie Burrows

❑ The Laird's Forbidden Lady – Ann Lethbridge

❑ His Makeshift Wife – Anne Ashley

❑ The Captain and the Wallflower – Lyn Stone

❑ Tempted by the Highland Warrior – Michelle Willingham

❑ Renegade Most Wanted – Carol Arens

Available at WHSmith, Tesco, Asda, Eason, Amazon and Apple

Just can't wait?

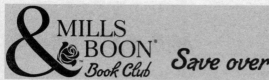